◆ ◆ ◆

"Pulls the rug out from under you with a professional snap. Together with Gores's sublimely comic, and utterly different, *32 Cadillacs*: a towering pair of back-to-back home runs."

—Kirkus Reviews

◆ ◆ ◆

"Exciting . . . Gores is a first-rate crime writer—in the same league as Lawrence Block, whose awards would fill a room."　　　　**—Houston Post**

◆ ◆ ◆

"This is one author who can write with a vengeance. DEAD MAN is suspenseful, and its violence is both frequent and gruesomely ingenious."

—New York Newsday

◆ ◆ ◆

"Total action. . . . The conclusion is a real page turner."　　　　**—Boston Sunday Globe**

◆ ◆ ◆

"A stunning climax. . . . Plenty of plot twists, violence and sex. . . . An updated, slightly self-reflective, comic detective story with a hero both hard-boiled and sensitive, who finally recovers his soul."

—Publishers Weekly

◆ ◆ ◆

"Excitingly paced."

—Atlanta Journal & Constitution

◆ ◆ ◆

"Not since Hammett and Chandler has anyone written quite as well as Joe Gores."

—Ross Thomas

◆ ◆ ◆

♦ ♦ ♦

"Gores has established himself securely as one of the best and most versatile authors of crime novels."
—*Twentieth Century Crime & Mystery Writers*

♦ ♦ ♦

"A chilling tale. . . . The redemptive power of death permeates the action. . . . Gores tells his original story in an original way."
—*San Jose Mercury News*

♦ ♦ ♦

"Reading Joe Gores's novel is like wrestling a bull bare-handed. . . . You succumb to the brute force of his writing."
—*Charlotte Observer*

♦ ♦ ♦

"A marvelous writer."
—*Cleveland Plain Dealer*

♦ ♦ ♦

"Plot twists and turns and a shocking surprise ending. . . . This is a terrific book. The characters are colorful, exciting, and real."
—*I Love a Mystery Newsletter*

♦ ♦ ♦

"Gores has mastered the hard-boiled Hammett irony . . . Taut, colorful, stylistically convincing, and satisfyingly complex."
—*Detroit Sunday News*

♦ ♦ ♦

"One of the very few authentic private eyes to enter the field of fiction since Dashiell Hammett."
—*Anthony Boucher*

♦ ♦ ♦

Books by Joe Gores

NOVELS
A Time of Predators (1969)
Interface (1974)
Hammett (1975)
Come Morning (1986)
Wolf Time (1989)
Dead Man (1993)*

DKA FILE NOVELS
Dead Skip (1972)*
Final Notice (1973)*
Gone, No Forwarding (1978)*
32 Cadillacs (1992)*

*Published by
THE MYSTERIOUS PRESS

JOE GORES

DEAD MAN

THE MYSTERIOUS PRESS

Published by Warner Books

A Time Warner Company

Grateful acknowledgment is given to quote from the song "I Am a Rock" by Paul Simon.
Copyright © 1965 by Paul Simon. Used by permission of the publisher.

MYSTERIOUS PRESS EDITION

Cover design by Jackie Merri Meyer
Cover illustration by Jeff Fitz-Majorice

The Mysterious Press name and logo are registered trademarks of Warner Books, Inc.

Mysterious Press Books are published by
Warner Books, Inc.
1271 Avenue of the Americas
New York, NY 10020

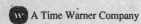 A Time Warner Company

Printed in the United States of America

Originally published in hardcover by The Mysterious Press.

First Printed in Paperback: September, 1994

10 9 8 7 6 5 4 3 2 1

For my beloved
DORI
who walked through snakes
so I could get it right

and in memory of

SHENZIE

I am a rock, I am an island.
And a rock feels no pain,
And an island never cries.

Paul Simon

No man is an island, entire of
itself; every man is a piece
of the continent, a part of
the main.

John Donne

I

EDDIE

Baghdad by the Bay

THE PRIMARY CLEAR LIGHT
SEEN AT THE MOMENT OF DEATH

O nobly-born, the time hath now come for thee to seek the Path. Thy breathing is about to cease. The Clear Light is like the void and cloudless sky. At this moment, know thou thyself; and abide in that state.

THE TIBETAN BOOK OF THE DEAD

1

Sherman Rare Books was a narrow elegant storefront across Post Street from the side entrance to the St. Francis Hotel. The steel gates padlocked shut in the recessed entryway at night were now, in midmorning, folded open for trade. The books were in locked breakfront hardwood cabinets; in recessed alcoves between them were original oil paintings. An unhurried place, sybaritic in its appointments, rugs, and furnishings, where the book was at least as important as its selling.

Eddie Dain sat on an antique Chippendale chair in a perfect lotus without even being aware of it. He was twenty-eight years old, with a strong, almost Sioux face and pale blue deep-set eyes, six-one, lean and springy, 140 pounds. A supple beanpole with a mind that had led Richard Feynman to write all over his papers while he was at Cal-Tech, arguing points with him. He wore a white cotton shirt, wash pants, running shoes, a windbreaker.

The phone spoke Marie's voice into his ear. "R—R1ch."

"K–Kt1," Eddie said to the receiver.

Marie's voice answered, "R–R2."

To Eddie, she had always been this wondrous being who had entered his life at Cal-Tech, became his best friend, stupendous lover, then wife. Even now, after five years, he still went weak in the knees whenever he looked at her, still was always peeking up her skirt or down her blouse like a horny teenager.

"Well?" she demanded.

"I'm *thinking*," he said, the old Jack Benny radio line.

As he thought, he happily drummed his fingers on Doug Sherman's antique oak desk, ignoring the endgame Sherman had laid out with yellowed-ivory chess pieces. He was still young enough and naive enough to treat everything in life as a game.

"R $\times$ P," he told her finally.

Doug Sherman was at the little table behind the desk, his back to Eddie, removing the steaming paper cone from his Melitta coffee dripper. Sherman was tall, lean, fortyish, barbered to perfection, as elegant as the embossed endpapers of his antique books. Below a balding crown his narrow face was sad in repose, with beautiful eyes and sensitive lips. His suit was superb.

"How's this one?" said Marie on the phone. "KP $\times$ R."

"You're kidding." But then Eddie started to think about it. "You're *not* kidding. Okay, R–Q1."

Sherman turned to Eddie, said, "Coffee?"

Eddie shook his head without turning as Marie giggled in his ear, "R–Q1? Bad move, baby. P–K6."

Sherman sat down in his swivel chair, leaned forward over the steaming cup, eyes half-shut as he savored the aroma. He sipped. He leaned back and sighed in perfect aesthetic comfort.

"You don't know what you're missing," he told Eddie. "French Roast and Guatemalan blend. Superb in every respect."

"So is Marie," said Eddie, then into the phone, "R–B1."

"What was that you said?" demanded Marie.

"R–B1."

"No—something with me and superb in the same sentence."

"Oh, that—I told Doug you were a superb cook but a lousy chess player."

"Just for that, $P \times R$–Qch." There was laughter in her voice.

"Damn!" He made his final move a question. "Um . . . $K \times Q$?"

"Gotcha, kiddo! R–RS. And you know what that means."

Eddie laughed delightedly. "I fall upon my sword."

"Since I'm a superb cook, I know I'll see you for dinner."

Eddie hung up, kissed a forefinger, touched it to the phone. Feeling Sherman's eyes upon him, he grinned sheepishly.

"*Now* how about some coffee?" said Sherman.

"You know what I want. *The Tibetan Book of the Dead*. Very beautiful, very old, very leather-bound. The Oxford Press First Edition that Alexandra Neel had bound in calf's hide. I know it's out there somewhere and I know you can find it. In a couple of weeks I'm renting a house on the beach out at Point Reyes for Marie's birthday. Candles, flowers, soft lights—"

"And *The Tibetan Book of the Dead*. For her birthday." Sherman shook his head, then chuckled. "His wife can read the juicy bits aloud to private eye Eddie Dain between stakeouts—"

"A lot of good my stakeout on Grimes did," Eddie said ruefully. "He goes on board his boat at the St. Francis Yacht Club with me watching, and . . ." He threw his arms up and wide, exclaimed, "*Fwoom!* No more Grimes."

"Or too much Grimes," said Sherman ghoulishly. "All over everything. Everyone else believes gases accumulated in the engine compartment ignited when Grimes pushed the starter, but does Eddie the gumshoe? No. No accident for him. Eddie the gumshoe will pursue the evildoers to their lair—"

"Their corporate office, more likely." Eddie grinned; it made him look eighteen instead of twenty-eight. He leaned across the desk. "I really want that book for Marie's birthday."

"Eddie, your Marie is very sweet, very bright, very gentle—but she's also a certifiable New Age California nut.

She's into Tibetan Buddhism, she's into T'ai Chi, she's into Iyengar Yoga, she's into—''

"—computer science and engineering, running the office now that I'm out in the field so much, raising our three-year-old son, beating me at chess, especially phone chess, and—''

"All right all right." Sherman had his hands up, palms out, to stem the spate of words. "Rub it in. She beats you at chess, you beat me at chess, and I would give almost anything to master that boardless phone chess you two children play with such casual idiocy. She's the most remarkable woman ever born, okay? But I'm not sure I can get that specific copy of *The Tibetan Book of the Dead* you want in the time you're giving me." He paused, indicated the chessboard on the desk. "Now *this* . . .''

But Eddie had caught sight of the seven-foot grandfather clock in a shadowed corner of the shop, masticating time with its slow pendulum jaw. He unfolded like a stork as he stood up.

"I'm due at Homicide in fifteen minutes."

Sherman said seductively, "Gaprindishvili versus Kushner, Riga, nineteen seventy-two? She did fine 'til she abandoned the Grunfeld Defense for the Nimzo-Indian, then Kushner . . .''

Eddie, on his way to the door, suddenly swerved, moved one of the black pieces as he went by the board.

"Kushner did that, obviously," he said. "R–R6. Just as obviously, Gaprindishvili then had to resign."

Sherman was studying the board with furious concentration. "Why resign? Why obviously? Why can't she—''

"Work it out yourself." He went across the thick Oriental carpet toward the door with DOUGLAS SHERMAN— RARE BOOKS backward on the glass in elegant script. He added, "Think Tibet."

"All right, goddam you, you'll have your *Tibetan Book of the Dead,*" Sherman called after him. "At full markup!"

But he was speaking to an empty room. He hesitated, tipped over the black king with a push of his finger, shook his head sadly, and poured himself another cup of that superb coffee.

*   *   *

In San Francisco, Inspector is a plainclothes grade between Detective and Lieutenant, equivalent perhaps to warrant officer in the army. Inspector Randy Solomon suggested to Eddie, "Have some of our coffee. It kills the AIDS virus."

Homicide's coffee, brewed in a filthy percolator beside the water cooler, was so horrible that cops from as far away as San Jose and Danville dreamed up things they had to "consult" with SFPD Homicide about, just to get a cup. If they survived it, went the legend, they could return home and sweep the streets clean of criminals because obviously they were men of steel: bullets and switchblades would bounce harmlessly off them.

"Doug Sherman told me SFPD has come up empty," said Eddie.

"How does that guy find *out* everything so fast?" Solomon rumbled in mild irritation.

He was in shirt sleeves, very large, very well conditioned, an African-American the color of *caffe latte*, easily as tall as Eddie's scrawny six-one but ninety pounds heavier, with none of it around his beltline. His voice was *basso profundo*, his laughter could rattle window glass. He had met Eddie on a handball court at the Y the previous year, they now played three days a week.

"Doug knows everybody, he's a born gossip, women like him," said Eddie. "People tell him things. The ultimate go-between."

"Why the hell doesn't he just stick to selling books?"

"Censorship," said Eddie. "Police brutality. Fie on you."

They went into one of the interview cubicles, glassed from the waist up: voices, phones, and rattling printers made conversation in the squadroom as difficult as resurrection. Randy sat down in a chrome and black plastic chair, sausage-thick brown fingers interlaced on his gut. He sighed.

"Anyway, Close and Bill on the Ronald Grimes case—not that it ever was a case except in our Sherlock's pig-headed—"

"You're wrong, Randy, my case is very much open.

Ronald Grimes lived far too high for our post-junk-bonds era.''

Randy squirmed around so the snubnose Policeman's Special in his belt holster would quit digging into his hip.

"Correct me if I'm wrong, but didn't his partner hire you just to see if Grimes was skimming from their brokerage firm trustee accounts? Grimes wasn't, right? So, end of story."

"*Start* of story. Grimes had *some* unknown source of illicit income. When I started nosing around, he died in an apparent accident on his powerboat. In his sleep—okay. In an explosion on his boat—no way."

Randy sighed and heaved his bulk out of the chair. "C'mon, Sherlock, let's you buy me some lunch across the street while I explain the facts of life to you."

They had the elevator to themselves except for a couple barely out of their teens, despairingly intertwined as if the descending cage were a spaceship capable of blasting them out of this space/time continuum. He wore black leather and hack boots and acne; she wore tearstains on her sallow cheeks.

"Got a continuance but he's goin' away," muttered Randy. They faced the doors to give the couple what little privacy the elevator offered. "Why are you out doing this shit really? Beautiful wife at home who loves you, cute little kid, a good business as a computer research source. Man, I had that going for me, I'd be down to Silicon Valley makin' beaucoup bucks . . ."

"Would you?" asked Eddie doubtfully. "Why are you a cop?"

Randy's gesture encompassed his size, his blackness, the hardness of his wide ebony face. "What else?"

"Plenty else. You're a cop because you're *good* at it. Because you like it. Because it's got you."

They crossed the terrazzo floor and went out through heavy brass-framed doors into the bright windy May sunshine, jaywalked across Bryant Street to Boardman Place.

Eddie said, "Well, it's got me, too. Detective work. I didn't want to be just another microchip in the Silicon Valley game, so I started researching stuff by computer for other

Cal-Tech students. After graduation we came up here and I kept going and all of a sudden I was making a living at it. Only my clients weren't students any more—darn little pure research. They turned out to be mostly P.I.'s hired by attorneys to check out jurors, witnesses in court cases, even the lawyers' own clients.''

They went down Boardman past storefront bailbondsmen to a *taqueria* with a big sign above it, ABIERTO 24 HORAS. Inside the narrow crowded room a jukebox played Mexican music filled with sad horns. A brown chunky Aztec-looking waitress brought Tecates instead of menus to their table; they ordered the special with the carelessness of long familiarity. The room smelled of hot oil and frying tortilla chips and red pepper and salsa spices.

"But," persisted Solomon, "if you could do it faster and cheaper with the computer than they could in the field, why—"

"I got my own P.I. license to cut out the middleman—it was just good business. But then I found out fieldwork is fun, too. The computer is still the core of my operation, but it can't ask just the right question at just the right moment. Of course once I get an answer, I use my laptop to interface through the car phone with the data base in my big computer at home.''

The waitress returned with huge platters of enchiladas, tacos, burritos, *refritos y arroz*, salad to go with their second beers. Randy jabbed a forkful of beans in Eddie's direction.

"So, Sherlock, what's your move now on Grimes? More 'fun'? Ring some doorbells? Go sit in your car across the street from the yacht basin with a magnifying glass and a deerstalker hat?''

"Right now, nothing—I've got other cases need work. Eventually, start massaging the data bases—*somebody* had him killed, there have to be tracks the computer can pick up.''

"You slip in that assumption about somebody having Grimes offed just so damn neat. But it was a gas leak got him.''

Eddie shook his head. "Professional hit.''

"You think the arson investigators screwed up?'' demanded Randy scornfully. "The explosion was in the engine compartment, right where you'd expect it to be. Forensics, fire department, insurance company—everybody says accident except Eddie Dain."

"Did they run a probabilities program on that particular make, model, and year of Chris-Craft to see how hull shape and engine-compartment size would affect a gas-leak explosion?"

"Why in hell should they, when everything points to—"

"I did—I developed the software program for it myself." Eddie waved a bulging bean burrito around under Randy's nose. "Flash point was seven-tenths of a meter from where it should have been for gas fumes, and a couple of intensity probability screenings I ran suggested C-4 *plastique*. Which means—"

Randy silenced him with an impatient paw.

"Wait a minute, Sherlock. If it *was* a hit, why pro? Why not gifted amateur?"

"Because all you professional law enforcement guys buy into it as an accident. I figure only a pro could fool everybody except the computer. After we get back from Point Reyes, Marie and I will work the data to find those footprints, then—"

"You ever think that if you're right it might be dangerous? If somebody *is* out there, and you start getting close to him—"

"I'll call a cop," said Eddie.

And he laughed and took a big bite of burrito, and, cool dude that he was, squirted brick-colored pinto beans and red sauce all down the front of his crisp white cotton shirt.

2

When Eddie crossed the Golden Gate to their modest two-bedroom bungalow in Marin's Tamalpais Valley, he found the household in an uproar. Or at least found three-year-old Albie (christened Albert, in honor of Einstein) in an uproar. Marie was her usual placid self.

"A kitten," she explained.

Marie was Eddie's age and tall; barefoot, only four inches shorter than his six-one and as limber as he, with the supple, beautiful body produced in certain women by intense devotion to yoga. Her taffy-colored hair was worn long and straight down her back in defiance of current fashions, her very clear hazel eyes were too large and wide-set under stern brows for absolute beauty—but she also had the soft rounded cheeks and rosebud mouth of a fairy-tale princess.

"Kitten?" Eddie looked around the narrow kitchen as he stripped off his burrito-stained shirt. Albie was hanging on his pantleg telling him about it also. "I don't see any kitten."

"It shall return," she said with placid resignation.

"How do you know, if—"

"Albie knows."

He believed her. Marie was a very sensual being, in touch with her body and the bodies of those she loved. In bed they made each other come so hard and so often that he sometimes thought there must be something to her reincarnation musings: it seemed that a love this rewarding spiritually and this intense physically just *had* to extend back through several lifetimes.

But now, Wisking the burrito stain before putting the shirt into the hamper, he said, "If the kitten does show up again, we just can't keep it. You know that, don't you, darling?"

"I know."

"If it's a stray, it'll be dirty and diseased—"

"I know."

"Then we'll just have to explain to Albie that—"

"I know." Then she kissed him, a long kiss that made him want to get Albie to bed early. She stepped back and patted the front of his pants and made a silent whistle, and laughed, "Tell you what, big guy. *You* explain to Albie why he can't have that kitten, and I'll give you something nice later."

"You cheat!" exclaimed Eddie with feeling.

But after supper, he and his son sat out on the redwood deck he'd built the year before, at the same time that he'd built an eight-foot-high wall between the driveway and the garage they'd converted to an office. The wall had a door that was locked, so Albie could play in the backyard while Marie worked at the computer and kept an eye on him through the office window.

The deck was low, ideal for sitting on the edge with your feet in the grass. Albie sat in rapt attention beside him, staring solemnly up into his face, swinging stubby legs as Eddie explained why they couldn't keep the kitten.

"Even if he does come back, he probably belongs to someone who'll want him to come home to them."

"He's black and white," observed Albie.

"Or his mother was a cat gone wild. In that case he'll be a feral cat himself and won't want to live with us because—"

"His whiskers are white." Albie held out demonstrative hands a foot apart. "Real long."

"That's long," admitted Eddie. He shook his head in admiration. "But wild kittens have all sorts of diseases—"

"Mommy says he's a puss-in-boots kitten. Black legs, white feet." Then he added, in case Eddie was as dense about books as he was about kittens, "Like in the fairy tale."

"Even a puss-in-boots sort of kitten would be . . ."

He trailed off because his son had jumped off the deck and was running on stubby bowed legs over to the wall. Thrust through the two-inch gap left under the fence for rainy-season runoff, a tiny delicate upside-down black arm with a white paw was making what looked like beckoning gestures.

"It's him!" cried Albie. He squatted and patted at the paw with one hand. The tiny paw convulsed about his finger, held on without claws. The kitten started to mew. Piteously.

"Open the door, Daddy!" cried Eddie's son. Piteously.

If he opened the door, Daddy knew, all was lost. If he didn't open the door, Daddy knew, all was lost. So macho Daddy said forcefully, "But it has to stay in the kitchen until we can housebreak it. And it goes to the vet's tomorrow and . . ."

Marie stood in the darkened kitchen, watching her husband cave in to her son about their new kitten and chuckling deep in her throat. So even though they had to make up a box with an old towel in it for the kitten to sleep on, and feed it, and of course hold it, when they did get to bed she gave Eddie something just as nice as she'd promised. More than nice and more than once, in fact, and then told him she loved him because he was a kitten freak in public while being a tiger in bed.

The kitten was little and skinny and black and white and full of fleas and scabs and rickety from lack of food, so for two weeks it was touch-and-go. It could keep down milk but then immediately had diarrhea, every time. Dysentery, dis-

temper, a massive flea allergy, eye infections . . . All plans
were put on hold pending its survival or the sad eventuality
of its death.

Ten days later the dysentery was gone. The distemper was
cured. Its eyes cleared up. It strode instead of wobbled. It
meowed! instead of mewed. Suddenly it was a delicate de-
mented huge-eyed black and white furball tumbling around
the house.

The day they knew it would survive, they named it Shenzie. Shenzie was a Swahili word Eddie had got from Randy
Solomon, meaning crazy—but crazy in a goofy, nutty, odd-
ball, wonderful sort of way that fit the kitten perfectly.

His survival ensured, Shenzie would watch by the hour
when they played chess, sitting on the edge of the coffee
table where the board was permanently set up, his skinny
black tail, white-tipped, loosely curled down around a table
leg.

"Think he's trying to learn chess?" asked Eddie.

"He's studying the way it works," said Marie firmly.
"He wants hands instead of paws. He wants to be an engineer."

Shenzie was Albie's cat, of course, but on nights when
Eddie was out in the field on his backlogged cases, and
Albie was asleep, he would lie below the screen on the computer box while Marie worked, and go to sleep—purring. If
she was reading, he would climb up on her chest and go to
sleep—purring.

"He never does that with me," said Eddie darkly. "Except for Albie, you're the only person in the world he trusts
enough to sleep on."

"We can take him to Point Reyes!" crowed Albie.

But this time Eddie was firm. "No we can't," he said
sadly. "It might be a little too tough on him—he's still
pretty shaky. Or he might get lost in the woods so we couldn't
find him again. You wouldn't want that, would you, Tiger?"

"Well, no, but . . ."

"Or get all wet in the ocean and maybe get pneumonia?"

"No, but . . ."

"Uncle Randy's going to take care of him while we're

gone," said Marie with comfortable finality. "That way, you'll have him to come home to."

"Okay," said Albie in charming capitulation. He kissed Shenzie on the nose and put him into the cat carrying case, a plastic one with holes, through one of which Shenzie's black and white paw immediately came out to begin groping about. That patented paw-grope was one of his best tricks to date.

While his wife still had been tossing her paycheck into the pot, Randy Solomon had scraped up the down on a tall skinny Victorian on Buchanan just above Fell. Even after his wife left him (cops' divorce statistics are horrendous), he managed to hang on to it and even get it painted and fixed up outside and in.

Eddie climbed the exterior front stairs and rang the old-fashioned doorbell. He was carrying Shenzie in the plastic cat case. Randy opened the door and stepped back so Eddie could enter by him.

"The famous Shenzie, huh?" He'd been hearing a lot about the kitten on the handball courts during the past two weeks.

"Himself," said Eddie, as he put the carry case on the couch and started to open it.

The living room was beautifully furnished in an African motif. An elongated ebony head four feet tall, carved by the Pare in Tanzania, dominated one corner; across from it was a 'Kamba drum made of stretched zebra hide, the cords that kept it taut made from thin rolled strips of antelope hide. Graceful cranes carved from Masai cattle horns stood on top of the TV cable box; there were Kisii stools carved from rounds of tree trunk with tiny bright beads pounded into the soft wood in intricate patterns. On a clear wall was a long Kalenjin spear and a handmade knife in a red hide scabbard.

Eddie gazed around, impressed as he always was, while getting the carry case open. Delicate puss-in-boots Shenzie leaped out with a pissed-off *meow!* Randy shook the windows with his laughter and, quick as a synapse, scooped the tiny furball up in his arms to cradle it upside down against his chest.

"Shenzie, my man, we gonna cook you for supper!" But Shenzie, knowing a soft touch when he felt one, merely purred. Randy laughed again and stooped to set him right side up on the floor, asking Eddie, "Got time for a beer?"

"Marie and Albie are down in the car."

Shenzie was twining himself back and forth around Solomon's ankles. Randy laughed again.

"Guess me an' old Shenz'll get along just fine."

"Thanks for taking him, Randy—I mean it. I've written out the direction to the place at Point Reyes if you think you can get away for a weekend—"

Solomon snorted as he crumpled up the directions. "Listen, the way people are killin' each other off in this city, I ain't gonna get any time off. An' if I did, I'd spend it chasin' gash rather than snipe or some damn thing at the seashore . . ."

He started walking Eddie to the door, then stopped, suddenly serious.

"Truth be told, Sherlock, I'm worried about this case of yours. You've sorta halfway convinced me that maybe somebody did make old Grimes's boat blow up. If you're right, we're talking murder for hire here."

"I sincerely hope so," grinned Eddie.

"Ain't funny, Hoss. If—"

"If I turn up a hitman where you guys and the underwriters and the fire department thought there was just an accident, I'll be the hottest eye in town."

"Or the deadest. You'd best remember what a hitman does for a living."

"He won't even know I'm there," grinned Eddie.

"Aw, hell, you're impossible." Randy laughed and stuck out a big paw for Eddie to shake. "Just don't make any moves while you're at Point Reyes, okay? Wait until—"

"We're not even taking the laptop. Total downtime. But when we get back—watch out!" He started out, then turned back again. Shenzie was atop the TV, sniffing one of the horn birds with brow-furrowed suspicion. "Anyway, Randy, hitmen aren't supermen—just guys with strange ideas about a fun time."

Randy stood in the open doorway at the head of the stairs with a worried look on his face, watching Eddie bound back down to his car with the bike rack and two mountain bikes on the roof. He waved at Marie through the window, she waved back. He could see little Albie in his car seat in the rear.

He sighed and went back into the house. Shenzie was waiting to ambush his ankle. "Hey, crazy cat!" he exclaimed. "You're bitin' the foot gonna kick you you keep it up!"

Shenzie didn't care. Eyes bugged out and wild, flopped on his thin black side, he sought to disembowel the side of Randy's size 13 leather shoe with pumping back feet while holding onto the highly shined and therefore slippery toe with his front feet.

By definition Shenzie was, after all, nuts.

But Randy loved it. He laughed so hard he almost fell on the floor. He dug the little mulatto dude. Mulatto—black and white. Get it?

Maybe he'd get himself a cat like this Shenzie one of these days. They sure were a lot more fun than he'd expected. Since his wife had left he hadn't been having a whole lot of fun. Just working, fucking when he could, with maybe a little moonlighting thrown in on the weekends for some extra cash.

3

Life in the rustic cabin at Point Reyes quickly fell into wondrous routine. Wake up spooned together for warmth in the old-fashioned double bed, whisper lazily until curious hands and mouths found familiar pleasure points, then the rising arc of passion until they fell back panting to the sounds of Albie stirring on his little bed in the next room.

No phones to answer. No computers to work. No friends to visit. No television to watch. Just books to read. Incredible salt marshes to tramp through. Sometimes at dusk as the fog rolled in, a driftwood fire on the beach in the lee of a washed-up log, trying to identify night noises out of the darkness.

"I think it's a . . . big bird!" Albie might exclaim.

"Tree frog," Marie, raised on a ranch in the California coastal zone, would say with great authority. She would hold finger and thumb half an inch apart. "About that long."

"But it makes a bigger sound than that!"

Once they heard a dog bark, but Marie said it was a fox—

a gray, you didn't find reds down by the ocean. Next morning, Eddie, up before dawn, saw the animal's tracks: dainty little pawprints hardly larger than those Shenzie might make. Fox.

Other nights, Albie asleep and the wind sighing in the trees behind the house, they would yawn over the chessboard until finally falling into bed themselves. Only to feel fatigue drop magically away for velvet moments in the dark of the night, soft cries of completion that never woke their son.

Perfect vacation days, with Marie's birthday the most perfect of all. It dawned clear and warm and bright, without a wisp of fog, and Eddie bare-legged in front of the open fridge calling out items for the grocery list.

"I think we should have steak tonight in honor of the occasion. And baked potatoes—"

"No oven."

"Okay, write down aluminum foil for the potatoes so we can stick 'em in the coals. And corn on the cob if that little grocery store is up to it—"

"And whatever crucifer they have fresh there."

Eddie turned to his son, who was waiting for the piggy-back bicycle ride to the store. "Eat your broccoli, dear," he said.

"I say it's spinach and I say to hell with it," said Marie like the little boy in the old *New Yorker* cartoon. They laughed, and Albie crowed; though he didn't understand it, he loved that one for some reason, almost as much as he disliked crucifers.

Eddie shouldered him and his outsized crash helmet, almost as big as he was, for the four-mile wobbly ride to the little corner store. And told Albie that he had only one year left.

"Year for what?" the boy asked the top of Eddie's head.

"Before you compose your first symphony. That's what Mozart did when he was four."

Albie thought about it. Not knowing what a symphony was, he finally said, "I'll wait."

When Eddie got back, Albie still on his shoulders and the food in saddlebags over the rear wheel, they all went exploring through the salt marsh to the beach. The narrow trail led down into a big area of pickleweed, a lanky plant whose woody segments held water the way ice plants do.

A shadow shot across them, making both Marie and Eddie duck. It struck the ground thirty feet away with a thump, extended claws first, then flapped up again with a tiny rodent wriggling in its talons. It was a foot-long handsome bird with hooked beak and heavily barred tail.

"Daddy! Look!"

"We see, Albie. It's a . . ." He turned to Marie.

"Harrier hawk," she said. "With a harvest mouse."

"He gonna kill the mouse?" demanded Albie.

"I'm afraid that's what he does for a living," Marie said regretfully.

Further in, the pickleweed was replaced by bright orange splotches of parasitic dodder and stiff triangle-leaved saltbush. Marie broke off a stem so they could bite it and taste the salt.

"Could the hawk kill me?" said Albie suddenly.

"Not a chance, Tiger, you're too big for him," said Eddie. "In fact, there's nobody around big enough to kill you."

"That's okay, then," said Albie.

There had been heavy surf the night before, so out on the beach they found great washed-up strands of kelp, its strange broad indented streamers looking as if they had been stamped out of green tin. The thirty-foot stalks, as big as a wrist, had heads like bulls' testicles. All smelling of salt and the sea and not unpleasantly of the deaths of the tiny marine creatures clinging to it when the giant seaweed had been washed ashore.

Looking at the shredded, ragged leaves, Eddie was reminded of one of Marie's favorite poems.

" 'Soul clap its hands and sing, and louder sing,' " he quoted, " 'For every tatter in its mortal dress . . .' "

"Except these tatters are on purpose," she said. "They split under the force of the waves so the holdfasts won't be pulled off the rocks down below. But these were anyway."

Eddie put his arms around her. "Let's always hold fast," he said to her in sudden inexplicable fierceness.

She laughed up at him. "Okay, big boy—forever."

"That's okay, then," he grinned, in imitation of Albie talking about the assassin hawk's activities.

Soaked in Bullfrog-36 to counteract depleted ozone, they sunbathed on a tiny wedge of sand available only at low tide, with occasional forays into the frigid surf. Albie wanted to be carried in each time also, game to their last icy dash back out of the water shrieking with frozen laughter.

Wrapped in towels, they watched a flock of sandpipers run seaward at the foot of each retreating wave, run back up at the lip of each advancing wave, moving almost in close-order drill as they pattered about stabbing sharp slightly up-curved bills into the sand for tiny living things.

Finally, they ate sandwiches and drank hot tea from a thermos, were waked from their nap by raucous western gulls squabbling with two crows over a dead striped bass without any eyes. Sun-dried and salt-crusty, they explored a tidal pool in slanting late-afternoon sunshine, moving down to it gingerly through the so-called black zone caused by lichens and blue-green algae. The gelatinous coat that kept the algae moist between their twice-monthly spring tide soakings made for treacherous footing.

Albie was in his glory here, being a touchie-feelie sort of guy, totally unsqueamish, as usual finding the tidal pools the high point of his day along the water.

"Mommy, what's this?"

He was squatting on the algae, holding up a tiny, spiral-shelled creature for Marie's inspection. He had long since learned that Eddie was next to useless in identifying either living or dead things on the beach.

"That's a periwinkle snail," she told him. She squatted beside him. "They eat the algae by scraping it off the rocks." She turned the shell over, pointed. "See? Rows of teeth."

"*Lots* of rows of teeth," said Albie solemnly.

"Thousands of them," agreed Marie. "When the rocks wear the teeth down, the snail just rolls up a new set, sort of like the teeth are on a conveyer belt."

The barnacle zone was mostly acorn barnacles, their close-packed flinty white cones making the rocks also look white.

"But when a barnacle dies his shell gets taken over by periwinkles, or little bitty shrimp, or limpets . . ."

Back at the cabin at dusk, Eddie put briquets on the hibachi and grilled the steaks while foil-wrapped potatoes baked in the coals and sweet corn roasted in its own husks. To Albie's delight, no crucifers. But there was ice cream and a chocolate Sara Lee with a single candle in it, and the cards and little presents they had picked out for Marie.

Finally, plates scraped and washed and leftovers in the fridge, Eddie started the fire laid in the stone fireplace. Albie was suddenly asleep, tipped over on his side. Marie carried his small sleeping form into his bedroom as Eddie went outside to bury the garbage in the mulch heap. Tree frogs trilled, branches rustled, something of consequence moved through the brush flanking the sandy track leading in from the main road.

He looked back at the cabin under the cold pale blue light of a waning moon. Smoke swirled from the chimney with the night breeze. Light shone from the windows. He shivered, somehow felt lonely even though everyone he truly valued— except for Shenzie—was just inside.

Watchman, what of the night?

He went back into the cabin, hungry for Marie. She held out fisted hands with chess pieces hidden in them.

"Left," said Eddie.

She opened her hand. "You get black."

"Black's good. I can do black." He sat down at the table and offered her a shameless bribe. "If I win you get your *real* birthday present."

She gave him a bawdy grin. "And if you lose?"

He brought out the book, beautifully wrapped by Doug Sherman, and laid it on the table beside the board.

"You get your *real* birthday present."

"Ah-hah! Win-win for Marie!"

But when she sat down at the board, her face lovely in the flickering firelight, she was concentrating too hard on her usual pawn first move, and spoke too casually without looking up.

"You know, honey, maybe Randy's right." When he didn't immediately react, she sought his eyes. "Maybe you're treating the Grimes thing a little too much like just a game.''

''You know that all investigations *are* just a game, sweetie—move, countermove, just like chess.''

''But what if it isn't just a game to somebody else?''

''You and Randy.'' He shook his head in mock despair.

''You didn't see Randy's face when we left. I did. He's worried, Eddie. Really worried.''

He reached across the chessboard for her hand. ''Okay, when we get back I'll just Close and Bill on Grimes, and forget him. Like Randy says, I was only hired in the first place to find out if he was skimming or not.''

Her eyes glowed at him. She squeezed his hand. He grinned at her and picked up the wrapped package and gave it to her.

''Now that's out of the way . . .''

The somber moment had passed. Marie always opened presents in the same way, starting sedately as if to save the wrappings, then suddenly losing control and turning into Albie, ripping the paper to tatters no matter how beautiful it might be.

> *An aged man is but a paltry thing,*
> *A tattered coat upon a stick . . .*

She went still, staring at the leather-bound *Tibetan Book of the Dead*. She turned it over and over, her eyes huge stars.

''Oh my God, Eddie,'' she whispered, ''it's Alexandra Neel's own copy! Oh my God! It's the most beautiful . . . I don't . . .''

She stood, eyes brimming, opening her arms to embrace him.

The cabin door crashed back against the wall. Two bulky men, silhouetted by moonlight, charged in with sawed-off shotguns in their hands, heavy boots grating on the bare planks. Silver ring glinting on a finger. One, sunglasses, sandy hair. The other, ski mask.

Eddie leaped up against the sudden sticky molasses slowness of terror as his conscious mind cried, No no no, stop, it's just a game, I don't need to keep on with the investi—

He heard the roar even though he didn't feel the shot pattern shred his shoulder, and rip his chest, and pop blood out of the side of his neck, and burst his cheek so his teeth were bared all the way back to the jaw hinge.

He crashed down, upsetting the table, as the shotgun belched yellow flame to smash Marie back and up, her mouth strained impossibly wide, her eyes wild, her hair an underwater slow-motion swirl, the black hole between her breasts blossoming red, her feet coming up off the floor with the force of her death. Her face thudded down a yard from his, her utterly dead eyes staring into his with inanimate patience.

Through cotton, Albie's voice came faintly up the hall.

"Mommy! Mommy!" With terror in it.

No, Albie had never known terror. Mustn't know terror. Eddie began a crabwise scrabble toward the voice. He couldn't raise his head, so he could see only Albie's stubby legs appear in the doorway, hesitate as he surveyed the room.

A question this time. "Mommy?"

"*Run*, Albie, *ru*—"

The second shooter blasted Albie's legs back down the hall out of sight. No blood, no pellets striking flesh. Just the legs disappearing as the door frame was splintered and pocked and ripped by the edges of the shot pattern.

A voice croaked despairingly, "I wasn't ready . . . Oh Christ . . . I wasn't ready . . ."

The first shooter fired again, almost casually. The twin charges of buckshot swept Eddie's body back against the legs of the table like a surge of floodwater. A widening red pool spread beneath his chest. His groping hand closed around *The Tibetan Book of the Dead* knocked from the table, held it.

His view was narrowing and darkening. His ears were failing. The voices were through steel wool.

"They . . . They all . . . dead?" Second shooter.

First shooter. "Yeah. We'll check if he has any notes here, a computer . . . then we'll burn the place down . . ."

Darkness. Silence.

Silence. Darkness.
I wasn't ready . . . Oh Christ . . . I wasn't ready . . .

Not a voice. A thought. A bed. Harsh antiseptic smell. *Shush-shush* of rubber-soled shoes in the corridor outside.

He knew he was in a hospital. He just didn't know why.

But then voices. Real voices.

"Goddammit, when *can* I see him? Every hour—"

"Every hour he lives is a miracle, the blood he's lost, the mess they made of him. He's alive only because a neighbor saw the flames and dragged him out before the place collapsed. Right now he won't remember anything anyway, Inspector. Why don't you let it go? Leave him alone."

"How about I just see him as a friend?"

Sounds. Movement. The voices were stereophonic now because they were on either side of his bed.

"Will he ever remember any of it, Doc?"

"This much massive trauma, who knows? He should be dead, he may be paralyzed . . . Physical survival is fifty-fifty at best, who can tell about memory?"

"Fifty-fifty? Was me, I'd make it," said Randy's voice thoughtfully. "I'd have too much to live for to check out yet."

"In his condition, what could he possibly have to—"

"Death, Doc." A pause, then Randy's voice added, softly, "Was me, I'd be plannin' a whole lotta other people's deaths."

Hearing that, knowing it to be true, Eddie died.

Leaving only Dain to live on.

Not that Eddie Dain knew any of this. The only thing functioning was his ancient lizard brain, nestled down there at the base of the cortex. Hunger, fear, survival—those were what the lizard brain knew about. And only one of those, survival, meant anything just then. If the organism could survive, the rest of what it needed would follow.

Because now some part of Dain had something to live for.

A whole lotta other people's deaths.

II

DAIN

The Windy City

THE SECONDARY CLEAR LIGHT
SEEN IMMEDIATELY AFTER DEATH

O thou of noble-birth, meditate upon thine own tutelary deity as if he were the reflection of the moon in water, apparent yet inexistent in itself. Meditate upon him as if he were a being with a physical body.

THE TIBETAN BOOK OF THE DEAD

4

Weight, 100 pounds. For two years, pain.

Constant. Low and throbbing, like drums. Or high and shrill, like red-hot irons laid lovingly against his flesh by medicine's benevolent sadism.

Start with the bones. Pins here, steel rods there.

Then, muscles and tendons. Slow, careful reconstructions.

Finally, the flesh. Operate, wait for the scar tissue to heal, operate again.

Now, the physical therapy. Move this finger. Wiggle that toe. Wonderful! Can you move that arm? Can that leg support . . .

No no, that's fine. Falling down is part of the therapy. One, two, three, four, rest. Let the pulse slow . . . One, two . . .

Two years. Weight, back up to his original 140.

5

For the year after that, Las Vegas. At first he'd thought Phoenix, Santa Fe—just so it was desert. He thought he ended up in Vegas only because more buses went there. Hot sun, dry air, burn out the pain that, often, had him sitting on the edge of the bathtub with a razor blade against the inside of his wrist.

Not just the physical pain, though that was bad enough.

two bulky men charged in with sawed-off shotguns

Fragments of nightmare.

the shotgun belched yellow flame to smash Marie back and up

Razor blade. A couple of swipes against the wrists, and . . .

Albie's legs disappeared as the door frame splintered

But—these were not nightmares. These were memories sent to him by God. The half-formed idea of doing something about their deaths started small, grew with the nightmares.

To do what you ought to do, you had to survive. So he started getting up before dawn each morning to walk along the road out into the desert. Half a mile, out and back. A mile. After a while, that led to trotting. Two miles, four. Jogging was the next logical move, skin brown, legs and arms pumping, sweat rolling, three, five, eight, twelve miles a day.

Six months in, he found himself other disciplines. Health club. Boxing gym. Karate dojo.

Weight, 160.

Carrying a book to strengthen his hands—the heaviest he had was a leather-bound fire-singed copy of *The Tibetan Book of the Dead*. Clutched in his hand as he was dragged from the fire.

I wasn't ready . . . Oh Christ . . . I wasn't ready . . .

So, strengthening not just his hands, but also his resolve. Until on the last morning of that first Vegas year, three years after it had happened, he was physically ready. Maybe emotionally he was still screwed up, maybe he couldn't remember any of it without black swirling rage, but physically ready to . . .

To what? To find the people who had done it, of course. After that was still hazy, but . . .

Hey—find them how? How do you find two anonymous hitmen hired to kill you three years ago . . . *hired!*

Somebody had hired them! So simple, yet in three years he hadn't thought of it. Easier to find him than the hitters, because he *wasn't* anonymous. Had to have a connection with Grimes . . .

Also, had to be tied into organized crime. The Mob. Mr. Average Joe, no matter how pissed off, didn't know anyone could blow up a boat and make it look like an accident even to the experts. Didn't know shotgunners for hire who . . .

Then he realized why he had come to Vegas. The mob still ran it, no matter how many layers of cotton candy you laid over them. The old men who played golf, the young men who protected them with watchful, venal eyes. Just because he was there recuperating, for the past year Dain had been studying them. He'd learned the players, the rules, without knowing it. Had watched the watchers without being watched himself, because he hadn't known he was watching.

So maybe he was ready to start looking instead of watching.

Weight, 180.

His assets: he didn't care if he lived or died; he didn't care about legalities at this point in the game; he was a genius with a computer; he was physically ready. Maybe not emotionally, but at least he would be *doing* something about what had been done to him. Final asset, they didn't know who the hell he was.

Even as Eddie Dain, he'd just been a fly to be swatted, so with a new name, a Vegas name . . . Travis. Travis . . . Holt. That was good. No elaborate disguise needed, but why be careless? Nonprescription glasses, colored contacts, rinse-away hair coloring, a neat goatee and mustache.

To go with the new name, a rock-solid new life. His laptop massaged Travis Holt into other people's records. Gave him dead parents, schooling, a rather no-account brother named Jimmy, put him into the Las Vegas National Guard— this last a precaution just in case he had to disappear without making waves.

As Travis Holt he was just a guy looking for a casino that needed a bookkeeper for its legit books. Big guy, thirty, maybe thirty-two, close to 200 pounds, moved quick, didn't drink, smoke, gamble, chase broads. Or guys. When he wasn't at work he was out jogging or at a gym somewhere. Physical fitness freak. And could you believe, a computer nerd. Genuine, complete nerd. The connected P.I. who checked him out joked that he probably whacked off at night watching his reflection in his computer screen.

It took Travis Holt only six months to make himself indispensable to the casino that hired him. Creative ideas about bookkeeping. Always available for overtime. Always willing to fill in for vacations. And a real whiz with the numbers. Pretty soon they had to give him access to the sensitive files.

Dangerous to give him access? Shit, no, man. Checked

him out back to the cradle. Family gone except for one brother in Vero Beach, Florida, fucking commercial fisherman when he works, which isn't often. By the records a drinker, can't hold a job . . .

Anyway, Chrissake, Holt is showing us things about figures make the accountants shoot their load. Legit ways to move money around, lose it, find it, turn it into goods and services—by the time it comes back in from the Bahamas it's as clean as Tide Concentrate. And he knows he ever tries to get into files he isn't authorized for, he leaves tracks right back to his terminal and we pound him headfirst into the desert and light his feet.

Knows better than to fuck with us.

Of course he knew better, knew all about the buried codes that gave warnings when access was effected. But he didn't care. Once he was inside, his obsession deepened. Sometimes, alone at night in his office, trying to find the man who had ordered his family murdered, he thought he might be cracking up. And still didn't care. The search gave him focus, eased his nightmares.

As for that access the wise guys thought impossible, at Cal-Tech he had learned all about the back doors always left in computer systems. Had designed viruses that would take security checks out and put them back when he was done. At Cal-Tech he had built his own computer, designed his own computer language, created his own software, broken into half the federal security mainframes in D.C. just for the hell of it.

So latenights, weekends, overtime, his computer made love to the mob's, stuck its tongue down their system's throat, lapped up their data. The books behind the books, the offshore skim accounts, the secret sauna meetings to move millions . . . The feds would have killed to know what he knew, but he cared nothing about that. Let the feds make their own cases. All he sought was to name the nightmares that rode through his sleep.

the door crashed back against the wall, two bulky men charged in with sawed-off shotguns in their hands, heavy boots on bare planks . . .

Long after midnight, almost four years after it had happened, he found a name, buried deep in the belly of the beast, that meshed with all the givens of that June night.

Mario Pucci. Los Angeles.

Pucci's specialty was bringing in drugs from Mexico on other people's private powerboats. Like Ron Grimes's. In fact, he and Ron Grimes had been yacht club cronies, had played poker together. What more natural, Grimes bringing in drugs for him? But maybe a scare from the Coast Guard had made him panic, want out . . . or maybe he'd gotten greedy . . .

A phone call from Pucci, a specialist gets on a plane, Grimes's yacht blows up with Grimes on it. Accident. End of story. But unknown to Pucci, a private eye named Eddie Dain had been hired by Grimes's business partner fearful Grimes's black money was coming from their company accounts. The private eye confirmed that it wasn't—and then kept going on his own with his computer, like a kid with a new toy, thought it was all just a big fucking game, wouldn't quit poking around . . .

Dain saw himself reflected in the computer screen, panting, sweating as with fever. He'd read the joke in the P.I.'s report on Travis Holt, about him watching his reflection in the screen as he jerked off . . . Was that what he was doing here? Mentally masturbating into this goddamned machine?

He sure wasn't acting like a normal human.

Goddammit, he *wasn't* a normal human being. He was a man who had been blown to pieces and fit back together again like a jigsaw puzzle. A man whose wife and child had been blown to pieces with him, then burned up without the chance to be fitted back together. Anything he did was all right, was justified . . .

He eagerly punched more keys. But when the machine spoke again the fire went out of his eyes, his jaw went slack, he sank back in his chair shrunken in size and density.

Mario Pucci had died of a heart attack on top of his mistress in a fancy Beverly Hills hotel two years ago. Had left no records in anyone's computer of who he might have called to swat that bothersome fly at Point Reyes.

Dain settled slowly back in his chair. It was over. All finished. It all died with Pucci. He had nowhere else to look.

Nothing else to do. No more reason to go on living. By habit, he backtracked out of the maze, reset the bypassed traps, logged out of the legitimate files, closed down his computer just as if he were coming back. But he knew he was all finished.

Out in the desert the sun was just up. Empty, brilliant, still. Saguaro cacti, Joshua trees, rocks, sand. Cry of a distant hawk, dry moan of the wind. A good day to die. He left his car, ran at a steady pace out into the desert. He would run until he died, like the runner bringing news of the victory at Marathon. His was a defeat, but his death would be as good, as clean, in the desert. A Hemingway death: grace under pressure.

Finally, miles from the road, where tumbled rocks rose to a ridge shaded by a big Joshua, he indeed fell. Collapsed facedown on the sand. A minute, ten, twenty. But he didn't die, clean, in the desert. He didn't die at all. He just felt hot, sticky, tired, irritable. He rolled onto his back. Lay there, arms wide, chest heaving, staring up into the clear blue sky. High above, wings motionless, dwarfed by distance, a turkey buzzard rode the thermals, binocular eyes seeking dead meat.

What had he done? Trained too well? Forged a body and a will that knew no despair? But Mario Pucci, like the vulture's meal, was dead meat. Along with Pucci, Dain's planned revenge was also dead meat. Tears ran down the sides of his face to the sand at the thought of it.

Finally he sat up, forgotten arms still outstretched. Scrambled to his feet. Began dancing to some silent inner music. Faster and faster, like someone stoned, twisting, rhythmic, sensual. Improvising, sweat flying.

If he couldn't run himself to death, he would dance himself to death.

He whirled in a circle, fell, leaped up, face transfigured, carried outside himself. Any moment now he would fall down dead of heatstroke. He ran right up a nearly perpendicular rock face and did a perfect backflip, a graceful parabola to land backward in the sand and do a back roll to shoot straight up into the air like an arrow, come down crouched—and freeze.

Dry deadly rattle. Lying on an exposed rock in the new sun, a massive rattler five feet long, red-brown with pale diamond markings. Still just slightly sluggish, but already drawing into its coiled striking position, tail vibrating visibly, vertical pupil slits in pale yellow lidless eyes almost closed against the direct sunlight. Red diamond rattler. Enough venom in its fangs, desert old-timers said, to fell a bull.

He stared at it, motionless. Even better. Totally sure. Let the snake kill him.

"All right, goddam you, do it!" he cried.

The rattler hissed but was motionless.

He began to move again, once more slowly, oh so slowly, slowly around the rattler, challenging it. Any moment now . . .

The snake hissed and rattled warningly, but did not strike.

Dain sprang in and out like a boxer dancing in and out to jab an opponent in the ring. That was it, a game. Once he had been a great, a tremendous games player. At chess. With his computer. With Marie's and Albie's lives. Now the game was to piss off the snake, so the game would have the ending he sought.

Belatedly, the snake struck. But because the man was already moving away it missed, went out full length off the rock to thump down on the sand. Dain yelled again, eyes wild.

"Yes! Yes! Goddam you, do it!"

The snake, aroused, was striking repeatedly, as quickly as it could coil and release. But Dain was beyond rationality, into the game obsessively. Once the snake's fangs struck the sole of his shoe as he whirled with one leg extended. He was shouting with . . . what? Madness, perhaps.

He tried a pirouette, his foot slipped in the soft sand, he fell just as it struck again, fanging the air a foot above his descending head. It landed across him, he bucked and rolled, throwing off the bewildered rattler even as it tried to coil and strike again in midair.

Venom was dripping off its fangs, its timing was gone. Its strikes were slower. It was running down like a cobra fighting a mongoose. Which is what the mongoose waits for.

Here, now, this man was the mongoose, pure energy, the years of training in every discipline he could find coming together and paying off. He whirled about the rattler, reached in a lightning hand to give its smooth sleek hard body a tweak, leaping back and away in the same motion, too quick, the snake too exhausted, the inevitable coil and strike didn't come within four inches of him, *Dain was winning the game.*

The snake, overheated, finally lay stretched out on the hot sand. If it had been a pit bull it would have been lying on its belly and panting. The man stopped, hands on knees, head down, panting himself in huge gulping breaths. He had won!

Won? *No!* He had lost! He was supposed to die . . .

Then he realized that his canteen full of water was on his belt. If he had really planned to die in the desert, why had he strapped on the canteen? He took it off his belt, opened it. Poured sweet cool water over the snake, then over his own head, down his throat. After long moments, the rattler slid away between a creosote bush and its sunning rock and was gone.

Dain saluted it. He started walking back toward the distant car shimmering in the desert heat. Began to trot. To run. The dance with the snake had sweated out his madness. No longer Saul struck blind on the road to Damascus. The scales had fallen from his eyes and along with them, his blindness.

Pucci was dead, but of course the two men he had hired wouldn't be. And Pucci wouldn't have dealt with them directly anyway, he would have used a go-between.

Dain's excitement was growing, but he had to face certain realities. He'd treated what was serious as a game. He'd been a computer nerd who'd wanted to be Sam Spade. Marie and Albie were dead because he'd been a fool. Accept it, go on from there.

Accept also that, despite his new designer body, down deep he was still just Eddie Dain. With that shell of muscle and reflex around the old core, he'd thought he'd be the Terminator. But he was Eddie Dain, and Eddie Dain couldn't do it.

Unless he could make other people *think* he was as hard, as impervious as he looked. Then, perhaps . . .

Making a game of life had gotten Marie and Albie killed, but how about making a game of death? He had been a private investigator of sorts when it had happened; now he had to make the mob think he was the greatest eye at finding people who had ever lived. He was smart and he was superb with the computer: he would learn how to find people nobody else could.

For the mob. His months with organized crime had shown him they'd become company men like everyone else. Easy for him to create an aura, a mystique, make himself the man the mob came to when nobody else could find who they were looking for. He'd need a go-between of his own, heighten that air of mystery that would move him through the underbelly until, someday, somewhere, he would run into three special men.

Would he know them if he did? Would they know him? He didn't know, didn't care; but he knew he wouldn't find them here.

So first he had to get away from Vegas clean.

A week later, orders came for Travis Holt to report to the National Guard's 72nd Military Police Company for two weeks' "summer camp," as the annual training is called. Holt dutifully took the order to his boss in casino bookkeeping; the 72nd had fought in the Gulf War, guarding Iraqi prisoners, so it was a popular outfit in Vegas. Permission was readily given for him to take his training without losing his accumulated vacation time.

Ten days after training was done, while the casino thought Holt was on vacation, a hand-scrawled letter from his brother Jimmy in Vero Beach informed the casino that Travis Holt had been killed in a training accident during the 72nd's summer desert exercises. Was any back pay due? Send it to his bereaved brother if there was.

Holt fortunately had passed his ideas along to the beancounters, so his death was no real hardship to the casino. A letter went to the asshole brother assuring him that no back pay was due, and the casino, shaking its collective head over slimeball relatives, closed the personnel file on Holt.

Who worried about dead men?

But even before he had died, Travis Holt had broken his tinted glasses, flushed his colored contacts, shampooed the dye out of his hair, shaved his mustache and goatee, and had left Vegas to become Dain. Yes, Dain.

Because he had realized that the only three men alive who knew a contract had once gone out on Eddie Dain were the same three men he wanted to find. If they found him first, that was fine. Just so he had a chance to meet them—and had a chance to see if he could play the Terminator for real.

6

The game started, as the best games always do, with playacting. Dain wanted Doug Sherman to be his go-be-tween, because Sherman loved gossip, loved intrigue, ached to be in the know, *au courant*. Loved playing a role himself, loved games, could be bitchy, was excited by power, by domination; being a go-between would push all his buttons at once.

But Dain would have to con him into it, because he could never be told that Dain's ultimate game was the killing game, not just getting back into the detective game. Dain had to make him *want* to be a go-between so he would never think to ask the questions Dain couldn't answer.

When Doug Sherman arrived to open the bookstore that June morning, a big quick stranger was waiting for him. Six-one, 210, 215, burned dark by desert suns, hands thick and knuckly from breaking boards. An Indian face, craggy and strong-boned.

The stranger said, "Hello, Douglas," in a voice Sherman almost knew. The voice was deeper than the remembered one, and there was no playfulness in it.

Sherman, elegant as ever, was caught up short. He stared. "I beg your pardon?"

"Dain," the man said. Flat voice, flat eyes. Something dead in them, also something intensely alive.

"Eddie Dain! My God, man . . ."

Sherman tried to embrace him, but Dain stepped quickly back out of his arms, callused hand extended to shake instead. It was like grasping a rock.

"It's . . . good to see you . . ." said Sherman lamely.

Dain nodded but didn't respond. Sherman kept busy unlocking the door and deactivating the alarms while casting covert sidelong glances at Dain. Keeping up a running chatter to cover his embarrassment and his scrutiny.

"Where have you been? After you checked out of Marin General I couldn't find any trace . . ." The door was open. Dain walked through it ahead of him, a leather-bound book under one arm. Sherman caught himself stammering inanely, "I . . . I'm sorry, I . . . didn't . . ." He went around behind his desk. "I'll make coffee . . ."

"Coffee would be fine."

Sherman busied himself with the Melitta, talking over his shoulder as he measured out fragrant ground beans into the paper cone, covertly watching Dain's reflection off a glass-protected Greek icon of St. Nicholas above the table.

"What's the book?"

"Ever the dealer," that deeper voice rumbled. Dain almost smiled. Held it up to see. "*The Tibetan Book of the Dead.*"

"The same one that I got you for Marie's—"

"The very same," said Dain without apparent emotion. He lifted a shoulder. Muscles slid beneath his smooth hide like the muscles of a tiger. "Physical therapy. You carry a heavy book around all day, it strengthens your hands and forearms." He chuckled. "So you'll be ready."

Sherman had recovered. "Ready." He nodded as if he

understood what it meant, added, "Of course. Ah . . . and so, these past four years . . . where have you . . . ?"

Dain put his leather-bound book down on the edge of the desk and sat down in the same chair he had habitually sat in four years earlier, but there was no unconscious lotus pose this time. He still looked flexible enough to do one, but now he was solid, hard. Prepared. Power seemed to come off him like heat.

But he only said, conventionally, "Hospitals, mostly."

The water was heating. Sherman sat down behind the desk which had, as always, the inlaid chessboard with a classic problem laid out on it. For the first time, Sherman's sad, beautiful eyes studied Dain quite openly.

"And?"

"And nothing." Dain almost shrugged. His smile was very slightly lopsided from the tiny white plastic surgery scars on one side of his face. "Lots of operations, lots of pain, lots of physical therapy. All of which cost a great deal of money."

Money. Familiar ground here. Doug Sherman knew all about using money to control situations. And he wanted to control this one. This Edgar Dain made him feel defensive, uneasy, perhaps a little frightened. Talking to him was like stroking a tiger.

"I can imagine. If there's anything I can . . ."

"There is."

A statement so bald startled the aesthete in Sherman. He felt almost embarrassed for Dain; such a blatant pitch for charity diminished the man's power. The kettle started to sing. He poured boiling water to the top of the paper cone.

"Listen, Dain, I don't have a great deal put by, but . . ."

"Not money." Dain stood up, started to pace. It was the impatient padding of a tiger about its cell. "Business."

Intriguing. "I'm in the book business." He suddenly thought he knew where this was going. Needed money, too proud to ask. He gestured toward the book. "That would be worth a good deal of money . . . and it must be painful psychologically to . . ."

"It's not for sale."

Sherman sighed, nonplussed. "A pity. But then, what
. . . ?"

"I'm going back into private investigations." Dain
paused, staring at a new painting in one of the alcoves. A
Magritte original, he was sure. He shivered slightly, picked
up his thread again. "For . . . unconventional clients. I know
of no other way to make the kind of money I need relatively
quickly." He looked over at Sherman. "I need a front man.
A go-between."

"I don't think I understand."

"Sure you do. I want heavy-money clients on the shady
side who will pay a lot to find someone they need found
without questions asked. I don't want anyone else as clients.
So I need a cutout, a go-between to screen out the un-
wanted."

"But how can you . . . I mean, four years ago you
were . . ."

"Naive? Inexperienced?"

"Bluntly . . . yes." He poured coffee into two exquisite
Meissen china cups, set out cream and sugar in solid silver
bowls. "Why would anyone in that . . . underbelly sector of
the . . . um, American experience, say, want to hire you?"

"You're right. I was a fool. I wasn't ready. But that won't
happen again." Dain had stopped pacing. His face, voice,
eyes, had lost their impassivity; there was an almost guttural
intensity to his words. "Now I know how to create the sort
of reputation I want. Trust me on that. With a screen, a filter,
I can say no easily. That's all I need from you."

He sat down with that looseness of muscle that typifies all
big predators off duty. Both men sipped their coffee. They
exchanged pleased looks over its quality.

Four years ago Sherman would have laughed in his face if
Eddie Dain had come to him with such a proposition. But
not now. Now he couldn't even think of him as Eddie any
more. He spread his hands in deprecation.

"Even if everything you say is true, why do you think I'm
the man for this sort of thing?"

"You were born for it. Everybody knows you, you know
everybody, you love to gossip, you love intrigue. And I can
trust your judgment. Maybe I even can trust you."

"I'm flattered by your confidence," said Sherman coldly.

Dain ignored his pique. "If a recovery of some sort is involved—skim money, stolen narcotics, whatever—my fee will be ten percent of recovery against a twenty-five K floor. That's sixty-two hundred fifty minimum per case for you—tax-free."

"Do you really think you can . . ." Sherman paused. He rubbed his eyes. He fidgeted. The offer was actually intriguing, not for the money, but . . . but he didn't want to show he was interested. "The thing is . . ."

He fell silent in midsentence. He knew he was going to do it. Dain was right, it was the sort of offbeat situation he couldn't resist. To *know* all the dangers beforehand . . . to ride the tiger . . . Yes! Absolutely delicious . . .

"Well . . . against my better judgment . . ."

Dain didn't do any cartwheels. There was that cold center Sherman hadn't adjusted to yet. He merely picked up his book from the desk and stood up. Standing, he drained his cup.

"Wonderful coffee," he said.

"Another cup—"

He shook his head. His eyes sought the tall grandfather clock in a shadowy corner of the room. Something flickered momentarily in those eyes, then was gone. Some feeling that might have been described as deep purple had it been a color.

"I'm due at Homicide in fifteen minutes," he said.

Sherman was on his feet also. "*Deja vu.*"

Dain nodded. He stuck out his hand. Sherman took it. He was delighted with the way he had handled himself. He loved the image of himself at the edge of the precipice. He gestured at the chessboard.

"Did you notice this endgame problem? The thirteenth game of Fischer versus Spassky World Championship match at Reykjavik, nineteen seventy-two? Extraordinary encounter." He moved eagerly to the nine pieces left on the board. "Look here—"

Something flashed in Dain's eyes that drove Sherman back an involuntary step as if the tiger had suddenly crouched to spring. But Dain spoke in flat, almost disinterested tones.

"I don't play chess any more," he said mildly.

Sherman was silent, measuring him for a long moment, pushing it, relishing it. Riding the tiger! He nodded slightly.

"Of course," he said. "A pity."

So it had worked with Sherman, the tough-guy image behind which Eddie Dain could live and function. He felt uneasy to be using his friends this way; but the gamesman part of him was excited by his initial success. Sherman's lively imagination had done a lot of Dain's work for him, but Randy Solomon would be different. To enlist Randy's cooperation for information only the cops could provide, he had to project the same stainless-steel image using very different tactics.

Homicide had a new percolator. It made good coffee, so the trade from out-of-town departments had slacked off. And sure enough, according to the load of bullshit Lieutenant Randy Solomon was trying to sell a trio of Homicide dicks when Dain walked in, out in the boonies the bullets and switchblades now were finding their mark with disconcerting regularity.

Four sets of indifferent cops' eyes swept over Dain, making professional assessment without interest since no threat was perceived. Three sets turned away. One set remained fixed on him. Staring hard. Harder. Suddenly Solomon broke away from the water cooler gang and went across the bullpen toward him.

"Jesus Christ! Eddie Dain! Where in the hell . . ."

Like Sherman, he moved to embrace Dain. Unlike Sherman, he was attuned to physical rather than intellectual threat signs in people and so managed to turn the bear hug into a handshake without embarrassment on either side. He jerked his head at the big office dominating the far end of the room. They went in. His name was on the glass, with

LIEUTENANT
HOMICIDE

under it in capital letters. Randy sat down behind the desk.

"Congratulations on the promotion," said Dain. "I didn't know. Nobody could ever deserve it more."

"That's what all the boys say." Sherman leaned across the desk and said, "Thanks just a fuck of a lot for all those cards and letters over the past four years. Where the fuck you been?"

Dain waved a dismissive hand. "Around."

"Not around here."

Dain shrugged. He leaned forward. There was a whipcord quality to the movement, as if he could pluck a fly from the air with his bare hand if he wished.

"Hospitals, mostly. Here you know about. Stanford. Arizona. The Big Apple. Even Mexico."

"That's a lot of hospitals."

"There was a lot to fix," said Dain.

Randy said darkly, "Got a hunch wasn't just double-ought buckshot that hurt you, Hoss." He gestured. "But you look like these days you could knock down a bull with a good right cross."

Dain was silent. Randy leaned back in his swivel chair and locked his hands behind his big square black head and chuckled.

"What ever happened to Shenzie the wonder cat?"

"Older but no wiser. I left him with Marie's folks down in La Jolla while I was . . ." He stopped, considering his word. "Recuperating. I brought him back up with me when I came back."

"They glad to see you?"

"Their daughter's dead. Their grandson's dead. I'm still alive. Would you be glad?"

"Fuck 'em they can't take a joke," said Randy without heat or apology. He paused. "So you're stayin' a while."

"Foreseeable future."

The cop in Randy made his face and eyes get elaborately casual. "Plannin' on doin' what, exactly?"

"What I did before. Private-eye stuff."

Randy suddenly got up and went to the door and made

sure it was shut, then came back and leaned his butt against the edge of the desk, so he could speak in lower tones than his usual pane-rattling decibels.

"It'd be my ass the department knew, Eddie, but these four years I been looking. Not every day looking, y'know, but . . . Anyway, I got a sort of a hint that maybe a guy down in L.A. ordered that hit. But shit, Hoss, you gotta go dig him up you wanta do anything to him. He died two years ago."

"Mario Pucci," said Dain. Randy stared at him for a long moment, then nodded and went back around the desk and sat down again. Dain went on, "Grimes was running dope up from Mexico for him in his powerboat. I imagine Pucci wanted him blown up to keep him from talking, and the boat blown up so nobody would find the compartments the dope had been stowed in."

Randy opened his arms like a priest giving benediction, but his face wore a puzzled expression.

"Guess I ain't tracking, Hoss. If the man's dead—"

Dain was on his feet, leaning across the desk to grip Solomon's forearm with a force that made the big man wince. But Solomon did not try to pull his arm away.

"The shooters aren't dead," said Dain. His low-pitched voice somehow was like chalk on a blackboard. He let go of Solomon's forearm. He sat down again. There was a sheen of sweat on his forehead. "At least maybe they're not dead."

Randy sighed. "One way, I'm glad. It's what I'd be doin', was me, lookin' for the fuckers. But the other way, I ain't glad, 'cause I can't help you. I don't think anybody can. Pucci was like all these guys now—about ninety percent legit."

"Too legit to quit," murmured Dain.

"You got that right. If he did have some old-time shooter around for laughs, he'd have him up in Washington State picking Granny Smiths in front of three hundred school kids when the hit went down. What's that phrase those fuckers in Washington love? Deniability?"

"Tin mittens," said Dain.

Solomon chuckled.

"I ain't heard that one since I was a kid. My grandfather used to say it."

"I had a lot of time to read a lot of old detective novels while I was recuperating," said Dain. "Who would Pucci use?"

Some cop's hardness came again into Solomon's face. "You ain't gonna make the same mistake twice, are you, Dain?"

"I'm not going to make any mistakes at all."

Solomon nodded. "Good enough. Somebody good, it'd be, from one of the families back east. Contract guys, fly in, bang! bang! fly out the same night. With Pucci gone, you got nobody to pressure. They'll of been paid out of some corporate slush fund somewhere with only Pucci knowing what they were gettin' paid for. May as well chase a fart in a whirlwind for all the chance you got of finding 'em."

"That's the way that I had it figured, but I had to ask."

"What now, Dain?" He had started to say "Eddie," but somehow the name didn't fit any more.

"Dialing for dollars. I got a lot of medical to pay off."

Dain stood up. He seemed quite recovered from the emotional turmoil of a few minutes before. He stuck out his hand to Solomon. They shook.

"Thanks, Randy. For everything. Now and four years ago."

"Shit," said Randy. He brightened. "Handball?"

"I'll call you," said Dain.

Randy stared at him for a long moment. "Sure you will, Hoss," he said.

He walked Dain to the door of his office. Stood there watching him thread his way out of the room between the desks.

He went back and sat down. Heavily. And sighed.

7

His first commission didn't come until three months after Sherman had started acting as his go-between. Six months before, a drug-money courier had skipped with the cash he had been carrying between New York and Chicago. Dain found him in two days on the Caribbean island of Curacao, and had a lot of sleepless nights over the man's unknown fate.

But it got him a rep. What cemented it was a Mafia don's private pilot who had testified against his boss and had gone into the federal Witness Relocation Program two years before. In seventeen days, Dain found him on a fishing boat in Alaska.

After that he had more of his curiously specialized work than he could handle, and in the intervening months had really become much more the image he projected: harder, colder, more indifferent to the fate of those he found. Still plenty of sleepless nights, but not over them. They were all scum. Just not the scum *he* was seeking.

Then, a year later almost to the day, Dain's game began—although he didn't know it at the time.

It was 9:01 a.m. in Chicago on a bright glary summer morning headed toward the century mark by midday. An early-thirties man went into the First Chicago Bank of Commerce on South Wacker a few blocks from the Chicago Mercantile Exchange. He was slender, weak-chinned, bespectacled, suited, carrying an attache case. His eyes were close-set, which weakened the face even more.

He went to the window with SAFE DEPOSIT BOXES over it. Unlike the tellers' windows, there was no line. Holding a key in his hand, he fidgeted until a round-faced girl in a frilly blouse came over to use her twangy Midwest accent on him.

"May I help you, sir?"

He displayed the key. "Six-two-three-eight."

The teller riffled the signature cards. Took one out.

"Adelle Lorimer or James Zimmer are authorized to—"

"James Zimmer—obviously."

His chuckle was so nervous it was almost a cough. She compared his signature with that on file with the bank, then pushed the buzzer to let Zimmer into the vault area. They went through the double-key ritual. Zimmer shut himself into one of the private cubicles with the long oblong green metal box. As he opened both it and his attache case, he had to wipe sweat from his face with his display handkerchief.

From the box he took a dictionary-thick sheaf of bearer bonds. From the attache case, a much smaller stack of bonds. Laboriously and individually he checked their numbers against the larger stack, winnowing bonds from it until apart from the original he also had two small stacks that were, bond for bond, identical. He substituted new for old, returned the doctored sheaf to the not-so-safe deposit box, put the originals removed from it into his attache case.

Zimmer emerged from the bank moving briskly and with confidence, case in hand. Starting to cross a quarter block short of the crosswalk, he had to wait for a grimy Cicero bus to pass. A tip-nosed Irish meter maid following the bus and blue-chalking tires from her three-wheeler yelled at him.

"Hey—you!" She revved her engine beside him a couple of times. "Didja really think you could get away with that?" Zimmer stared at her through spectacles that, luckily for him, darkened in bright light so she could not see his wide and terrified eyes. "Didja ever hear of crosswalks?"

"No, I . . . I mean, yes, sorry, Officer, I was just . . ."

But she was gone. The minute hand of a big wall clock on a brick building across the street jerked solidly forward to 9:24. At the corner he crossed with the light, turned right, trying to regain his casual, jaunty stride; but the encounter had left the hand holding the attache case white-knuckled with tension.

He looked around rather furtively, then ducked into an alley. A kid carrying a cardboard tray of Styrofoam cups had to make a matador-with-the-bull move, the cover came off a cup to slop hot coffee over his wrist.

"Jesus Christ, man, why don't ya look where ya . . ."

Zimmer, oblivious, scuttled down the midblock alley at the far end of which a dirty and dented five-year-old red Porsche was parked facing the street. A lush-bodied platinum blonde in her mid-twenties, exotic as a tropical bird, was adding blood-red lipstick to full, sensual lips by the tipped-down interior mirror. Her dark and magnificent eyes were almost obliterated by too much mascara and liner, but even so she was vivid, alive.

A swarthy short-order cook came from a greasy spoon's kitchen door to dump something into a garbage pail with a nasty splashing plop, and the passing Zimmer leaped two feet in the air. The blonde shook her head at his antics in the driver's side mirror, pressed a Kleenex between her lips to blot them.

Zimmer got in beside her and put his attache case on the floor. Now that danger seemed past he was high on excitement, a hell of a fellow.

"Smooth as fucking silk." His lips curved around the dirty word his squeaky voice didn't quite fit.

"My mighty hero of romance," she said lightly.

Her irony was lost on Zimmer. He leaned over to kiss her. She pushed his face away with the back of her hand.

"What's the matter with you, Vangie?"

"What's the matter with you? This was the easy part."

Her skirt had ridden up as she worked the pedals, exposing long, beautifully muscled dancer's thighs in sheer black pantyhose. She tapped the horn twice as she edged the low red car out across the sidewalk. Zimmer, the coolest dude on earth, put his hand up between her legs.

"In an hour, sweet thing, I'm going to—"

Vangie slammed on the brakes so hard he bounced off the dashboard, thus effectively removing the offending hand. She glared at him with glacial eyes.

"Touch me again when I don't want you to, sweet thing, and you're going to need a prosthesis to pee."

A black teenager just coming out of a clothing shop with a mop, pail and squeegee heard Vangie's voice carry through the open window and started to laugh. She winked at him, then goosed it to send the beat-up little red Porsche zipping from the alley mouth.

Zimmer was angered by the black boy's laughter. As Vangie skillfully threaded the car through Loop traffic under the cool shadow of the El on Van Buren, he sneered, "No guts, baby? Shit, I *did* it, while you sat here peeing your pants! I'm—"

"Just what did you do, Jimmy?"

"I ripped off two million bucks in bearer bonds from T. J. L. fucking Maxton!" he exclaimed with defiant triumph.

She looked over at him and her face softened.

"Oh Jimmy-honey, don't you get it? When Maxton realizes what has happened here and picks up his telephone, somebody very good at finding people is going to be on the other end."

Dain still lived in the modest bungalow in Tam Valley, but now also leased a convenient loft over a dilapidated pier next to the firehouse on the San Francisco waterfront. The loft had a bed, dresser, wardrobe in one corner, bathroom in another, a kitchen in between. At 8:30 A.M., two hours after he had fallen asleep, the phone jerked him upright out of nightmare.

Albie's legs were blasted back down the hall out of sight as the door frame was splintered and pocked and ripped by the edges of the shot pattern

His shoulders slumped. His eyes became human again.

"Bad one, Shenz," he said.

Shenzie the wonder cat, his head sideways on the pillow and his front paws over the top of the blanket like a sleeping person, got up with a huge jaw-creaking yawn, stretched fore and aft, and stalked off in search of kibble as the phone rang again. Dain had not heard him purr since the day, five years before, when he'd been dropped off at Randy Solomon's Victorian.

Dain blew out a big *whoosh!* of breath, fumbled for the phone with one hand while dashing sweat from his face with the other.

"Dain."

"Sherman here. A call just came for you."

Dain sighed. "One hour."

He stood. He was nude, lean but tremendously muscular, his right shoulder, upper chest, and side of his neck peppered with small round white marks. On his left arm, rib cage, flank, and thigh were innumerable well-healed surgical scars.

In a gym area furnished with an Olympic bar set, racked dumbbells, benches, pulleys, rings and horses, mats, Dain selected two 70-pound dumbbells. He began doing warm-up cleans and presses with them. As his skin flushed with the added blood, the fishbelly scars stood out starkly.

Fifty minutes later, he settled into his usual chair across the desk from Sherman as the bookseller reached out a long arm to stab playback on the cassette recorder.

Sherman's voice said, "Three-four-six-two."

"I want to talk with Edgar Dain."

"Mr. Dain is not available for phone calls."

The other voice blustered. "Yeah, yeah, I know, but this is different. Very sensitive, large issues at—"

Dain cut the voice in midsentence by punching off.

"Midwest, maybe Chicago. Asshole, maybe an attorney."

Sherman said, "Oh, well, that's that, then. If the man is an attorney, Dain couldn't possibly do any work for him."

As their arrangement had blossomed, they had fallen into a professional relationship devoid of the personal. Dain executed the commissions he accepted through Sherman without discussing them or ever filing any written reports, facts Sherman found almost unbearably unprofessional.

"Attorneys lie a lot," said Dain. "Always at the wrong time to the wrong people."

Sherman began to prowl. He'd believed that being Dain's go-between would be tweaking the tail of the tiger. Instead, the tiger stayed in its cage. He scooped up the invariable leather-bound book from the corner of the desk. *The Tibetan Book of the Dead*. He almost slammed it down again.

"Still drugging your mind with lunacies five years later."

"It's my mind."

"And don't give me any crap about physical therapy. You use it to remind yourself of . . ." He paused, fearing he had gone too far, but Dain did not react, so he asked, "So, what do I tell T. J. L. Maxton when he calls again?"

Dain raised his eyebrows. "That was Teddy Maxton?"

"You know him?"

"Of him. Chicago investment attorney who does occasional legal work for some minor mob figures."

"You amaze me, Dain. Sometime I'd like to know what you were really doing during those four lost years."

"Recuperating."

"Where? In the Witness Relocation Program? You know more arcane facts about obscure organized-crime individuals than—"

Dain came to his feet in a single swift movement. "Maxton, huh? Let's step on his tail, see if he squeals."

Sherman felt the familiar delicious thrill of excitement.

"If Maxton's really connected, is that wise?"

"Is living wise?" Dain countered as he stalked out with his *Tibetan Book of the Dead* under one arm.

* * *

Two days later, 7:30 A.M., Dain was at the World Gym in Kentfield near the College of Marin, doing a circuit workout that built cardiovascular capacity while strengthening the five major muscle groups. The few dedicated bodybuilders in the basement free weight room at that hour were too busy with their own workouts to pay any attention to Dain, as he in turn ignored the morning-long shadow that climbed across him.

"Dain? Edgar Dain?"

Dain was doing barbell curls with two hundred pounds, grunting with the effort. He finished, pouring sweat, the planes of his chest shifting under his black sweatshirt with each heaving breath.

He said rudely, "Outside in an hour."

When Dain emerged, the man was waiting on the sidewalk in front of the gym, legs slightly apart and heavy features set in an angry scowl. He was a fleshy well-conditioned late- forties, five-nine, 190, with mean blue eyes and a stubborn jaw. Raymond Burr during his early career as movie villain, with something of Burr's indefinable dynamism that held the eye. Dain figured he would make a lot of a certain kind of woman go weak in the knees.

"Theodore Maxton," Dain nodded without offering a hand. "You'd make a good politician. Plenty of physical presence."

"How the hell did you know who I—"

"I spotted your hired flunky following me around, followed him last night to the St. Francis. You're in suite nine-oh-one."

His car was parked in the lot of Taqueria de Marin, which didn't open until eleven. Maxton had to trot or be left behind. Dain pressed WALK for the three-way light at College Ave.

Maxton said almost reasonably, "Don't be so damn difficult, Dain. Everybody likes money. I want you to find James

Zimmer for me—until a week ago he was a law clerk in my legal firm.''

The light changed. They crossed. Dain said, ''How much did he steal, how, and from whom?''

''Who said anything about stealing? I just want him found.''

''How much did he steal, how, and from whom?''

Maxton snarled, ''A client, Adelle Lorimer has—had— five million dollars' worth of her late husband's undeclared bearer bonds in her safe-deposit box. Mrs. Lorimer is on an extended tour of Europe, our firm has power of attorney, Zimmer was her attorney of record so he had access to the box. He extracted two million worth of the bonds, substituted forgeries, and disappeared. Since the money is undeclared, Mrs. Lorimer does not want publicity that would bring IRS scrutiny.''

Dain paused beside the '84 Toyota Corolla in which he had driven Marie and Albie to Point Reyes five years before.

''Why was a law clerk her attorney of record, and why did he think he could get away with the theft?''

''Mrs. Lorimer knew his parents. As for the theft, in the normal course of events, the bonds probably would have remained untouched in the box until Mrs. Lorimer's death.''

Dain unlocked the car door. ''I'll be in touch,'' he said as he slid into the car. ''Or I won't.''

''Hey, wait a goddamned . . .''

He stood in the deserted parking lot, glaring after Dain's car and muttering curses under his breath. But Dain, driving away, already was considering which data bases would give him best access to T. J. L. Maxton's affairs. About the fugitive Zimmer he thought not at all, except to wonder if Maxton's definition of drastic might include hiring a hitman for him. Perhaps a hitman who, years before . . .

That sort of slim chance was all Dain lived for.

8

Teddy Maxton's office was in the penthouse of a new high rise with a good view of Sears Tower and the Chicago River snaking through the Loop. The office was expensive without distinction, relentlessly modern, reflecting a designer's tastes rather than Maxton's. The lawyer was on the phone with a client when the door was opened by Jeri Pearson, his thirtyish executive secretary. Maxton looked up, irritated.

"I told you no—"

"A Mr. Dain? He seemed to think—"

Maxton, mollified, made a beckoning gesture. It was after 4:00 P.M., so he had a drink at his elbow. He said into the phone, "Something's come up, I'll call you back tomorrow."

Jeri ushered in Dain, shut the door as she left. Dain was dressed in a conservative business suit and a Sulka tie. In his left hand was his usual leather-bound book. He stopped in the middle of the room as Maxton moved his glass and raised an eyebrow, almost smirking to see him there after all.

Dain shook his head, wiped away Maxton's self-satisfied look by saying, "I get ten percent of anything recovered against a twenty-five K guarantee. I cover my own expenses."

"*Ten percent!* I told you he stole two million dollars. Ten percent is an absolutely outrageous—"

"My fee is not negotiable."

Maxton came around the desk, his hands clenched and his face dark with anger. "Everyone's fee is negotiable."

Dain sat down in the visitor's chair, laid his leather-bound book on the edge of the desk. After a moment, Maxton went back behind the desk to get his drink, jaw aggressive.

"You had two other P.I.'s looking for him for a week before you came to me, and don't even know which rest room he uses."

"You mean he's a fucking *fag*?"

"No. I mean that you know nothing about him, yet you handpicked him to be Lorimer's attorney with power to cosign on that box with her. Who or what made him desperate enough to steal from you? Was he being blackmailed? If so, over what? Was he a gambler in debt to a shylock? Is he a cokehead? In love?"

Maxton exclaimed, "How do you expect me to know anything like that? He's a fucking *law clerk*, for Godsake!"

"Exactly. You said the substitution probably won't be discovered until Mrs. Lorimer's death, if then. Does she know about the theft? Do you plan to return the bonds to her?"

There was a long silence. Maxton finally turned to the window behind the desk, stood with his face so close to it that when he spoke his words left small puffs of steam on the glass.

"Zimmer agreed to substitute forged bonds I supplied for two million worth of the genuine ones. He was to get a hundred thousand, tax-free, for that service."

"And just in case, you made sure you couldn't even get into the box—only Zimmer," said Dain. "That way, if the substitution was discovered, Zimmer would take the fall."

Maxton turned back into the room. "That's right."

Dain leaned forward with a friendly look on his face.

"So the question is, why did *you* have to steal the bonds?"

Maxton slammed his empty glass down on the desk so hard it cracked in his hand. He threw it into the wastebasket.

"None of your fucking business."

"I'll tell you why," said Dain. "Your wife found out you were fooling around and filed for divorce. She wanted the usual—alimony, house, car . . . But I'm assuming she also wanted a lot of tax-free cash under the table—*or else*."

Maxton said softly, "Or else what?"

"Normally I'd expect her to wake up dead in a garbage pail somewhere, but instead you trot out and try to steal two million bucks to keep her happy. So she's really got something— probably something the fraud division of the IRS or your playmates with the *ini*-names would like to know. So she's got an edge on you." He suddenly snapped the words. "Does Zimmer?"

"I *told* you, the man's a fucking law clerk. That's why I chose him for this—he wouldn't dare try a double cross."

"But he did," said Dain. He stood abruptly, picked up his book, headed for the door. "I'll be in touch."

It was the week before exams on Northwestern's hundred and sixty green hardwood-dotted acres bordering Lake Michigan. Undergrads sprawled on the grass like terrorist victims. Dain, in his three-piece suit and power tie, wearing clear-glass horn-rims that made him look professorial, stopped a worried-looking coed for directions to the law school. She had a chocoholic complexion and a stack of books under her arm that listed her to port like a sailboat beating into the wind. When he spoke to her she dropped her books. He caught them before they hit the walk.

"The law school?" he prompted gently.

"Oh, ah, yeah." She half turned, pointed beyond the U-shaped concrete admin building with its signature clock tower to another building half-hidden by the green leaves and startling white trunks of some birch trees. "The red brick? With the white window trim?"

"Many thanks. Good luck with the exams."

An hour later, in the pleasantly secluded Shakespeare Gardens, he stopped beside a bench on which a sternly attractive brown-haired woman was correcting papers. She wore a tweed suit with a skirt short enough to show several inches of very shapely thigh. There was a great stack of lawbooks on the bench.

"Dr. Berman?" She squinted up into the sun; Dain shifted so he blocked it from her eyes. "They said at the law review that you often came here in nice weather to correct papers."

She took off her glasses, said rudely, "I'm faculty advisor for the review. Who are you?"

"James Zimmer," said Dain as if the name were an answer.

The irritation faded. Her eyes softened with memory. "Jimmy Zimmer! God, I haven't thought of Jimmy for . . ." She caught herself, said sharply, "I asked who *you* were."

"Mr. Zimmer has applied to the United States Justice Department for a position as a federal prosecutor. In such cases there is a routine investi—"

"Jimmy? A federal prosecutor?" She stopped just short of an unexpected giggle. "We were law students here together . . ." Sternness tightened her face. "I doubt if I can tell you anything that would be of interest to the Justice Department."

Dain put a shoe on the edge of the bench. "How about if Jimmy made the law review or not?"

She looked startled, then burst out laughing. "You're good at this, aren't you?"

"I hope so," said Dain, and moved her books aside enough to sit down beside her on the bench.

When he left a half hour later, he knew that on his own Jimmy Zimmer would have had neither the imagination, wit, nor courage to plan the bond theft from Teddy Maxton.

*   *   *

That evening at Zimmer's apartment building he gleaned a second possibly useful fact from a snide overweight born-again in the laundry room. She described a woman Zimmer had been "shamelessly intimate with" for several weeks that past winter.

"Nights at his apartment?"

Her eyes flashed. "Whole weekends. It ended around the middle of January."

"And after that?" Dain's voice was insinuating.

"He had a peroxide floozie up one time, a month ago, but I put a stop to that." Her uncolored lips curved in righteous triumph. One plump cheek even dimpled. "I called the police and told them harlots were working out of his apartment."

Dain asked God to bless her, and left. Her description of the blonde was "cheap"; her description of the winter lover was that of Maxton's executive secretary, Jeri Pearson.

A cooling wind off Lake Michigan was puffing its way up the skyscraper canyons to swirl old newspapers against pedestrians' legs and tug at women's dresses. If Marilyn Monroe had been out in it, her skirt would have been up around her ears and poor old Tom Ewell would have had to strap down his hard-on.

As the minute hand on the clock a block down from the First Chicago Bank of Commerce leaped forward to 9:23 A.M., Dain exited the bank. He had traded his leather-bound book for a clipboard. In the guise of a state bank examiner he already had talked with the woman who had let Zimmer into the safe-deposit box. She hadn't remembered him, but her records had: clocked in at 9:03, clocked out at 9:22.

A city-grimed Cicero bus farted past Dain; he made a notation on his clipboard. Behind the bus, a red-headed Irish-faced meter maid was chalking tires. Another note for her. Near the corner a postman opened the letter box and began putting the mailed letters into a big canvas bag. Dain made a note.

He crossed the street, stood on the far corner. His eye was

caught by a doughnut truck pulling away from KARL'S
KOFFEE KUP KAFE midblock to his right. He scribbled a
note, went down that way. A boy exited Karl's with a tippy
cardboard tray of coffee in plastic-capped Styrofoam cups.
Dain wrote.

Beyond Karl's was an alley. He glanced down that way,
then stopped, utterly still. Foot traffic flowed around his
solid immobility. Yes. It was what he'd do. He started am-
bling down the alley, stopped again. Him, but not Zimmer.
Zimmer, alone, just about here would be thinking, *still time
to turn them over to Maxton* and get his 100-K and live happily ever after.

As he was passing the back door of a cafe a short-order
cook came out to dump some garbage in one of the pails. It
went in with an ugly wet plopping sound. Dain stopped
again, abruptly.

Zimmer would have given Maxton the bonds, but he hadn't.
So if he'd come down this alley, something stronger than his
fear of Maxton had driven him on.

Or drawn him on.

Belatedly, he made a note on the Hispanic cook as a wino
careened past him up the alley. No note for him. Winos saw
a lot, but their sense of time and reality was elastic, and in
hopes of a bottle of muscatel they would tell you not what
they'd seen, but what they thought you wanted them to have
seen.

He emerged from the far end of the alley, looked around
casually. Here is where he would have parked if he'd been
waiting to pick up Zimmer and the bonds.

A black teenager had just finished washing and squeegee-
ing the front display windows of a men's clothing store.
Dain made a note and strolled on, noting a florist truck, five
secretaries exiting a building for a coffee break, an old
woman staring down through lace curtains from a third-floor
apartment window.

He quit for the day at the end of the block. Ten minutes
max was as long as Zimmer would have been in the vicinity:
after that he would have walked away, caught a bus, a taxi,
driven off himself in a car, or been picked up by someone
else.

For the rest of the week, Dain left the front of the bank each morning at 9:23 to canvass in a different direction until he was satisfied that he had covered all reasonable possibilities.

Records could tell him all about who Zimmer had been up until the day he stole the bonds. Records could tell him Zimmer had accessed the Lorimer safe-deposit box at 9:03 A.M. and had left at 9:22 A.M. There the records stopped.

But Zimmer had kept going. So Dain did, too. He now had his raw data: now he could begin to work it. This was like a chess game. The same almost infinite number of choices; the same implacable logic. And it absorbed him to be working someone else's backtrail, so he wasn't thinking about

Marie going back and up, mouth strained wide, eyes wild

Yes, only Dain could work the backtrail. In person. Which was his salvation. Using the computer made him unbearably sad; as for chess, even looking at a board, even now five years later, made vomit rise in his throat.

On the coffee table in Mill Valley was the unfinished game he and Marie had been playing before they had left for Point Reyes five years before. He hadn't been able to put it away.

"You know, honey, maybe Randy's right. Maybe you're treating the Grimes thing a little too much like just a game . . ."

And he, pretentious asshole that he was, had said, *"You know that all investigations are just a game, sweetie—move, countermove, just like chess."*

And she had died. And Albie had died.

Sometime, maybe, someone else would die. Oh God, please let him find someone else he could make die . . .

9

Next morning, Dain caught the Cicero bus three stops short of the First Chicago Bank of Commerce, stood right behind the driver talking to him under the sign that said DO NOT TALK WITH DRIVER WHEN THE BUS IS MOVING. Nothing. A bill changed hands and Dain got off at the stop beside the bank.

Meg Crowley, in uniform and with her citation pad sticking out of a back pocket, turned from the counter with a coffee and turnover to cannon into a man just emerging from the rest room. Hot coffee cascaded down the front of his shirt.

"No milk or sugar next time," said Dain with a wry grin.

Meg already had set her turnover and empty coffee cup on the corner of a table and was ineffectually dabbing with paper napkins, trying to blot up the stain; he was a hunk. They sat beside a window that needed washing. He told her about the missing heir he was *that* close to finding, son of a woman dying in Bangor, Maine. He described Zimmer, with attache case . . .

"I remember him!" exclaimed Meg suddenly, her face lighting up. She laughed. "I've got a Mick temper on me, and he jaywalked right in front of me as if I didn't exist . . ."

The postman looked like a ferret but was worthless. He had no fixed schedule for picking up the mail from the drop-box on the corner, couldn't remember his pickup on that particular day, and only saw letters, not people on his route. A dead man walking.

The next morning, twenty bucks bought Dain three blocks' worth of conversation with the doughnut truck driver who delivered to Karl's Koffee Kup Kafe just short of the midblock alley. He had seen nothing, or if he had, didn't remember it.

Chuck Gilette was a sandy-haired kid who delivered coffee and Danish from Karl's to offices around the neighborhood. He wanted to go to college but his grades weren't all that good so his salary and the tips he made went into the old college fund.

For Chuck, also, the missing heir and his dying mum.

"Sure I remember him, Mr. Dain. He sort of darted into the alley just as I came out of Karl's, so I had to make a move . . ." He sprang backward in demonstration, like a batter getting brushed back by a close pitch. "The cap flew offa one of the cups, hot coffee all over my hand." He grinned sheepishly. "I started to cuss him out, but he didn't even know I was there."

A $50 contribution to Chuck's go-to-college fund.

Pablo Martinez, sneaking a cigarette behind the greasy spoon, got uneasy when Dain showed him a $20 bill.

"Four day' ago you come down the alley," Pablo accused.

"I'm not *la migra*," said Dain quickly. He described Zimmer, his clothes, face, the attache case in his hand. "I want to know if he walked past you last week and where he went . . ."

The man Pablo had bought his green card from had assured him it was so close to genuine it would pass any immigration scrutiny, but Pablo was not convinced. As a short-order cook illegally in the country, he had learned to be a pessimist.

"I doan see nothin', man."

Dain gave him the twenty anyway. Pablo's reaction had confirmed he'd seen Zimmer passing by.

The black teenager who washed down the haberdashery windows each morning was on break, so Dain went through the motions with his other possibles even though reasonably sure someone had been waiting for Zimmer in a car at the end of the alley.

The five secretaries who went for coffee at 9:30 each morning were like the three monkeys: hear no, see no, speak no.

The old woman who hung out of her third-floor window had seen nothing she could remember on the day in question.

The florist truck driver, intercepted on his route, said he only remembered cars that he was able to look down into from his truck's height advantage and see women's legs.

"Saw a broad driving a 280Z stark friggin' naked, once." He was gesturing, excited. "Saw another broad giving a handjob to a guy in a Caddy Seville once, he was stopped for a red light on South State Street, middle of the friggin' day . . ."

Colorful, but about as useful as the wino in the alley.

When he got back to the haberdashery, Dain found Zeke White stacking sweaters in a row of bins across the back of the store. The place smelled of wool and leather and shoe polish. Zeke had bright eyes with almost bluish whites, a high-bridged nose more Hamitic than Bantu, and hands too big for the rest of him, hands like those of 49er wide receiver Jerry Rice. He wore his hair buzzed, with his initials shaved into one side. His jeans were baggy, his hightops red with the laces undone.

"I saw you doing the windows four mornings ago."

"Zmah job, man," said Zeke with great economy of speech.

Dain described Zimmer. Zeke kept folding sweaters. "I'm trying to find out if he came down the alley one day last week when you were washing the windows."

"Didn't see the dude, man."

Dain took a flier. "Maybe getting into a car?"

Suddenly Zeke started to laugh, a big deep man's laugh though he was still just a teenager.

"Blonde in a red Porsche," he said. "Parked in the alley. Car was a beater, real muddy, she took a lot better care of herself than she did of that car. I'm doin' the store windows, all of a sudden she come outten there like she be drivin' the Batmobile. Was a cat with her but I couldn't see him 'cause he was on the other side of the car, y'dig?"

"Sure," said Dain.

"Dude put his hands on her down where I couldn't see, an' she slam on the brakes so hard he hit his head on the dash." He gave his booming laugh again. "Man, she tell him, You put yo hands on me again I don't want you to, you gonna need a plastic dick t'piss.'"

The woman? Really blonde, platinum like, man, with a really pretty face messed up with too much eyeliner an' mascara, real red lipstick, didn't really need it all, sure, it made her sexy, but also made her sorta . . . cheap like. Which she wasn't.

"She winked at me, man, when she said 'bout him pissin'. She call him sweet thing, but she doan really mean it."

Another $50 for Zeke. He was worth it.

* * *

So . . . a blonde in a beat-up old Porsche almost certainly had been waiting in the alley to pick Zimmer up after the theft of Adelle Lorimer's bonds. Like the Wizard of Oz with the cowardly lion, she'd given Zimmer his courage.

Jeri Pearson? Platinum didn't fit her hair color, exotic didn't fit her face. But she might know the exotic blonde—probably her successor with Jimmy Zimmer, maybe the one-night stand at his apartment before the bluenose had gone to the cops.

Meanwhile, it was Friday. Dain flew back to San Francisco for the weekend. He was missing Shenzie and the summer fog, and he had to analyze all of the data he had gathered.

Wearing only an old pair of blue cotton workout briefs, Dain was using a coiled spring exerciser with all five stainless- steel coiled springs in place. Through the open loft windows came cold wet foggy night air, the wash of small oily waves against the pilings beneath the pier, at intervals the far sad cry of the Alcatraz foghorn.

For the twentieth time without pause, Dain brought his arms down from straight overhead with agonizing slowness against the tension of the opening springs. When the arms were straight out from his shoulders at either side, the fully extended springs were stretched across the back of his shoulders and neck.

Dain gasped out, "What . . . do you think . . . cat?"

Shenzie, who was sitting on the edge of the bed watching him, said *meowr* and batted Dain's hand lightly with one paw.

Dain's arms started slowly back up. His face was contorted with effort, his torso flushed with blood. The pale pock scars on his shoulder, chest and neck were very visible. As the spring contracted above his head, his lats sprang out on the sides of his body in a tremendous V-shape spread.

When the springs were finally closed, he let out a gasping breath that carried "Twenty" with it.

He lay down on the floor parallel to the bed, his head toward the head of it, his feet pointed toward an artist's portable easel with a 19-inch by 24-inch sketching pad open on it. The hand-lettering in Sharpie permanent marker on it said:

LAW SCHOOL
    former profs
    former students
APARTMENT
    landlady
    tenants
OFFICE
    exec secretary
    receptionist
    other secretaries
BANK
    teller
    meter maid
    postman
    doughnut truck
    delivery boy
    short-order cook
    window washer
    secretaries
    old woman
    flower truck

Dain, still panting, began to do twisting crunches, hands locked behind his head, shoulders off the floor, bicycling with his legs, twisting to touch each elbow to each opposite raised knee. He did fifty on each side without stopping, letting his eyes sweep across the drawing pad open on the easel with each rep.

When he was finished he bounced to his feet, went to the board, with the Sharpie drew a line through every item under each of the headings, save one. Sweat formed a wet circle around his bare feet as he stood there on the plank floor.

"Cat, we have to find out who the peroxide blonde is."

Shenzie yawned prodigiously, but had nothing to say. He

began giving himself a professional wash job on the edge of the bed. Dain tapped the unlined item on the drawing pad—*exec secretary* under OFFICE.

"Only one easy shot left, Shenz."

He phoned an airline, made a reservation for Chicago, then got down to do clap-hand push-ups, giving a sharp shove as he came up off the floor at each rep so he could clap his hands twice before his body started down again. Despite his grunts and the sweat rolling off him, they looked effortless. The only other sounds were the waves breaking against the pilings fifty feet below, and the occasional muffled bellow of foghorns.

Shenzie padded the length of the bed to the bedside table, curled himself around the telephone as if Dain's call had made it warm, and went to sleep.

10

Chicago, like San Francisco, is a town where umbrellas routinely get turned inside out when it rains. Monday evening was blustery and Dain was relying on a rain slicker and rain hat as he entered the Sign of the Trader, just inside the West Jackson Boulevard entrance to the Board of Trade Building. He went through the heavy wood and glass door, the noise hitting him like a subdued echo from the trading pits that had closed several hours before. He tossed his rain-wet slicker over one of the coatracks lining the coatroom.

The bar/restaurant was dark-lit, richly appointed, with deep carpets and leather-lined booths and heavy wooden chairs and tables for the diners. Indirect pastel lighting enhanced the look of a never-never land where no opening bell ever rang—an effect negated by the strip of green electronic futures quotations running endlessly around the room just below the ceiling. Snatches of conversation flowed around him as he tried to pick Jeri Pearson out of the traders, runners, and company people crammed three-deep at the bar.

"I hear you sucked some gas this morning," said a sandy-haired man to a beautiful brunette in her early twenties.

"I didn't give much back," she objected. "Maybe a K."

"I made twenty-three K today," said sandy-hair. He still wore his sweat-soaked trading jacket.

She chuckled. "Good. You can pay for the drinks."

Dain spotted Jeri at one of the tables set back from the bar. The tide of milling humanity swirled him that way; he slid in opposite her. She had a lush body and a dissatisfied face. She caught the sleeve of a passing waitress.

"Bloody bull for the gentleman!" she yelled over the din.

The waitress nodded and moved on.

"Thanks for meeting me!" Dain boomed.

She shouted something back that contained " . . . *mystery man* . . ." and " . . . *intrigued*" in it.

He nodded as if he had understood. She stood, leaned down so her face was close to his ear and she could speak normally.

"Now you're here to hold the table, I'm going to the little girls'. I'll be right back."

It was interesting that Jeri had chosen this place when he had called her for a meeting. Very public, very noisy, both of which would discourage not only intimacy, but questioning as well. Interesting, too, the trip to the ladies': a chance to report to Maxton by phone that Dain had arrived?

"Seven-twenty a bushel?" said a twangy voice above him. "The guy is nuts. Me, I'm dreaming of beans in the teens, like the drought year of eighty."

The voices moved off. "Dream on. The bottom's going out of soybeans when the new Ag report comes out."

Jeri slid in across from Dain just as the waitress set down his drink—a bloody mary with a shot of beef bouillon in it.

He lifted it to toast her, somebody jammed an elbow against his hand in passing, spilling the squat heavy glass across the tablecloth, moved on without apologizing. Dain set about wiping up his spilled drink with the cloth napkin.

"Quite a place!" he yelled politely. *"You come here often?"*

Helping with her own napkin Jeri shouted back, *"Used to!"*

Dain leaned toward her so he was speaking almost into her ear as she had done to him earlier.

"So what happened to you and Jimmy?" he asked.

"I don't know what you mean." She tried to pull back from him, but he had one big hand clamped around her fore-arm.

"The fat born-again in his apartment building knows."

"*That* bitch!" She tried to wrest her arm back from his grip. Dain was unmoving. She jerked her head. "C'mon, let's get the hell out of this dump."

"Your place or mine?" asked Dain without humor.

Despite the thunderstorm, Jeri's one-bedroom, forty min-utes from the Loop by bus, had been close and humid after being closed up all day. The rain had stopped, so Dain had thrown open some windows and sat on the couch with his feet on the coffee table while Jeri had made drinks.

Jeri came out of the bedroom, her steps languid; she had changed into a negligee that showed her dark nipples and pubic triangle through the thin shimmery material. She was carrying a little glass vial in one hand, a single-edged razor blade in the other, was performing meaningless little dance steps to some inner music. She plopped on her knees be-tween the coffee table and the couch, beside Dain's ex-tended legs.

"Gonna do me a little itsy-bitsy line," she said. "You in-terested?" Her voice was clear, but her movements liquid.

Dain answered only with a slight negative movement of his head, watched moodily as she chopped and rowed the coke. She used a plastic straw cut in half to snort the first line. She shook her head, then giggled and reached up to knock a fist gravely on his temple.

"H'lo! Anybody home in there?"

Dain was silent, waiting her out. He couldn't afford to feel anything for Jeri Pearson. He needed to use her and lose her. She shook her head as if in wonder.

"Life of the party. When he first walked inna Maxton's, I thought, Mr. Stud has come to town . . ."

She stopped and rubbed some of the coke on her gums. She giggled. She started to cry. Then her face smoothed out. She giggled again. She leaned back against his outstretched legs.

"You aren't interested in me, are you? Jus' in what I can tell you."

"Tell me what happened to you and Jimmy. You and Jimmy were good together."

"Jimmy?" A giggle. "Somebody t'do, that's all." She sat with her head down, staring at the coke on the coffee table. "Not a nice girl, that's me. Nice girls don't work for Maxton."

"Why not?"

"Work for Maxton, gotta give him head under his desk when he's on the phone." She started to cry again. She leaned forward to snort the second line on the glass tabletop. "Was in love with him. Maxton. He dumped me. For an exotic dancer."

"Exotic dancer?" asked Dain. "Peroxide—"

"Try whore instead." She wiped her nose with the back of her hand, leaned back against his legs again. "No peroxide. Black-haired bitch, I could kill 'er! Real long black shiny hair down to her ass. Real pretty, goddam her, jugs out to here . . ." She pantomimed in front of her own perfectly adequate breasts. "She an' couple others p'formed at the Christmas party . . ."

"That's when Maxton dropped you for her?"

"Chrissake, you aren't listening!" She peered at him blearily. "That's what he does. Focuses all that power . . . all that drive . . . all that energy on a girl 'til her panties get wet. At first he just *needs* you so fuckin' bad you feel you're the most special woman in the world. Then he drops you an' makes you feel like shit on a stick . . . *worse* than shit on a stick, 'cause he's furious with you 'cause he ever wanted you . . ."

"So he'd dumped you before the Christmas party."

"Two months before. Christmas party was first time I

saw *her*—one took my place.'' She looked owlishly at him. ''Firs' time *Jimmy* saw that slut, too . . .''

Dain's eyes had gotten sharp and bright, but his voice was very soft, almost insinuating.

''Tell me about her and Jimmy.''

Her eyes teared up. ''Two weeks after the Christmas party *he* dumped me for her. Ever'body dumps poor ol' Jeri.''

''Do you remember the dancer's name?''

''No.''

''Or where Maxton hired her from?''

''No.''

''Could you find out?''

''Why should I?''

When he didn't answer, she struggled to her feet, swayed, caught her balance, and looked down at him with bleary eyes, her negligee open so her naked body was on display.

''Want some of that?'' she challenged. Before he could answer, she said, ''Did it inna men's room once, backed up against the urinals . . .'' She giggled again. ''Guy banged me so hard the urinal flushed when he came.''

Dain was silent.

''Don' believe me?'' she demanded truculently.

She pulled up her negligee and straddled him, put her arms around his neck, started to French-kiss him as her naked crotch worked against him. Nothing happened to him. He wanted to get stiff. He wanted to feel something—excitement, lust, even anger. Nothing. Goddammit, wasn't five years long enough to mourn? Marie was never coming back to him.

Marie's mouth was strained impossibly wide, her eyes were wild, her hair an underwater slow-motion swirl, the black hole between her breasts blossoming red

Jeri suddenly stopped, drew back to look shyly into his eyes. ''I'm going to be sick now,'' she announced.

Dain got her off him and into the bathroom in time, held her head while she threw up. As he wiped her mouth with a wet washcloth, she passed out. In the bedroom he put her to bed, and after pulling up the sheet and a light blanket found himself kissing her on the forehead as if she were a little girl.

Dain walked all the way back to his hotel, half-hoping some half-wit would try to mug him, but the Chicago streets on that night were safe as a cathedral. He was empty as a pocket with a hole in it, was nothing, had nothing, except a lust for revenge and a cat who wouldn't purr.

11

"Great turnaround time," said Dain to Jeri when he found her behind her desk at Maxton's office at 8:30 the next morning. Her eyes were clear, her hair was brushed and shiny. She wore a wide-shouldered pinstripe suit and slacks, the suit jacket almost to her knees when she stood up. She looked terrific.

"Good genes. Dain, listen, I . . . I think I remember—"

"You passed out, I put you to bed. That's all."

In his private office Maxton was grunting into the phone. Rain-washed Chicago sparkled outside the windows. He covered the receiver, said sarcastically, "How nice of you to drop in. It's been over a week. My bitch wife is getting . . ." He uncovered the receiver, said, "Yeah, I'm listening," and covered it again.

"Who do you know drives a red Porsche?" asked Dain.

"Nobody."

"Who did Zimmer know drives a red Porsche?"

"I told you before—Zimmer was a fucking law clerk. We didn't have any social life in common."

"You'd be surprised," said Dain.

"What the fuck does that mean?" He said into the phone, "Then go into court and get a continuance, fuckhead."

"Platinum blonde," said Dain. "Mid-twenties at a guess, too much makeup, cool face, maybe beautiful, maybe just this side of beautiful. She was waiting for him when they grabbed the bonds. She's the one who planned the steal. Too bad you don't know her, I could have cut across, saved some time."

Maxton barked into the phone, "Yeah, yeah, you stupid fuck, I'm listening," then said to Dain, "A fucking broad? No way. Zimmer planned it."

Dain shrugged and was on his feet, his usual leather-covered book in hand. He looked down at Maxton, said, "Why does every male in Chicago think he's got to be Mike Ditka?"

In the outer office, Jeri Pearson, who had been listening on the intercom, bounded to her feet and kissed him on the mouth.

"Nobody's ever told him off before! They're all too scared of him." She stepped back, suddenly shy. "Listen, I remember you holding my head when I was sick last night and—"

"It never happened," said Dain.

Jeri said, "The dancers were from the Cherry Bomb."

The Cherry Bomb was in Rush Street's strip-club district, two blocks west of and parallel to Michigan Avenue. A huge barn that stank of stale beer and stale sweat and cheap perfume and disinfectant and testosterone. There was dim lighting for the tables, indirect lighting for the bar, spot lighting for the stage with revolving red, yellow, blue and green gels for the three women in G-strings and pasties who writhed, danced, and gyrated to canned music.

At the empty end of the bar furthest from the action, Dain waited with a $50 bill, folded lengthwise, nipped between his extended fingers. It quickly brought the bartender to him.

Over the music, Dain yelled, *"Dancer. Real pretty. Great breasts. Black hair to her butt."*

The bartender eyed the fifty and made a fly-away gesture.

Mercifully, the music ended, the women left to scattered applause and rebel yells. A manic aging emcee bounded onto the stage. He rolled eyes like stones and flicked his tongue after the departing strippers in their G-strings and pasties.

"Put a dollar bill on their heads," he yelled into his cordless mike, "and you got all you can eat for under a buck!"

"Any friends?" asked Dain.

Another trio of strippers was taking the place of the first. The bartender jerked his head toward a long lithe black woman. "The tall one. Cindy."

Dain dropped his fifty on the bar, crossed to the stage as the emcee's overamped voice yelled, "Anyway, welcome to the Cherry Bum—I mean Bomb, the only place in town where the girls wear underpants to keep their ankles warm!"

The music suddenly blared, the black woman started to dry-fuck one of the fire poles set up onstage.

Dain yelled over the music, *"Cindy!"*

She turned her head and he held up two fanned $100 bills, then stuffed them down the back of her G-string.

Dain was leaning against the brick wall of the alley when Cindy emerged from the stage door at 4:07 in the morning. She wore running shoes and tight jeans and a long-sleeve red T-shirt with DANCE THEATRE OF HARLEM stretched across her breasts.

She stopped dead at the sight of him, sighed, and nodded as if winning a bet with herself.

"Don't ever anything come free in this world of ours," she said. "Now, mister, I know you laid a double-century on me, and I know you spect something for it, but—"

"Just a walk and a talk," he said. "I don't want to know where you live, I don't want a free sample."

She looked deep into his eyes for a moment, asked, "You weird?" then answered herself before he could, "Wouldn't tell me if you was, would you, Mr. Sad Man?"

They started walking together; she was tall enough so they made a striking couple. In the street at this hour there was only silence, contrasting with the tumult of the Cherry Bomb. Their meandering unsynched footsteps were the only thing breaking the immediate silence around them, though the slow breathing of the city formed a background curtain of sound.

Cindy gave a deep laugh. "You don't want nothing, Mr. Sad Man, you must be that Good Samaritan the preacher talk about on Sunday, layin' a pair of C-notes on me like that."

"I didn't say I didn't want anything," said Dain.

"Oh yeah, right, right. Walkin' an' talkin'. Y'want me t'talk dirty? 'Bout what I'd like you to do to me, or what I'd like to do to you? Or maybe cry a little an' tell you all about what a nice girl like me be doin' in a place like—"

"I want to talk about you and your friend with the long black hair entertaining at Teddy Maxton's Christmas party."

Cindy dumbed down her face and put a whine in her voice.

"Was just a gig, man. Dude paid us a century each to do the same show we do at the club—"

"The long-haired one who took off with Jimmy Zimmer."

"Look, man, I don't know nothing about it. Even if I did know something about it I wouldn't know nothing about it."

Dain said, conversationally, "If they catch them, Cindy, they'll snuff her. Right along with him."

"Snuff?" she cried in alarm, her black eyes shocked in her strong-boned brown face. "What you talk snuff? Vangie—"

"If I get to them first, I can give her a break."

She grabbed Dain's arms and started trying to shake him. It was like trying to shake an oak tree.

"What you talkin' 'bout? *Who* you talkin' about?"

"Maxton. His friends."

She let go of his arms. A slow shudder went through her. She stared at the sidewalk. Dain gently took her arm and urged her along. The streetlights were on automatic, blinking yellow caution in four directions at each intersection.

Somewhere far to the south a siren rose and fell, rose and fell.

"Straight she went off with Jimmy Zimmer? Mr. Creepo?"

"Straight. And they took—"

"I don't wanna hear it." She hugged herself as they walked, as if suddenly cold. "I don't wanna be havin' this conversation."

They crossed on a crosswalk; there was no traffic.

"Vangie who? From where?"

She didn't say anything for a quarter of a block, finally said in a rush, "Vangie Broussard. From I-don't-know-where. Never talked about 'did'—only about 'gonna.'" She gave her sudden deep laugh again, her fears for a moment forgotten. "That girl had the biggest collection of gonnas I ever heard."

"Gonna what?"

"Gonna make a big score. Gonna get took care of *right* by Maxton. But that Christmas party . . ."

She fell silent. Dain prompted, "What happened?"

"Maxton wanted her to take some important client into the private office during the party and fuck his brains out." She looked over at him, burst out, "She was in love with the dude, man, he say he love her, an' he ask her to do that! Was a couple weeks after that she started hittin' on Jimmy Zimmer—he already had his tongue hangin' out down to his shootops . . ."

They walked. Dain said, "Anything else you can tell me?"

"We roomed together, but she was a loner, didn't do a whole lot with the other kids. I came home one afternoon, must be like two weeks ago now, she was gone. The place spotless, a month's rent for her *and* me on my pillow, but not even a note . . ." She looked over at him, said suddenly, "We partied a couple times with Zimmer and his buddy, I never saw nuthin' in either one of 'em, but Vangie asked me."

"Tell me about the buddy."

"Bobby Farnsworth of Farnsworth, Fechheimer and Farnsworth. Mr. Cube." Her sudden urchin grin shaved ten

years off her age. "Boooo-o-o-ring. I'm not really into IRAs
and all that jazz, but like to him, *The Wall Street Journal* is
Rolling Stone."

"Stocks and bonds?"

"Chicago Board of Trade all the way, baby." She
stopped in front of a run-down brick apartment building.
"You walked me home after all. It's six floors straight up
unless they fixed the elevator, but if you want a cup of coffee and ain't afraid of heights—"

"You don't want to know me, Cindy," said Dain. "I'm
bad news. Even my cat won't purr."

She looked at him for a long moment, then nodded and
leaned forward and up to kiss him on the cheek.

"Goodbye, Mr. Sad Man," she said.

12

Before starting through the newspaper, Dain called Farnsworth, Fechheimer and Farnsworth. The receptionist sounded bored enough to be doing her nails behind the switchboard. He told her, "I'd like to make an appointment with Mr. Farnsworth to discuss setting up a rather substantial investment account."

"Mr. Farnsworth Senior or Junior?"

"Junior."

"Mr. Farnsworth Junior is in our San Francisco office for three months' training. If anyone else—"

"No. But his San Francisco home phone number might help."

He wrote it down, hung up. San Francisco. Could Zimmer and the woman, Broussard, also be in San Francisco? No. They would be hiding in Broussard's life, not Zimmer's. But a good coincidence for Dain just the same. When the time came, Farnsworth would be Zimmer's best bet for moving the bonds.

But first, Broussard. Cracking the Chicago police computer with his laptop would take longer than direct action, so he quickly scanned the morning newspaper, finally stopping at an item on the local news page.

COP IN COMA AFTER BRUTAL BEATING

When he got off-shift this morning at 4:00 a.m., plain-clothes detective Seth "Andy" Anderson of Central Station made the mistake of stopping off at a coffee . . .

Dain's ballpoint pen underlined *Seth "Andy" Anderson* and *Central Station,* then hand-scrawled a letter on a sheet of hotel stationery cut in half so it was memo size. Dain used the half without the letterhead, dating it five days earlier.

Andy:
I don't want to go through channels on this one, since it's about Vangie Broussard, that black-haired "exotic dancer" I been humping since she left Chicago. I think she was involved in a 187PC out here a couple nights ago, and if she was, I wanta bust it myself. I'll be in Chi on the 14th, can you pull her package to give me a look when I get there? Thanks, pal.

He scrawled *Solly* below the note as a signature, then added a handwritten postscript:

P.S. I need a sweetener in the Department since you-know-what.

Dain addressed an envelope to Andy Anderson at Central Police Station, Chicago, then paused to run a mental check. It was okay. Randy Solomon wasn't due back from vacation for two more days, so he put Solomon's SFPD return address in the upper left corner, stamped it, set the date on a self-inking rubber stamp for five days previously, and canceled the stamp.

Finally, he put in the letter, sealed it, opened it again

raggedly with his finger under the flap. He stuck the letter and an SFPD lieutenant's shield in a leather carrying case into the side pocket of the cheap, rather shabby suitcoat he had bought at the Salvation Army, and left the hotel.

Chicago's Central Police Station was old, ill-kept, angry-looking, as if it never got enough sleep and took a lot of Tums. At a booking desk from the days when Al Capone ran the city, Dain flashed his SFPD shield. In his off-the-rack suit and unshined shoes, an old-fashioned fedora mashed down on his head and an unlit cigar screwed into one corner of his mouth, he looked like fifteen years on the force.

"Yeah, welcome to Chicago," said the booking sergeant. "How are things out there in fruit and nut land?"

"That's L.A. We're the cool gray city by the bay."

"Yeah, Herb Caen. What can we do for you, Lieutenant?"

"Anybody awake in Vice at this hour?"

"Prob'ly ain't gone home yet." The sergeant grinned and handed him a visitor's badge that he clipped to the breast pocket of his suitcoat. "Elevator to the third floor, turn left."

Dain thanked him and rode the elevator up, not to Vice, but to the Detective Squadroom. Various plainclothesmen were at the battered desks, typing reports, interviewing complainants, witnesses, suspects. Off in a corner a black youth with dreadlocks was being fingerprinted by a Hispanic woman in a crisp blue uniform. Smoke blued the room. Dain's eyes found an empty desk with a DET. ANDERSON name block on it.

Going down the room drew Dain no more than a casual brush of eyes from the busy cops. He hooked a hip over the corner of the desk, in the same movement slipped his letter, envelope clipped to the back, underneath the top folder in Anderson's In box. He then leaned toward the man typing at the next desk. His nameplate read DET. KALER.

"Hey, pal."

The cop kept on typing. Unlike the stereotype, he was

good at it. Dain leaned over and tapped him on the shoulder. Kaler swung toward him, angry, pale eyes flashing.

"Andy, he's out for coffee 'r somethin'?"

Kaler began, "Listen, asshole, when—" then his cop eyes took in the policeman ID included on Dain's visitor's badge. He shrugged in wry apology, swiveled to face Dain. "Tough morning. You know Andy?"

"Y'know." Dain shrugged in turn. "I wrote I'd be in town, he was supposed to be pullin' a file for me to look at."

Kaler leaned back and locked his hands behind his head in a lazy manner. "Well, I got some good news and some bad news. Andy's in the hospital. Seems he stuck that hard fucking Swede head of his into something wasn't any of his business, and somebody tried to knock it off."

"What's the bad news?" asked Dain, deadpan.

Kaler gave a short hard bark of laughter.

"Yeah, you know our Andy, all right. Bad news is he'll live." He came forward in his chair, the unoiled swivel creaking when he did. "I can snoop Andy's desk for your note, and—"

Dain said very quickly, "No need to do that . . ." Then he seemed to catch himself. He seemed to make himself relax visibly. He shrugged. "Sure," he said.

Kaler checked the In box, found the note, read it standing over Dain. "I like it," he said finally, "especially all that you-know-what stuff. Tell me about that, and maybe I can . . ."

His voice trailed off. There was a $50 bill on the corner of the desk that had not been there before. He turned away, the trailing fingers of one hand sliding over the bill, palming it.

"I think I can find that file for you, Lieutenant Solomon."

Kaler returned with the BROUSSARD, EVANGELINE file: every stripper passed through police hands a time or two. On top were the Broussard mug shots, front and side, her fingerprint cards, a thin sheaf of report forms. They leafed through it together. When Dain carelessly flipped the file closed, his fingernail flicked off the paper clip holding her mug shots in place.

"Shit, nothing here. Couple soliciting busts . . ."

"Yeah," said Kaler, "couple indecent exposures when we hit a joint where she was dancing, couple of priors for the same thing down in New Orleans . . ." He gave a hearty laugh. "This chick has a hard time keeping her clothes on, don't she?"

"You've no idea," said Dain. He sighed. "Hell, it was worth a shot." He stood up. When he did, his hand hit the file and knocked it off the edge of the desk. "Shit."

Bending to retrieve it, he grunted slightly as if with effort. With his left hand he palmed the mug shots that had slid from the folder, stuck out his right to Kaler. They shook.

"Anyway, many thanks. What hospital's Andy in? I gotta fly back this afternoon, but maybe—"

"Wouldn't do any good, he's still in intensive care."

Dain shook his head. "Fuck of a note. Well, anyway, give him my best when you get in to see him."

"Sure thing."

Dain spent half a day working the O'Hare parking lots and shuttle buses with Broussard's mug shots, then spent most of his flight to San Francisco studying them. Even with the flat police lighting and the dehumanizing circumstances, her beauty shone through. Exotic was a good word. Deep tan or dark skin, dark eyes that challenged the camera, the cops behind the camera . . . The surname suggested a reason for her dark rather wild beauty. As did the soliciting busts in New Orleans.

It was going to be another routine operation. He would find them, Maxton would get his bonds back, Zimmer would probably get roughed up a bit, and that would be that. He might as well be working for legitimate clients on the right side of the law for all the good this was doing him.

Who would need a hitman in the Jimmy Zimmer bond caper?

Homicide had been jumping all morning. A tourist from Cincinnati had wandered into Emergency at S.F. General complaining of a headache, then had fallen dead on the floor. They had found a .22 slug in his brain. The cabbie who delivered him to the hospital had picked him up on Eddy Street in the Tenderloin.

A thirteen-year-old shot a fourteen-year-old dead with an A/R on full automatic in the parking area of one of the Western Addition housing projects in an argument over a crack concession.

When police arrived at a rather nice Victorian on Elizabeth Street on a neighbor's complaint, they found a seventy-three-year-old man watching *Santa Barbara* with a self-righteous set to his jaw and a bloody claw hammer in his hand. His sixty-eight-year-old wife lay on the floor in front of the TV. She had wanted *One Life to Live*.

In his private office Randy Solomon was working on the preliminary paperwork on the three killings. He was wearing a short-sleeved shirt, his jacket over the back of his chair.

Dain came through the open door. He was wearing horn-rims and a conservative three-piece suit and was carrying a slim attaché case. Randy hadn't laid eyes on him for over a year. His face hardened as he did an exaggerated double take.

"Well, well, the big private eye. A whole year, nothin', then here comes Jesus Christ. Down here slummin', white boy?"

Dain sat down in the visitor's chair.

"Why the hardnose, Randy?"

Solomon detoured around Dain to close the door, then came back so he could lean down into Dain's face. He said softly, "I knew a guy once—young, sharp, good mind, good investigator. Sweet wife and a nice little kid. Just getting started on his own . . . looking for that big case . . ."

"And they all lived happily ever after," said Dain.

Solomon ignored this. His voice was openly hostile.

"Know what I see now? A whore in a three-piece suit."

"I do what I always did, Randy. Find people."

"For the sleaze of the earth," snapped Solomon hotly, "with that fag bookseller pimping for you."

Dain was suddenly on his feet.

"What am I supposed to do, for fuck sake? Repos and wandering wives? The fuckers killed my family! Where else will I find them except outside the law?"

Solomon looked surprised, then chuckled and went around behind his desk. The tension suddenly went out of both men.

"Shit, I might of known. You getting anything?"

"Another day older and deeper in debt."

"So why the fancy getup?"

"I've been at the stock exchange cavorting with the bulls and the bears."

"Who's winning?"

"This morning, the bulls. To be exact. Robert Farnsworth of Farnsworth, Fechheimer and Farnsworth out of Chicago. Daddy sent him out here for three months of seasoning before giving him more control of the family brokerage business. Bobby-boy is best buddies with a guy I am seeking for a sort of connected Chicago lawyer named Maxton. This guy and an exotic dancer—"

"Teddy Maxton?"

"Yeah," said Dain in surprise, "you know about him?"

Randy waved a vague hand. "He comes out here as consulting defense counsel every once in a while. He's damned good in front of a jury." His voice, eyes, hardened slightly. "Our Teddy the kind of guy hires a hitman?"

Dain shook his head. "I'm just paying the bills with this one." He leaned forward in his chair, cleared his throat. "But I, ah, need a good wireman, Randy."

"You know that stuff isn't admissible in court," chided Solomon. "And it sure as hell ain't legal."

"Admissible in court I don't need, legal I don't care about. I just think this Zimmer will be calling Farnsworth and I want to be listening in."

Solomon tore a sheet from his memo pad, began writing on it. "Remember Moe Wexler?"

"Pensioned off six or seven years ago on a medical disability? Had a leg broken in about eight places . . ."

"That's Moe. Here's the address of his electronics shop." He handed Dain the memo slip with a wink. They stood. "How's my boyfriend? Shenzie the wonder cat?"

"Don't ask. You might get stuck with him again for a few days if this Farnsworth thing pans out. The neighbor lady in Mill Valley who usually takes him is out of town . . ."

Solomon gave his deep chuckle. "Anytime for the Shenzie cat." They shook hands, Dain started for the door. Randy spoke to his back. "How about some handball?"

Dain turned and looked at him. Suddenly grinned.

"How about tomorrow? I'll whup your ass."

"That's my man," said Randy happily. "The hopeless romantic to the bitter end."

13

Arched across the front window of the narrow storefront in Clement Street was MOE'S ELECTRONICS PLUS. Under this in smaller letters was, TVs—VCRs—Recorders—Radios, and under that in even smaller letters, *repair & service*. Dain pushed open the door, jangling a small brass bell fixed to a spring inside the top of the door. There was a wooden counter with an old-fashioned cash register, behind that a doorway to the work area covered with a heavy brown curtain.

The curtain was shoved aside by a big easygoing man running to fat. He had a cute little mouth and hair in his ears and ex-cop written all over him. He moved with a slight limp.

"Hello, Moe," said Dain.

Wexler studied him for a moment, then smiled genially.

"Eddie Dain," he said. "You're looking fit. Randy Solomon called, said you might be around, or I'd of thought somebody was sending an ex-49er tackle around to bust my other leg.''

"How's the first one?''

"Still busted.'' He hesitated. "I'm sorry about your wife and kid.''

Dain was silent. Wexler raised a hinged flap of countertop and went to the door to twist the bolt lock at the same time that he jerked down over the doorpane a small brown roller shade that had OUT TO COFFEE—BACK IN 15 on it. Dain had begun counting out $100 bills on the counter like dealing a hand of poker.

"One bug on the private phone of Robert Farnsworth at Farnsworth, Fechheimer and Farnsworth. They're a broker-age house on Pine across from the Pacific Coast Stock Exch—''

"You sure your call won't come through the switchboard?''

"My man is dumb, but not that dumb.''

Moe nodded. "They got a service door on Leidesdorff Alley with a lock on it you could open with garlic breath.''

"You ex-cops,'' marveled Dain. He counted out another sheaf of bills. "The second bug is at Farnsworth's apartment. He's got a three-month lease in that tall white stucco place on Montclair Terrace where Francisco—''

"Yeah. Gotcha.''

"Apartment three-C. We're looking for a call from a James Zimmer or anybody who could be Zimmer. I figure a week tops.''

Moe shuffled the bills together like a hand of cards.

"I can use an infinity mike at the brokerage house, can go back in for it afterwards. At the apartment I might have to go into the walls, that'd mean I'd have to leave the equipment.''

Dain gestured at the third fan of bills he had laid on the counter. "If you can salvage the equipment, consider the extra five bills a bonus.''

"A week gonna be enough?''

"If we've got no action in seven days, I'll have to rethink my premise.''

Moe started to pocket the folded bills, then hesitated.

"Randy says you're working for Teddy Maxton on this one."

"Randy's got a big mouth," said Dain coldly.

"We went through the academy together, what can I say?"

"What the fuck is it with Teddy Maxton and the SFPD? Mention his name and you all piss your pants in unison. Maxton's in Chicago, for Chrissake."

"He's got a long arm."

"That bother you, Moe?"

"It rains, my leg hurts, that bothers me. I can't get it up for the wife, that bothers me. Maxton don't bother me."

"Then why are we talking about him?"

Moe leaned forward slightly across the counter to look closer at Dain, as if confirming some rumor he'd heard.

"Watch your butt with this guy, Dain. He's one tricky son of a bitch."

Dain smiled for the first time since his wife and child had come up in the conversation.

"So am I, Moe. So am I."

Maxton got out of the elevator on the P-1 level under his office building and crossed the concrete to the Mercedes parked in his slot. It was another scorching Chicago summer afternoon, but Maxton, moving between his air-conditioned office and his air-conditioned home in his air-conditioned car, only felt the heat by his backyard pool, where he expected it.

He pushed the remote that unlocked the doors of the Mercedes, started to get in, checked the movement. Dain was sitting in the rider's side. Mozart's *Sinfonia Concertante*, K–64, was sweet as honey off the car's CD player.

"How the fuck did you get in here?"

Instead of answering, Dain said, "We're going out to O'Hare, I want to show you something."

"That'll take hours this time of day, and I've got two tickets to the Cubs game."

Dain said nothing. Maxton got in, grumbling, began fighting the rush-hour traffic out Wacker to the big convoluted freeway exchange that would put him on the John Kennedy north to O'Hare. Cars were stacked bumper-to-bumper, horns blared, exhausts fumed, light glared into drivers' eyes off polished chrome. The air conditioner whooshed softly under the Mozart.

"Zimmer and a peroxide blonde were booked on a flight leaving for Rio four hours after the bonds were taken," said Dain in a conversational voice.

This jerked Maxton's head around. "They left the *country?* How the fuck're you going to—"

"Remember last New Year's Eve office party? When you hired some exotic dancers to put on a show for the employees?"

"Of course. We'd had a good year, financially."

"Zimmer met her there."

"Who, goddam you?"

"The woman who planned this whole thing. You had a little something going with her yourself at the time, I hear."

Maxton said icily, "You hear wrong."

"She wasn't always a peroxide blonde. Think about it."

Dain slid down in the seat and shut his eyes. He didn't open them until the roar of a landing jetliner's engines penetrated even the Mercedes's vaunted sound-exclusion paneling, then he sat up suddenly.

"Get in the right lane, to long-term parking."

Maxton swung the wheel over, stopped at the striped arm, got his ticket from the machine, drove through. His voice was tentative, almost shocked. "You're saying it was . . . *Vangie?*"

"Evangeline Broussard," Dain nodded. "She planned the steal, she was waiting for Zimmer in an alley around the corner from the bank. Go down this row."

Maxton obediently drove down the long row of dusty cars.

"I don't get it, Dain. Why would Vangie—"

"You wanted her to fuck one of your business associates in the back room during the Christmas party, for Chrissake."

His bewilderment didn't lessen. "Yeah? So?"

"She thought she loved you, Maxton," Dain said in an almost defeated voice. "She thought you loved her."

"Loved her? She's a fucking hootch dancer, for Chrissake!"

"Stop here."

Dain walked over to Vangie's red Porsche; from the dust on it, and the dried rain-streaks on the windshield, it obviously had not been moved in many days. Maxton followed, still not knowing what they were doing there. On the far side of the Porsche, Dain leaned his elbows on the dusty top. Maxton faced him across the grimy red roof.

"And then?"

Maxton shrugged sullenly. "She did it, of course. A couple weeks later her gig ended, so we broke it off. But I gave her the money for a car since she was driving to New York . . ."

Dain patted his palms on the roof of the Porsche.

"This car. Right here. Vangie didn't expect anyone to connect her with Zimmer, probably figured the car would get stolen and that would be that."

Maxton started pounding his clenched fists on the car roof.

"Goddam her soul to hell! My money, my car! I'll see her dead, the rotten little bitch!"

Dain shrugged by raising one shoulder.

"That crap doesn't do any good, Maxton. Zimmer saw her at the party, fell hard. She saw him as a way to get back at you. She must have laughed herself sick when you decided to steal two million in bonds and handed them to Zimmer for safekeeping."

"And the fuckers are away clean! You may as well—"

"You ever consider what sort of trouble you'd have converting two million in American bearer bonds into cruzeiros in Brazil? When the rate is nearly four thousand to one and you don't even have the language? You can bet Vangie considered it."

"What . . . are you saying?"

"They never caught the plane. Doubled back to the city by airport limo, caught a bus to Texarkana, left it at some stop in between. Once they have you thinking South America, why leave the country? The bonds are legal tender in any brokerage house they walk into.''

"How do you know all this stuff?'' asked Maxton almost suspiciously.

"It's what I'm good at, remember?'' He walked around the car back toward the Mercedes, Maxton following.

"I'll get a list of the bonds to every brokerage—''

"No. You'll spook them. She's smart, I tell you.'' He stopped, opened the driver's door of the Mercedes. "She'll plan to wait a few months before cashing them in—''

"My bitch wife won't wait a few months, damn you! I'll put an army to work on the brokerage houses, we'll—''

"No army. Nobody. *Nada.* Zero. Nothing. Get it?''

Dain held the open door; after a moment's hesitation, Maxton slid in under the wheel.

"All right,'' he said, "I'll play it your way for the moment. What's your next move?''

"Go back to San Francisco.''

"San Francisco?''

"To wait. It won't be long, believe me. She won't be able to control him.''

"Wait is the goddamnedest stupidest idea I've ever—''

"It's time to quit looking for your prey and start looking for what your prey is looking for. In the dry season if you're a lion and your prey is a wildebeest, you wait by the water hole. If you're a red-tailed hawk and your prey is a field mouse, you soar over the—''

"You think she's in San Francisco?''

Dain slammed the door, walked away between the close-packed dusty cars. "Don't screw it up, Maxton,'' he said over his shoulder. "Wait for them to make their move. They will. Believe me.''

III

VANGIE

The Big Easy

THE SECRET OF
RECOGNITION

O nobly-born, that which is called death hath now come. Thou art departing from this world, but thou art not the only one; death cometh for all. Be not attached to this world; be not weak.

THE TIBETAN BOOK OF THE DEAD

14

Night—soft, warm, moist, seductive—handcuffed New Orleans to the Vieux Carré's blocked-off Bourbon Street like a kinky lover. Exotic underwear shops, crowded cheek by jowl with po'boy sandwich stands, displayed teddies and chemises and lace body stockings with open crotch panels for easy access. Traditional jazz poured out into the night from open doorways at the crowds of shirt-sleeve and summer-dress tourists.

Jimmy Zimmer strolled along a side street, stopped outside Carnal Knowledge where two strippers sprawled on straight chairs just outside the open doorway, loose meaty thighs spread wide to catch the cool outside breeze and the eye of passing males. He moved inside, stood near the stage, looking much seedier than he had in Chicago less than three weeks earlier. He seemed jumpy and determined, his eyes almost mean behind their horn-rims, his skin pale as if he spent all his time indoors.

Vangie's face registered consternation when she saw

Jimmy arrive. She was hand-cut crystal in a display of Coke bottles, her body moving to the music by its own volition. Rednecks shrieked obscenities at her, college boys made explicit suggestions, two black-leather lesbians moaned sexual dreams.

Through a gap in the fake plush curtains, Harry the Manager watched her as avidly as any john. He was a short man with a degenerate face; his bald pate, fringed with dandruff-flecked brown hair, gleamed with the urgent sweat of his thoughts.

When the music ended, Vangie came hurriedly through the curtain wearing only the required cache-sexe, her otherwise nude and magnificent body gleaming as if oiled. She had to corral Jimmy and send him hustling back to their room before her next show, and before he . . .

But Harry was right beside her, his short fat legs trotting to match her long muscular strides. "Baby, you're terrific! In two weeks you've almost doubled the gross!"

"So double my salary, Harry."

"Funny! Funny! Listen, baby, how about you be nice to me? I got friends. I can do you a lot of good in this town."

She had just enough time between numbers to do it if . . . But Harry's greedy fingers half cupped the ivory cone of one of her naked breasts as she tried to get through the dressing room door. She stepped back with a look of utter revulsion.

"Jesus, what a turd!" she said in a low, despairing voice.

Harry crowded her back against the door frame, grabbed her hand, pressed it against the bulging front of his pants.

"Feel it, baby! C'mon, feel it!"

She bent his little finger back, he squealed and let her go as she darted through the doorway and slammed the door an inch from his nose. She shot the bolt, yelled through the door.

"Go jerk off into a Handi-Wipe!"

Harry smashed the heel of his hand against the wall and turned away with a vicious, congested look. Inside, Vangie put her head down on her arms. Oh God, for just a little release from pressure! She raised her head and looked at her reflection in the mirror. The makeup lights made her look garish and cheap.

"They don't lie," she said aloud to her reflection.

She had $2 million in bearer bonds but still had to dance until four in the morning because it wouldn't be safe to cash them in for another six months. Two million! Freedom. A way out. Worth whatever it took, worth doing damn near anything. The music reverberated through the walls and she stood up.

If only Jimmy didn't bring the hunters down on them in the meantime.

Dain, backlit for a moment by the lights of a turning automobile, looked hulking and pitiless. It was ten o'clock and San Francisco's financial district was zipped up for the night except for a few old-style restaurants like Schroeder's down on Front Street. As he passed the Russ Building's inset entrance, Moe Wexler fell in beside him to hand over a small flat packet a few inches in diameter.

"Great work, Moe. But why all the cloak-and-dagger?"

Moe's eyes were constantly shifting, probing the empty street ahead and behind them. "When I went to check the apartment bug tonight, there was another one in place that wasn't there before." His roving eyes slid across Dain, were gone again. "Ah . . . what if we're talking Maxton here?"

"I thought Maxton didn't bother you any."

"Yeah, well, that was talk, this is the real world, like."

Moe peeled off into Sutter Street. Dain kept going down Montgomery to Market, his face thoughtful.

He sat on the edge of the bed in his loft, a yellow Walkman Sport beside his thigh, listening again to Moe's tape. Shenzie listened also, head cocked to one side as if waiting at a mouse hole. The voice talked of the bonds with remarkable clarity.

"Nothing wrong with them, is there?" asked Farnsworth in a jocular voice. "Not forged? Counterfeit? Stolen?"

"Good God no!" Zimmer's voice was high-pitched and full of fear. A voice that looked over its shoulder as it talked.

"Then take them to our Chicago office and—"

"I'm out of town."

Farnsworth's voice said, "Out of town where?"

"N . . . I can't tell you that."

Dain hit the stop button.

"Hear it, Shenzie? Hear the 'N' he didn't quite swallow?"

Dain punched EJECT to pop out the cassette. Shenzie reached out a sudden delicate paw and struck the Walkman three times, very quick light blows, then whirled and ran to the far corner of the bed where he crouched, glaring balefully. Dain ignored the histrionics.

"Just what I told you, cat. Hiding in her life, not his." He tapped the cassette thoughtfully against his open palm. "But just who put the other bug on Farnsworth's apartment phone?"

Shenzie said *meòw*, then relaxed his baleful stance to wash himself with a delicate pink tongue. Dain picked up the phone. "You're gonna visit Randy for a few days, cat. He volunteered."

In the Vieux Carré, Vangie and Zimmer walked away from the far sad dying sounds of Bourbon Street. It was four in the morning. Around them were darkened windows, rumbling garbage trucks, early delivery vans; ahead, a darkened movie theater marquee with light spilling out across the sidewalk beyond it.

"Jimmy, I thought we'd agreed you'd stay off the street until I could get together another traveling stake for us."

"I'm taking care of the traveling stake," boasted Jimmy.

Since the bond theft, their original sexual relationship had developed an almost mother/son dimension. Vangie grabbed his arm and hurried him toward the light laid across the sidewalk beyond the darkened theater.

"I don't want to hear this—but I've *got* to hear it."

They passed under the sagging marquee. Half its unlit bulbs were broken. It advertised a triple bill: *Caught from*

Behind, Stiff Lunch, Nympho Queens in Bondage. Beyond was the DELTA HOTEL—*Day—Week—Month—Maid Service*, with rooms on the upper floors above the theater.

In the rear of the lobby a sallow-faced clerk dozed behind the check-in desk. A huge slow floor fan was trying to stir around the heat and perhaps shove some of it out the open door. Two shirt-sleeved white men and three black men seeking some illusory coolness not to be found in their rooms sat there despite the hour, wide-kneed and slack. Vangie half dragged Zimmer back toward the elevator. Their eyes followed her across the lobby as most men's eyes would always follow Vangie.

Zimmer was babbling. "See, Vangie, what I did was—"

"In the room, honey."

"But you have to understand that—"

"In the room."

It was a room where love and hope would bleed to death, blessedly dark except for street light leaking around the drawn window curtain. Vangie locked the door, Zimmer switched on the single low-watt overhead. Vangie got a flat brown pint of bourbon from the dresser, at the sink poured some of it into the glass from the toothbrush holder, added tap water. She leaned against the sink to face Jimmy with glass in hand.

"Okay, Jimmy," she said wearily, "hit me."

"I called Bobby Farnsworth tonight."

Despair entered her eyes, but somewhere she found a smile to paste on her mouth. "What'd you call him?"

"You know what I mean, Vangie—on the telephone."

"Okay, what'd you *tell* him?"

"I didn't *tell* him anything. He told me things. What's the matter with you anyway?" His voice had a febrile hostility; since he'd found in Vangie the strength he could never possess himself, he had to rebel against it. "*I* got the bonds for us."

"Yes, Jimmy." She took a big gulp of her drink, made a face. "You got the bonds for us."

"Now I'm going to get us the money for the bonds."

"Or get us killed."

"Why do you always have to belittle everything I do?"

His face was petulant, his voice whiny. "I told Bobby I was out of town with some bearer bonds, and he told me how to convert them. I didn't even leave him a phone number or anyplace where—"

"We agreed we didn't touch the bonds for six months, didn't we, Jimmy?" Vangie set her glass in the sink. "Here it is less than three weeks, you're calling a broker already."

"It's easy for you. I'm stuck in this cockroach palace staring at the walls, while you . . ." His voice had been rising, suddenly he was shrieking, his face red, veins standing out along the sides of his neck. "While you get your rocks off shaking your titties for a bunch of fucking rednecks!"

Vangie seized her breasts and squeezed them cruelly. "You think having guys do this to you is fun?" she cried.

Then as fast as it had come, her anger was gone. She shivered and poured the rest of her drink down the sink.

"I know it's hard for you to be cooped up here, honey, but as soon as I've gotten us together a traveling stake, we'll move on, I'll get a waitressing job—"

"And make extra money on your back in the private room?"

She sighed and went to look out the window, standing with one knee on the edge of the bed, her other foot on the floor. It was an unconscious pose of great grace, a dancer's pose. Her voice was harsh and strained.

"Why don't I just split with the bonds and leave you here for Maxton to find? Who the hell needs you?"

"Vangie, don't talk that way!" He came up behind her, slid his hands under her arms. "Vangie, please, I . . . I love you. I want . . ." His hands cupped her breasts as he kissed the nape of her neck. "I need to make love to you, need to know that . . ."

She shook him off without turning, irritation in her face.

"Jimmy, Jimmy, there's somebody coming after us and all you want to do is fuck. Can't you feel him out there?"

"All I feel is your rejection of me."

He used his chastised-child voice. Vangie wasn't hearing.

"Once I saw a deer some dogs had been running, Jimmy. They lost its scent, he came down to the bayou to drink." She paused to lay her forehead against the cool window-pane. "Usually deer, they just stay on the bank, sort of nuzzle aside the lily pads and duckweed and dead vegetation to drink. But those hounds, they'd run this one pretty hard, he wanted fresh water. So he waded out toward the channel . . ."

"Vangie, I'm sorry, honey. Please don't . . . shut me out."

"Only the little regular splashes a deer makes walking are different from those a muskrat makes swimming or a raccoon makes wading, and a gator can tell the difference, every time. Up the channel came ol' gator, underwater. When the deer waded out to the edge of the channel and put his head down to drink . . . *Snap!*"

She slapped both hands, fingers splayed, against the glass.

"Ol' gator had him by the nose." Her palms left long wet smears on the glass. "He drug that deer into the water and gave a *jerk!*"—her hands jerked into fists pressed convulsively against her cheeks—"and the deer's neck was broke." She gestured down at the empty dawn street. "Out there somewhere is *our* gator . . ."

"Vangie, please . . ."

She turned to transfix Zimmer with a whisper.

"Waiting to break our neck."

15

After his 5:30 A.M. workout at World Gym, Dain swung back to Tam Valley to pick up Shenzie. He let himself in through the front door, got the carry case from Albie's now-deserted bedroom, and went through to the kitchen.

"What?" he exclaimed.

There was a scrabbling of paws as the bandit-faced baby raccoon who was eating Shenzie's kibble ran to squirm his fat little butt back out through the cat door in a panic. An outraged Shenzie was sitting on the kitchen counter watching the thief eat, his white whiskers standing straight out from the sides of his face like a radical acupuncture treatment gone awry.

Dain, fighting the morning rush across the Golden Gate, laughed at Shenzie all the way into the city. He arrived at Mel's Drive-in on Lombard just at eight. Mel's was a deliberate anachronism, an attempt to recapture the fifties feeling of the original Mel's on south Van Ness, which had been a huge circular barn of a place with roller-skating waitresses.

On the walls of this Mel's were black-and-white photos—
stills from American Graffiti; Marilyn Monroe at the original Mel's, sucking on a malt; waitresses with beehive hair-
dos, wearing slacks and Ike jackets, serving hamburgers to
grinning boys with duck's-ass haircuts and packs of Camels
rolled up in their sleeves. A lot of the boys would have died
in Korea.

Somewhere they had found old booths of cigarette-
scarred vinyl with miniature jukebox selectors on the back
wall. You could flip through deliberately dated original cuts
of Frank Sinatra, the Pretenders, Billy Eckstine, Frankie
Laine—pick your tunes, drop your quarters, and the Wur-
litzer gleaming in pastel yellow and purple and cherry red up
by the cash register would play them for you.

Doug Sherman waved a languid hand around when Dain
joined him in one of the booths. "How banal of you, dear
boy."

"Not at all," said Dain. "Lets you rub elbows with the
common man." He had been finding Sherman extraordinar-
ily smug as of late. "Have you ordered?"

"Just coffee. I figured once you'd had your little joke,
we'd go somewhere to get—"

"This is a great breakfast place, Dougie. The four basic
food groups—salt, fat, cholesterol, carcinogens. And *four-
teen* Elvis selections on the juke, including 'Hound Dog'
and 'Blue Suede Shoes.' On Tuesdays you can join the fun
with carhop waitresses. I think I've died and gone to
heaven."

"My, aren't we antic this morning," said Sherman snidely.

A waitress bustled up on thick ankles, wearing a rustling
black nylon skirt and white cotton men's-style shirt with
miniature black bow tie. She would have been about twenty
when the original Mel's had opened a few years after the
war.

"Coffee?" she asked.

"Yes." Dain decided to do the entire job on Dougie-
baby. "And I'm ready to order. Bacon cheeseburger with
fries, order of onion rings, a chocolate shake." He looked
over at Sherman's ashen face. "You ought to get one,
Doug—they're great!"

"My God!" breathed Sherman. "Do you realize what's in . . ."

The waitress chirped at him, "How about you, sir?"

"Nothing, er, ah, a refill on the coffee, and, ah, a glass of orange juice." She wrote, nodded, started away, Sherman called after her, "Is that O.J. fresh-squeezed?"

"Yessir," she piped, aged eyes bright, "I squoze it out of the carton myself just this morning."

Sherman repeated, "My God," then turned to Dain with a glint of anger in his eyes. "Why did you really bring me here?"

"I'm on my way to the airport, I've got something I—"

"Back to Chicago?"

"No."

"So Mr. Maxton's problem was resolved quite rapidly."

"Not resolved. Suspended. I've been waiting for the tape of a phone tap to confirm my next move. My man found someone else was tapping the same phone. Maybe Maxton is playing games with me, so . . ." He shrugged. "I wanted you to hear something, check my assumptions."

The waitress arrived with their food on a single big platter balanced on one arthritic hand. Sherman took a cautious sip of orange juice; Dain slurped his chocolate shake, began wolfing down golden-brown french-fried onion rings. The look on Sherman's face was worth it.

Munching away, he took the yellow Walkman out of his pocket and set it on the table, punched PLAY.

"Robert Farnsworth here. How may I—"

"This is Jimmy."

Sherman's hand darted out to hit *stop*.

"Are you *crazy*?" he hissed at Dain across the table. "Playing an illegal surveillance tape in a public place . . ."

Dain looked around. In the next booth were a tall trim brown-haired man with glasses and a short white-haired muscular overweight man wearing a red shirt in a Southwest American Indian motif. Whenever the jukebox paused to change tunes, they could be heard taking turns trashing publishers and bemoaning Hollywood agents who never returned their phone calls.

Back in the open kitchen the cooks, just out of their teens

and wearing tall white chefs' hats on top of too-long hair, bopped and jinked to Buddy Holly's stuttery "Peggy Sue." The air was heavy with the smell of frying bacon, sizzling eggs, french fries bubbling in hot grease. The place was jammed, the din atrocious.

"With the music going, you'd need a shotgun mike in here to hear what those guys are saying at the next table."

He turned on the Walkman again.

"Jimmy! I've been calling your office long-distance, they keep saying you're out of town. I want to know if you have any phone numbers out here in San Francisco for me. Girls like—"

Zimmer's voice interrupted. "Bobby, that . . . ah, client who has the . . ." he cleared his throat, "bearer bonds . . ."

Farnsworth was immediately all business. "These are the bonds you were telling me about in Chicago, Jimmy?"

"Yes, yes."

"Nothing wrong with them, is there?" asked Farnsworth in a jocular voice. "Not forged? Counterfeit? Stolen?"

Zimmer exclaimed in a near panic, "Good God no!"

"Then take them to our Chicago office and—"

"I'm out of town."

Farnsworth's voice said, "Out of town where?"

"N . . . I can't tell you that."

"Attorneys!" He sighed. "Okay, look in your local phone book and see if Farnsworth, Fechheimer and Farnsworth has an office in whatever city—"

"I already did. They do."

"Bravo! Take in the bonds and . . ."

Dain punched off the Walkman. "The rest is just verbiage."

"What's it all about?" said Sherman. "Who're the players?"

"Jimmy Zimmer stole two million bucks in stolen bearer bonds from our friend Maxton. Bobby is his stockbroker buddy temporarily in San Francisco. It was Bobby's phone I bugged."

"So the bonds were stolen twice."

"Technically, embezzled the first time. Anyway, Jimmy-baby is running around with a woman named Vangie Broussard. By her Chicago arrest record, her first busts were in New Orleans for dancing nude on barroom tables at the age of sixteen. So . . .''

''You're off to New Orleans?'' demanded Sherman in surprise. He gestured at the Walkman. ''On the basis of *that*?''

''That—and the second bug on Farnsworth's phone.''

''But why New Orleans? Because a woman dances on tables when she's a teenybopper—''

''It's on the tape—didn't you catch it?'' His food had gotten cold while they listened to the recording. Maybe he wouldn't have to eat it. ''When Jimmy was asked where he was calling from, he voiced the letter 'N' before he caught himself. 'N.' New Orleans. The brokerage firm has a New Orleans office, Broussard's first arrest was in New Orleans, it's home territory for her. Plus her name—Broussard. That's a Cajun name.''

''I suppose it fits.'' Sherman was staring at him as if seeing him for the first time. ''Have you ever considered what a very strange man you are, Dain?''

''I doubt Nielsen would choose you as a test viewer, Doug.''

Sherman chuckled and nodded. ''*Touché.*'' He leaned forward across the table. ''But even if by some strange event they should be there, how do you plan to—''

''She's too smart to let Jimmy cash any of the bonds this soon, so she'll be dancing in some topless joint in the Old Quarter to raise them a travel stake.''

Sherman hesitated, spoke as if with difficulty. ''Dain, I have a bad feeling about this one because of that second bug . . .''

Dain stood up, scooping up the check and leaving a too-large tip in its place. ''And I have a good feeling about it— because of that second bug.'' He stuck out his hand; Sherman shook it. ''I've got Shenzie in the car, I've got to drop him off at Randy Solomon's place before I go to the airport.''

''I'm surprised you'd leave your cat with that Gestapo thug. Will there by anyplace I can reach you if—''

''I'll reach you. If.'' He grinned again, pointed at the

Walkman with the Farnsworth tape still inside it. "Keep that for me until I get back. Just in case."

He left his car in his rented parking place across the Embarcadero from the loft, caught the shuttle bus to the airport, and was in New Orleans in time to watch the sunset.

16

Here the Mississippi was the classical Mark Twain river—lazy brown water, green banks, a churning paddle wheeler angled upstream to fight the current. On the landing dock was insomniac Dain, one of the few early passengers waiting to catch the deliberately anachronistic paddle wheeler's first trip of the day. His only lead was Vangie; he could only look for her at night. So he rode in a clopping horse-drawn carriage through genteel upper-crust neighborhoods, watched the Vieux Carré street life through wrought-iron filigreed balconies, listened to the music starting to strut from some of the clubs.

Dain went through the open passageway to the hotel court where the fountain burbled and brightly clad tourists sipped tall pastel drinks. From the courtyard, he went along Chartres to Conti, turned left toward the rising sounds of Bourbon Street. Wandered, pausing to look in windows, peering through open club doorways at the entertainment inside. Stood on a corner to watch black boys tap-dance for thrown coins.

A topless joint, the music not very good, leave without even making it to the bar for a drink. Stand on the sidewalk eating a po'boy and drinking beer from a paper cup. Then plunge back into the night world.

Better music, the hornman a Muggsy Spanier clone, nurse a beer through a whole round of floor shows, leave the bottle half-full behind him. Just another single male alone on his own in the big city. To bed at dawn, to not sleep worth a damn.

Another day to kill. He rode a streetcar named Desire out to the end of the line, rode it back in again, spent a half hour admiring the stations of the cross and the stained glass at St. Louis Cathedral, sat in a pew, feet on the kneeler . . . his eyelids drooped . . .

The black hole between Marie's breasts blossomed red. Her eyes were wild, her hair was wild, from her mouth, strained impossibly wide, came a hoarse masculine SCREAM, quickly muffled

Dain jerked erect, mouth-breathing, looked around quickly. A nun in a habit was staring at him from across the aisle. A little child was crying, pointing a finger. He almost fled.

At the oyster bar of Houlihan's, he watched a man commit murder on fresh dripping bivalves with great skill and a sharp knife. Couldn't eat, found a karate dojo, exhausted himself with two hours of the basic "forms" of his second-degree black belt—two *taikyoku* drills, five *pinans*, and the other "open hand" drills—*saifa, kanku, tensho* and *sanchin*.

Back at his room he lay nude on the bed, tried to justify his life. Whatever he did was meaningless. Lassitude gripped him. He was surprised to realize that he hoped Broussard would outwit him, but he knew she wouldn't. He was too good at the precise geometry of manhunting, she was a prey animal that

Between Marie's beautiful breasts the black hole blossomed red. Her eyes were wild, her hair was wild

Dain woke with a yell, bathed in sweat. He was falling to pieces. He took another shower; when he emerged, wet hair slicked back, towel around his waist, another night had fallen and the old-fashioned streetlights glowed from their cast-iron poles. Music drifted up from Bourbon Street to his small outside balcony, along with the clip-clop of a horse-drawn buggy in Rue Chartres. He leaned on the filigreed railing. Jasmine and mock orange filled the air with heavy fragrance.

He had to find her soon or abandon the search.

Midnight again. Dain leaned in the doorway of yet another exotic dance club on one of the side streets of the Quarter—for the moment he had exhausted Bourbon Street. How many had he hit tonight, how many more would he have to hit before he scored or admitted that his logic had been faulty—or was driven away by his now incessant nightmares?

Another hour, another joint. Different faces, different voices, different music, all the same. The gyrating woman was past her prime, like pheasant hung so long that the skin had a greenish tinge and when you shook it all the feathers fell out. When he left the mostly empty joint, he set his untouched beer on an empty table in passing. Somebody was gulping it down from the bottle before he cleared the doorway.

Directly across the narrow street was something called Carnal Knowledge. For some reason it was jumping, blaring, spilling customers out the open doors. Raucous rebel yells, groans, screamed sexual obscenities. If the two scantily clad women sprawled spread-legged in chairs outside the joint were typical, its success was undeserved.

Dain slid inside. Very good music pounded a wicked beat for the topless girl writhing onstage. Being tall, he could just see her over the silhouetted heads of shouting, arm-waving tourists and drunks. The dancer was Vangie Broussard.

She was magnificent, of body, face, movement. He felt an

irrational flash of sympathy for this bright wood duck among the mud hens as he turned away, edged back out of the crowd again. He felt an equally irrational flash of caution. Why? There was no reason anybody should be tailing him. But what reason had there been for that extra bug on Farnsworth's phone?

One of the resting dancers blocked his way with a meaty white thigh. "Don't like girls, baby? That one's hot stuff."

Dain patted her cheek. "So are you, darlin', so are you."

He went on, feeling the little momentary fierce joy he'd always felt the rare times he'd beaten Marie at chess. Nothing to do with winning: rather with the implacable beauty of

Marie, her eyes wild, her hair wild as her feet came up off the floor with the force of her death

Dain growled aloud, thrust the image away. No, goddammit, don't rob yourself of this triumph, minuscule though it might be. Make it pay off. Then maybe Marie could stop haunting his dreaming and—now—even his waking hours.

Deserted 2:00 A.M. street, the nightlife behind him, its raucous sounds dim on the air. He'd come this way deliberately, still wary, the same wariness that will make a leopard lay up on its own backtrail to ambush the white hunter he doesn't even know is tracking him.

Okay, deserted enough here. Dain took out the little pocket guide to the French Quarter he had gotten at the hotel desk, used it as an excuse to stop abruptly and gawp up at the next pair of street signs. Yes! An echo of sound scraped from the pavement—only it was not an echo because he had stopped moving. He squinted up at the signs, down at the guide, nodded and turned down Ursulines.

When he was out of sight, a tall spare man in excellent condition, with the coloring and weathered look of the outdoors, cut across Burgundy at an angle toward the corner where Dain had disappeared. His shock of sandy hair had natural curl and was shot with gray, he wore glasses with a half-moon of bifocal on the lower curve of lens. Like Dain, he was sauntering.

Moving through the bright lights and thinning crowds, Dain got fragmentary images of the tall spare weathered figure before it could slip off the edges of reflecting store windows. So, he'd been picked up on the street sometime during the evening. Dain felt totally alive for the first time since his snake dance in the desert. Hunting, he had become prey. Wonderful!

He turned off on Conti, went in through the archway to the hotel courtyard, in the tiny taproom was served by a black-haired girl in leather shorts and halter who dispensed drinks with a smile and a lot of cleavage. Leather-bound book clipped under one arm, he crossed the courtyard to a small round white wrought-iron table near the splashing fountain. At this time of the morning, he was the only person in the court. A gecko hung in sideways patience against the curved side of the fountain.

He set down the icy opened imported beer on the table, seated himself with his glass of ice water, the pastel lights from the fountain playing across his face. A chair scraped being drawn out. Dain spoke without glancing over.

"Pauli Girl. I took the chance you were a beer drinker."

The stalker tipped the glass to pour beer without getting too much of a head. His hands were big, strong, angular. He had a soft inviting Louisiana accent.

"You make me feel lacking in southern hospitality, Mr. Dain, buying for me in my own town."

Dain looked at him. He was a big man, big as Dain but without Dain's weight of muscle. His hard-bitten face had an inner calm behind the hardness. Dain matched his courtly tone.

"You have the advantage of me, sir."

"Keith Inverness."

Neither man offered to shake hands. There was not so much antagonism as wariness between them, mutual recognition by hunting animals whose territories happened to overlap.

"You still have the advantage of me, sir."

"Because I know who you are? A man in my line of work hears things from time to time, Mr. Dain."

"Your line of work." Dain made it a statement, not a question. Inverness smiled slightly.

"I guess you could say it's the same line of work as yours—except mine has a pension at the end of it."

Dain said pleasantly, "What if I told you that my line of work is rare books?"

"Like this?"

Unexpectedly, Inverness reached across the table to snatch up Dain's leather-bound volume. His big hands were remarkably quick. He riffled through it, allowed himself a small smile at its harmlessness as he laid it on the table.

"The things people keep in cutout books might surprise you, Mr. Dain."

"I doubt that."

With what seemed like genuine regret, but without any sudden moves, Inverness took a badge in a leather case from his pocket and laid it on the table.

"I guess you'd better make that Lieutenant of Detectives Inverness, Mr. Dain." He drank beer, wiped his lips almost daintily with one of the paper napkins on the table. "Like you, I track people down. But inside the law."

"That's okay with me," said Dain.

"I'm also New Orleans police liaison with the Louisiana State Commission on Organized Crime." Dain was silent. "We'd kind of like to know who you're looking for in New Orleans, and for whom."

"Not who—what," said Dain, suddenly misty-eyed. "And for me. New Orleans jazz. Dixieland. Storyville. The heart—*the soul*—of the blues. *My* heart and soul are transported back to those halcyon days when the Nigras all had rhythm and clapped hands and knew their place . . ."

Inverness nodded, unhurriedly stood and put his badge away. He said in an almost apologetic voice, "You're too good at finding people, for all the wrong people. You couldn't expect to remain anonymous forever. Enjoy your stay in New Orleans."

Dain sat unmoving, watching Inverness depart, his left thumb scraping idly down through the label of the empty beer bottle to tear it in half. The dancing colored water jet beyond his head made his profile very sharp and clear.

To hell with it. He already knew where Vangie worked;

just tag her to find out where she lived, make sure she was still with Zimmer, give Maxton the information, fade out . . .

But what would happen to Vangie then?

Goddammit, why should he care what happened to her?

Also, someone with a lot of clout had gotten the Louisiana Organized Crime Commission to send around a very good man to tell Dain, in essence, to get out of town. It couldn't be Maxton, checking up on him. Maxton didn't know he was here . . .

Wait a minute. Could *Maxton* be under investigation? Couldn't that explain Inverness? Organized-crime people in Chicago had Maxton under surveillance, they identified Dain, tagged him to New Orleans, notified Inverness . . .

That didn't work. Inverness would have known Dain had been hired by Maxton, wouldn't have asked. All right, what if Dain's presence was muddying the water so his superiors told Inverness to get Dain out of the picture . . .

But then Inverness would have known where he was staying, would have tagged him at his hotel rather than on the street . . .

No. Somebody knew he was in New Orleans, knew what he looked like or had pictures to send—Inverness had been able to pick him up cold—but was unable to tell Inverness where he was staying. Jesus, could he actually somehow have crossed the tracks of the killers who

Marie was smashed back and up, her mouth strained impossibly wide . . . Albie's legs were blasted back down the hall out of sight . . .

The bottle in Dain's hand exploded. He looked at it in surprise, opened his fingers slowly. It was shattered where he had been gripping it, the bottom and neck were intact. The glass had not cut his calloused palm. He shook his head to rid it of the shards.

Nonsense. But it had decided him. He checked his watch. Three-thirty A.M. He would keep on with Maxton's investigation, because something connected with it had stirred *something* up. So just keep going until he found out what and who and why. He'd checked for tails leaving the hotel before, had gotten careless through the long night, but he'd had that flash of apprehension and so had shown no reaction at all when he'd spotted Vangie.

So Inverness wouldn't be expecting him to go back out tonight, thus wouldn't still be tailing him.

Carnal Knowledge was dark and silent, closed. From down the street came the rattle-clash of garbage pails being put out. The door opened and Vangie and the dancer who had stopped Dain earlier that night emerged.

She said wearily to Vangie, "Another buck, another fuck. Wanna go get coffee, kiddo, or—"

"Home and to bed," said Vangie. "See you tonight, Noreen."

Vangie turned and started up the street, her heels loud on the sidewalk. Down the block ahead of her, on the other side of the street, a large muscular drunk shambled from a recessed storefront and staggered in the direction she was going with a too-much-to-drink pace unremarkable in the Vieux Carré at four in the morning.

17

It was midafternoon and the pitiless New Orleans sun struck blinding light from the chrome of passing cars, baked the sidewalks, softened the blacktop: a sweltering, shirt-sleeves kind of day. A clerk dozed behind the check-in desk at the Delta Hotel. The huge slow floor fan stirred around the heat. The same five old codgers in shirt sleeves were again—or still—sitting around with their faces and bodies slack. A sixth was sprawled with a newspaper over his face, gently snoring.

Across from the dozing clerk the elevator doors opened. Vangie came out wearing a light summer dress that showed little but suggested much, subtly touching and caressing her body as she crossed the lobby with her long dancer's stride. Half a minute after she had gone out into the street, the old codger under the newspaper harrumphed and hawked and sat up, crumpling the paper aside. He stood up, rubbing his eyes, and shambled out apparently still unsteady from his nap.

Vangie went into the cathedral where Dain had wakened screaming in his pew the day before. The old man waited outside on a bench in Jackson Square. Vangie emerged from the cathedral, bought a sandwich and a soft drink from one of the portable wheeled po'boy stands set up to catch the tourist trade. She went down St. Anne past the street artists and hawkers, bought two pralines in opaque paper slips from the store on the corner, crossed Decatur with the light, heading for the waterfront.

On the far side of the walkway across the railroad tracks, Vangie went down rough wooden steps to the brown Mississippi lapping over tumbled black rocks. She sat two steps up from the water, put her pralines and soft drink down beside her, in no hurry to eat. Instead, she watched the river traffic for nearly ten minutes, her unwrapped sandwich open on its waxed paper in her lap. At this hour she was alone on the steps.

When she finally took a big bite of po'boy, chewing without inhibition, a shadow fell across her. She didn't look up, not even when a man sat down on the same step five feet away.

"Think those prayers in the cathedral are going to do the trick?" he asked in a conversational tone.

She looked over at him hard with cold eyes, but he was not looking at her, was looking instead at a tow of barges being shoved up-current by a river steamer. He looked almost sad. Vangie was suddenly strident around her mouthful of sandwich.

"Blow it out your flutter-valve, Jack."

A big black Labrador that had been lapping water and scaring the fingerling rock bass around the half-submerged stones came up to thrust his dripping muzzle into Dain's hand. Dain fondled him behind the ears, still not looking at Vangie.

"Dain. Edgar Dain." He reached over, broke an edge off one of Vangie's pralines, told the dog, "No teeth!" as a warning against snapping at it, then offered the morsel to him. The dog wolfed it, ecstatic. Dain said, "Maxton sent me to find you. I've found you."

The girl gradually stopped chewing, like an engine run-

ning down. Suddenly the rich mix of spicy meats and
cheeses was cardboard in her mouth. She looked surreptitiously about, fearful of seeing bulky men in Chicago over-
coats coming down the steps after her. No one was close to
them, no one at all.

The man who had said his name was Edgar Dain was still
watching the water. His face was still sad. His hands had
given the rest of her praline to the dog, who lay down at his
feet, panting with his tongue out and a silly look on his face.

"Sorry. I fed one of your pralines to the dog."

Vangie shuddered as if the scorching sunlight had a wind-
chill factor. "Jesus, you're a cold-blooded bastard." No answer. "It was that goddam phone call of Jimmy's, wasn't
it?"

"That confirmed it, yes."

The river looked very peaceful. Downstream the same
side-wheeler full of tourists that Dain had ridden two mornings before bellowed raucously with its steam whistle. Dain
chose his words carefully, as if they were brittle and might
break.

"Maxton is screaming for blood, but I think if he had his
bonds back he'd not go looking too hard for you or Zimmer."

She began shrilly, "That fucker's screaming for blood?
What about . . ." She stopped, controlled herself. "Yeah, we
give you the bonds and they don't get to Maxton, and we
end up—"

"I don't want the bonds, Vangie."

"Oh sure, I believe you."

Dain scratched the black Lab behind the ears, stared out
over the slow brown water, shook his head, said patiently,
"You came in by bus, you're too smart to leave a locker key
with Zimmer, so if I searched you right now . . ."

Vangie had sprung to her feet at mention of a bus depot
locker key. This jerked the Labrador's head up, but she was
just standing there. He chuffed and put his head down again.
Slowly, uncertainly, Vangie sat back down.

"Maxton doesn't know where you are—yet." He turned
to look at her. "I stirred somebody up by coming here to

look for you—for my own reasons I want to find out who and why.''

''Maybe that I'd believe. Good old self-interest.''

Dain was stroking the dog's back absently. ''But I'm going to have to give him something pretty soon.''

She said despairingly, ''If I fuck you will you—''

''No.''

''Doesn't it bother you that we might be killed?''

''I stopped worrying five years ago about what happens to people.'' Smothered anger entered his voice. ''Especially people who ask for it.'' He stood up. ''If you don't give them back to Maxton I won't be able to help you, Vangie.''

''Jimmy won't do that,'' she said regretfully.

''Then *you* give them back.'' He was suddenly, harshly angry. ''You stole two million dollars from a guy who said he loved you and then offered you to his friends—''

''Yeah, so I stole his fucking bonds. And you know what? I'm *glad* I did if it gives that pig one sleepless . . .''

She ran down again, a startled look on her face as if she hadn't known she was capable of so much hatred. Dain nodded.

''That's terrific, Vangie. Some great revenge you're getting on him. *Think* about what can happen, for Chrissake! Keep the room you have, but have a friend rent you another room in your hotel under another name and sleep in that one. And keep Zimmer off the street—I might not be the only one looking.''

Vangie started to speak, stopped. Her spirit was gone.

''How do I get hold of you?''

''Call me at the De La Poste Motel in Chartres Street by this time tomorrow. I can give you that long.''

''Edgar Dain. De La Poste Motel. Tomorrow afternoon.'' As he nodded and turned to start off up the steps, she added almost wistfully, ''We almost made it, didn't we?''

Dain looked down at her bowed head for a long moment.

''You weren't even close,'' he said.

It was dusk, the huge high piles of cumulus on the western horizon were shot with pink, Bourbon Street was opening its doors and tuning up its music. Vangie sat on the edge of their bed in the Delta Hotel regarding Zimmer with resigned eyes. Between the edges of the curtains on the window behind her was the pornhouse marquee, the scattered lights on it still unbroken flashing intermittently.

"It's the only way, Jimmy. You know that when Dain tells Maxton where we are . . ."

Jimmy, a weak man scared, kicked over a chair. "*No*, goddammit, *no!*"

Vangie sighed, got to her feet, went to him. She put her arms around his neck, her face close to his. "Jimmy-honey, listen to me! You *know* we have to—"

He shook her off angrily.

"All I know is that I lose the bonds, I lose you!"

"Maybe, maybe not—but you won't lose your life."

"According to Dain."

Vangie controlled her anger. "*Not* just according to Dain. You know what Maxton is capable of—"

"I never knew Maxton as intimately as you did." He had worked himself up into a fine, nasty, self-justifying anger. "You'll end right side up, though—or should I say backside up? I bet you slept with Dain this afternoon and made plans to—"

"Jimmy, I have to go to work. I get paid tonight, we need the money. We'll talk about it when I get home, okay?" Zimmer was petulantly silent, refusing to meet her eyes. "At least *think* about giving them back. And *please* let's get another room like he suggested."

Zimmer replied in his childishly defiant way, "I'll do whatever the fuck I please."

At Carnal Knowledge, the musicians were just arriving, having a drink, looking to their instruments. A few local guys on their way home after work were having a quiet beer before the entertainment drove the prices out of reach. Two bulky men, Nicky and Trask, entered like matched, mobile, very heavy bookends. They moved in on the bartender in unison.

"Harry?"

The bartender jerked an indifferent thumb toward a dark corner by the end of the bar. Bulky guys asking questions were no novelty to him, and Harry was a pain in the ass.

"Him."

In the dark corner, Harry had Noreen crowded up against the wall, trying to caress her breast while talking earnestly about sexual matters. Noreen looked bored. The bookends closed in on Harry as if he were an encyclopedia of slime molds. Seeing them over Harry's shoulder, Noreen did a quick and grateful fade, then found something to talk about with the bartender, out of earshot but able to watch obliquely in the backbar mirror.

The one named Nicky, who had a whole lot of blond hair, said to Harry, "You phoned about a girl named Vangie." He tossed a photo of her on the bar. "Yes or no?"

Harry picked up the picture, studied it with a show of concentration. He had gotten a sly, money look on his face.

"Well-l-l . . . I can't be certain."

Trask, the one with short black hair, said, "Get certain."

"I ain't gonna get in trouble over this, am I?" asked Harry with belated caution. "I mean . . . how heavy is it? I mean . . . what'd she do?"

"Asked questions," said Trask.

Harry said hurriedly, "Ah, yeah, yeah, she's the one, all right, fellas, she dances here." He added in a smaller voice, "Stuck-up fuckin' bitch."

Nicky rolled two $100 bills into a cigarette-like cylinder and stuck the cylinder into Harry's shirt pocket.

"See, pal?" he said. "Easy money. Now just tell us where she parks her pasties and we'll be on our way."

Harry told them. As they started out of the place, Trask paused to finger Harry's shirt collar regretfully.

"Ring around the collar, Harry," he said. "Mention us around town, you got no collar. Maybe even you got no neck to go into the collar you ain't got. *Capisce*?"

He guffawed loudly and swaggered out after Nicky. He had really liked that TV series, *Crime Story*, about the old days in Vegas, and had patterned himself after the show's mob characters.

18

Noreen, in pasties and spangles, was doing an exaggerated and prolonged grind in front of the dressing room mirror. She added an exaggerated *bump*! to the grind that made everything jiggle, and winked at her own overmascaraed eyes in the mirror.

"So why ain't you rich, kiddo?"

A mile away in the porn palace next to the Delta Hotel, a couple of dozen male patrons of three races—white, black, Asian—sparsely studded the theater like chocolate chips on a store-bought cookie. Management didn't mind the nearly empty theater; it was only a money-washing operation anyway.

Zimmer, absorbing the raw sex and grunts and four-letter exhortations from the screen, fondling his own half-hard-on furtively like everyone else, jerked his hand away abruptly. Why was he here with these freaks and weirdos who couldn't afford a VCR, when he had something like Vangie waiting in his bed?

She wasn't waiting in his bed, that was the answer. She was out shaking it in a Vieux Carré sleaze joint, or maybe right now fucking the guy who was after them to rob Jimmy Zimmer of the bonds. For her own good, he'd force Vangie to give him the locker key, *he'd* control their destiny . . .

Zimmer emerged into the polyglot, swarming street crowd, no tourists, all local. When he turned in at the Delta Hotel, a bulky man sauntered in ahead of him. A bodybuilder, mirror athlete, all muscle and no guts, deep tan and a great shock of almost straw-yellow hair.

Another bulky man, equally large but with black hair cut Marine Corps short, turned away from the check-in desk to meet the blond man in front of the elevator. They shook hands noisily as Zimmer reached around them to punch the button. Cream puffs—these hulking overinflated guys were all fag for each other.

"Hey, man, what about this nightlife, huh?" black-hair asked blond as the elevator door opened.

"Yeah! Thompson's got the broads up at the room already!"

The three men got on. Zimmer, closest to the panel of floor buttons, pushed 6 just as the blond man said, "Hey, punch six for us, will you, buddy? Thanks."

Zimmer turned right, toward his room. The two big guys paused, debating which way their room was. They ended up following Zimmer down the corridor.

Heavy applause, rebel yells followed the distant music. Down the corridor from the backstage area came the approaching click of high heels; Vangie came in wearing only an exhausted expression, spangles, and sweat. She sprawled in one of the straight-backed chairs with her arms hanging limply at her sides. Through the half-open door came Harry's voice from backstage.

"Noreen, get out here! You're on next!"

"Her master's voice," said Noreen, but she made no

move whatsoever to get out of her chair in front of the
makeup mirror.

Nicky and Trask were coming up the hall behind him with
their loose drunken conventioneer laughs when Zimmer
opened his door. Trask shoved him hard between the shoulder blades. Jimmy ran across the room, arms flailing, to
smash into the dresser. Nicky shut the door as Trask pulled a
blackjack from his pocket. Zimmer turned to protest, but
Trask waved the sap in front of his startled eyes.

"Make a sound I splinter your nose."

Zimmer pressed himself back against the dresser, terribly
pale, his terror-filled eyes darting from one hulk to the other.
Nicky was at the phone, dialing 9 for an outside line. When
he had it, he dialed a local seven-digit number.

"Six forty-seven," he said into the phone, and hung up.

"Noreen! Get your fucking ass out here!"

Noreen went languidly to the door. She caught the frames
on either side of it to do a high kick out into the hall. She
stuck her head back in.

"I almost forgot, kid," she said over her shoulder, "couple creeps laid two C-notes on shithead earlier—both looked
like that Arny Schwartzynigger guy, y'know? Had a picture
that from fifteen feet away in bad light looked like you."

She was gone, leaving Vangie gasping like a netted fish.

"Noreen! Wait . . ." Noreen was still gone. "But . . . but
he can't . . . we can't . . ."

She ran almost blindly at the door, slamming it shut and
bolting it. Panting, she reached down the front of her *cache-
sexe* and took out a flat old-fashioned tin aspirin box. She
dropped it into her purse as she crossed on wobbly legs to
the pay phone beside the door. She dropped her quarter into
the slot and began tapping out a number, leaving the receiver hang on the end of its silvery flex so she could be
pulling on her street clothes with the other hand. She was almost crying.

"He . . . he promised me, tomorrow afternoon . . . it isn't fair . . ."

Zimmer's eyes darted toward the door at the discreet knock. His face looked flayed down to the bone. Maxton came in wearing an elegant summer-weight suit and open-throat raw-silk sport shirt. He looked a question at Nicky, who shook his head. Trask came out of the bathroom. Like Nicky, he wore thin surgical gloves. He also shook his head.

"Indeed." Maxton dragged a straight chair in front of the door, sat down in it backward so he faced the room with his arms on the back, said to Zimmer, "James, take off your clothes."

"*No!*" cried Zimmer in a terrified voice.

The phone rang. Zimmer jerked galvanically toward it. Maxton shook his head and said soothingly, "Just to make sure you aren't hiding some significant other in your shorts, James."

The phone kept on ringing, but it was now much too late for anything outside this room to affect events inside it. Zimmer began to unbutton his shirt with leaden fingers.

Vangie was buttoning her last button with one hand while slamming the receiver back on the hook with the other. She grabbed her purse from the dressing table, her high heels clattered down the hallway on her way to the alley door.

Maxton was out of his chair, leaning against the inside of the door with his arms folded on his chest, staring at Zimmer nude and shivering in the middle of the floor. Zimmer had thin arms and a sunken chest with a single scraggly tuft of brown hair growing over the breastbone. Nicky dropped the last of Zimmer's clothes on the floor.

"Nothing significant, Mr. Maxton." He snapped Zimmer's flaccid organ with a finger, chuckled, "Especially not in his shorts."

"So she *does* have the bonds. Dain was right." Maxton

spoke almost to himself. He turned an icy eye on Zimmer. "James? Talk to me."

"A key," said Zimmer eagerly. "Vangie has it. It was all her idea to take the bonds, Mr. Maxton. I . . . I didn't think until . . . until it was too late . . ." Maxton was silent. Zimmer cried, "Dain! Dain knows she has the key!"

Maxton's voice was a whip. "You spoke with Dain?"

"Vangie did."

"Key to what?"

"To a locker. At the bus depot."

Maxton was silent, then smiled and nodded. "Yes. I see. Thank you, James. You've been a great help."

"Can . . . can I get dressed now, Mr. Maxton?"

Maxton gestured to his men. "Goodbye, James," he said.

He turned away as Nicky and Trask began crowding Jimmy back toward the open bathroom door like driving a steer into the slaughterhouse chute. He clung to the door frame with despairing strength; their big athletes' hands tore his soft deskman's hands free like wet blotting paper. They shut the bathroom door behind them. Maxton could hear the muffled sound of water being run into the tub as he departed the hotel room.

Vangie came through the open street door at almost a run, slowed abruptly to a walk, trying to look casual and not making it. As she put out a finger to press the elevator button, it started down from the sixth floor. She ducked into the doorway of the emergency stairwell beside the elevator. Nicky and Trask left the elevator glancing around the lobby, seeing nothing of interest, strutting toward the street. Trask was telling Nicky a dirty joke, and they were guffawing.

Vangie cautiously opened the stairwell door to peek out into the hallway. Empty. She shut the door behind her, trying to stifle her panting from the six-floor all-out stair climb. The elevator descending from this floor didn't have to have anything to do with her and Jimmy. He probably had gone out just to bug her, and hadn't come back yet. That was all.

Still she hesitated before keying the lock with exaggerated caution. She let the door drift open on its own. The dim overhead was on, the bed still looked freshly made.

"Jimmy?" It was little more than a whisper. She moved in, shut the door behind her. "Jimmy?"

The closet was empty except for their clothes; she edged toward the bathroom door, cautious as a doe at the edge of a clearing. Turned the knob, feathered the door open, stuck her head in. The very narrow wedge of light let her see Jimmy's bent knees rising above the water in the nearly full tub. One arm, resting against the edge of the tub, was also above-water.

Vangie pushed the door wider and fumbled along the wall for the light switch. Relief made her voice buoyant.

"Why in heaven's name are you taking a bath in the dark?"

The room sprang into view. The water filling the tub was rosy with diluted blood, with Zimmer's bent knees islands above this pastel surface. Brighter, richer red had run down the forearm above the water from his slashed wrist.

Vangie reeled against the sink, gripping the sides with her hands, face contorted, mouth working. Somehow she kept from screaming, though she clapped a hand over her mouth as if to physically hold in the sound. She ran from the room.

The Delta's only bellboy, an aged man in his seventies with little hair and one cloudy lens in his eyeglasses, was leading an equally aged couple down the hallway outside with their suitcase in his hand. Vangie erupted from her room and knocked him down, bounced off the wall, eyes vague and unfocused, a hand still across her mouth. She lowered it to speak.

"Ex . . . excuse me . . ."

She ran away down the hall, careening from side to side like a car driven by a drunk. The bellboy braced one hand on the wall and with the help of the couple got shakily to his feet. He stared after Vangie, then turned and looked at the open door of the room. Back down the hall. To the room.

He started shakily through the open doorway.

19

The gypsy cab driver lit his cigarette, shook the match out and dropped it into the street. Vangie, after being handed a wig box by the woman behind the counter, came out of the exotic underwear shop in her very short skintight skirt and blouse with the top four buttons undone. She opened the rear door of the cab but the cabbie patted the seat beside him insinuatingly.

"Plenty of room up here, baby."

"Bus depot," she said, getting in the back.

He slammed the cab into gear, left rubber pulling away from the curb. He found her face in the rearview mirror. She had her head back against the seat with her eyes closed, Jimmy dead in their bathtub vivid against her eyelids.

"Stuck-up bitch," the cabbie muttered to himself.

The cabin door crashed back against the wall. Two bulky men, silhouetted by moonlight, charged in with sawed-off

shotguns in their hands. Heavy boots grated on bare plank
floor. Silver ring glinted on a finger. One, sunglasses, curly
hair. The other, ski mask.

"Doesn't it bother you . . . that we might be killed?"

Vangie went back and up, her mouth strained impossibly
wide, her eyes wild, her hair an underwater slow-motion
swirl . . .

A fist pounded on the door. Coming up out of nightmare,
he thought, *Vangie?*

Zimmer's tub was only half-filled with pink water because his corpse had been removed and laid beside it. Inverness crouched beside him, jerked back the wet-grayed sheet
to let Dain, crowded into the doorway behind him, see the
face.

"The murderer, confronted with evidence of his crimes,
broke down and confessed," said Dain in a toneless voice.

"No, nothing like that," protested Inverness.

"I never saw the gentleman before, dead or alive."

"I never said you did. It looks like suicide, but a couple
of things bother us, that's all."

In the bedroom, they stood facing the window so their
voices could not be heard by the busy crime-scene team; fingerprint powder covered most surfaces. Outside, the pornhouse lights winked on and off in sequence.

"No note, no hesitation marks," said Inverness. "Usually
a suicide with a razor, you'll have a couple of dozen nicks
where he's making up his mind."

"Make up *your* mind. Was it suicide or not?"

"He killed himself, close as we can tell. He was shacking
with a topless dancer name of Evangeline Broussard. Loud
argument earlier in the evening, Broussard ran from the
room just before the body was discovered. She has a juve-
nile package here in New Orleans. Kid stuff. She's Cajun,
from the bayou country—St. Martin's Parish a few miles out
of Breaux Bridge."

"Why couldn't this Broussard woman have killed him?"

Inverness gave him a quick slanting look, then looked
away.

"If he'd been unconscious when he went in the tub, maybe. But he wasn't. With him awake, no woman could have held him down while she slashed both his wrists. Damn few men could do it."

"If it wasn't murder, what am I doing here?"

Inverness was looking out the window again. He seemed to address the glass pane. "Chicago labels in their clothes."

Dain cast a quick glance around the room. The aged bellboy was sitting in one of the room's two straight-backed chairs, talking with a plainclothesman, his bony shoulder slumped, his gnarled hands clasped between his thighs.

"That's supposed to mean something to me?" asked Dain.

Inverness nodded, moved fractionally closer to Dain. "I think it does. I think you were looking for him for a client from Chicago."

Did Inverness know Maxton was his client and was just baiting him? That thing about Chicago labels in their clothes . . . But what did it matter? As organized-crime liaison, Inverness certainly would hear all the rumors flying around.

"I told you why I was here—"

"Yeah, yeah, the heart and soul of New Orleans. Get serious."

"Okay, if I had been looking for Zimmer, his suicide would have ended any interest I might have had in either him or Broussard. If I had a client, I would not have reported to him that I was coming to New Orleans and I would not have reported to him since coming to New Orleans. That serious enough?"

"You haven't really told me anything," Inverness objected.

The bellhop was on his feet, about to head for the door.

"You really didn't expect me to," said Dain. "I'll be in San Francisco if you have any more bright ideas about confronting me with evidence of my crimes."

He nodded and walked out, inevitable leather-bound book under his arm. Inverness stared after him, frowning.

* * *

Through the thin walls of the bus depot ladies' room came the echoing voice of a dispatcher calling a destination in what might as well have been Swahili. At this time of night the place was empty except for Vangie, in front of the vanity table mirror breaking the dark lenses out of a pair of cheap rhinestone-rimmed slanty sunglasses to leave just the rims. Next, from her aspirin tin she took a long-shanked locker key. Finally, she opened her wig box and reached inside.

The bellhop went arthritically down the hall. Mortality had come calling; finding the body had aged him. Dain caught up with him just after a turn in the corridor hid them from the eyes of the police guard on the door of Zimmer's room.

"The lieutenant said you might be able to tell me where St. Martin's Parish and a town called Breaux Bridge might be."

The old man's good eye gleamed at him shrewdly. "Now why would a city feller like you want to be going to a damn fool place like that?"

"Damned if I know," admitted Dain.

Trask was lounging against a pillar a short distance from the coin lockers in the walkway to the bus loading area. He was trying unsuccessfully to look like a bored husband.

In the waiting room, a fat black woman with two kids was just stepping away from the ticket window, to be replaced by a gum-chewing hip-swinging floozie with slanty rhinestone-rimmed glasses. Straw-blonde hair was piled high on her head. She set a hatbox on the floor by her feet.

"Ah want a ticket to Lafayette? One way?"

She had a rather hoarse voice with a backcountry accent unremarkable in any southern bus depot. The clerk took her money, gave her a ticket and some change.

"Just made it," he said. "That bus is loading in three minutes at Gate Three."

"Ah need someone paged, too?" The blonde Vangie set

the empty wig box on the counter. "She's supposed to pick up this here hatbox? Evangeline Broussard."

"Will do," said the clerk.

The peroxide blonde started down the walkway to the buses, chewing her gum and swinging her hips, then sat down on a bench opposite the bank of coin lockers and directly across from Trask. She sprawled so her legs would catch his eye, then crossed them first one way and then the other, each time giving him just a tantalizing glimpse of the shadowed delights between then. Trask actually licked his lips.

The loudspeaker boomed, *"Will Evangeline Broussard report to the ticket window? Ms. Evangeline Broussard to the ticket window, please. We are holding a package for you . . ."*

Trask, electrified, forgot the peroxide blonde's sexual endowments, lumbered some ten feet up the walkway to scan the waiting room. Vangie ran quickly and silently across the deserted walkway. In her terror she fumbled her long-shanked key, dropped it, caught it before it could hit the vinyl floor, shoved it into the correct lock with shaking hands.

Trask started to turn back toward her, but the loudspeaker boomed again.

"Ms. Evangeline Broussard to the ticket window, please."

This swung Trask away again. Vangie jerked Zimmer's attaché case out of the locker, eased the door shut, turned quickly away. Trask, with a snort of disgust, wheeled from the waiting room to look at the lockers he was there to guard.

The floozie blonde who'd tried to show him her snatch was walking down the sloping walkway toward the bus loading area; no one else was around. He turned regretfully away, dropping her from his mind as he leaned against his pillar again.

Dain pushed a wedge of hallway light ahead of him into his darkened hotel room, went between the beds to switch on the lamp. As he began to strip off his clothes, the balcony door opened and Maxton came through it just as Nicky, who'd been hiding in the bathroom, came around the partition beside the bed with a gun in his hand. Dain sat down on the edge of his bed.

"Terrific," he said in a disgusted voice. "You rented the room next door just so you could get in through the balcony and wave guns around at three in the morning. Just brilliant."

Maxton demanded, "Where is the little bitch?"

"On the run, I suppose. Zimmer killed himself tonight. She'd know that would bring you to town, so she'd run."

"Where are the bonds?"

"Last I heard, in a bus depot coin locker."

"I have a man at the bus depot."

Dain gave a short, harsh laugh. "He won't stop her." Sudden anger entered his eyes. "A man at the bus depot, huh? *You* killed Zimmer, made it look like a suicide!" He stood up so abruptly that Nicky's arm jerked up the gun. "You *asshole*! You had to come sucking around. Who tipped you off anyway? I'd have had your goddam bonds for you this afternoon, with nobody dead."

"I don't believe you," said Maxton. "Zimmer told me that you and Vangie—"

Dain scooped up the leather-covered *Tibetan Book of the Dead* from the bedside table and tossed it at Maxton. Maxton caught it, leafed through it, nonplussed.

"There's nothing in here. What—"

"Exactly."

Dain was throwing back the covers to show the empty bed. He lifted the mattress to show nothing was under it. Jerked the slips off the pillows to show only pillows were inside. Ran his fingers around the pillow stitching to show they were untouched. Maxton was spluttering.

"What are you . . ."

But Dain was undressing with the same maniacal speed, throwing each item of clothing in the direction of Nicky. When he was nude, he jumped into the bed and pulled up the sheet.

"I'm going to sleep," he said. "You do what you want."

Maxton's face had suffused with rage. There was also anticipation in his gaze. "Nicky, teach him some manners."

Dain sat up abruptly under the sheet when Nicky started forward. Dain's eyes were very cold and very steady.

"Not unless you want one of us dead."

Their eyes locked. Maxton suddenly realized that Dain's bone-deep despair was more dangerous than any bluster by men trying to mask their fears. He spoke in a strangled voice.

"That's all right, Nicky. Just search the room."

Dain lay back down, turned his back, pulled up the sheet. Maxton moved up between the beds and sat down heavily on the one still made. He had already realized the search was going to turn up nothing.

"You should have told me you were so close."

"I knew if I did, you'd come busting down and fuck it up. Which you did anyway. How did you know where they were?"

The second bug on Farnsworth's phone? Dain wanted to lay that question to rest. But Maxton ignored it again.

"My goddamned wife isn't going to wait much longer, you know!" he said aggrievedly.

"Kill her, you're good at that."

"She left a letter with her lawyer."

A half hour after Maxton had departed, empty-handed, Dain sat up again.

"*Fuck!*" he exclaimed aloud.

Vangie was in trouble. He was leaving her hanging out there, slowing twisting in the wind. If Maxton found her, he'd kill her. Kill her because nobody stole from Theodore Maxton, by God, and got away with it. And after doing Jimmy earlier tonight, it would be easier for him to kill again.

Or to have his goons do it, same thing.

Marie was dead because he'd been a fool, and now Vangie was popping up in Marie's place in Dain's nightmares. If he deliberately walked away from her, and she was killed . . .

He was scared, he realized. Hadn't been when Maxton and Nicky had been in the room, but he was scared of them now, sort of in retrospect. A week ago he would have said he didn't care if he lived or died. Now . . .

Maybe he still didn't, but *something* was changing in him. He was involved in life somehow. Maybe just in Vangie's life? Maybe he just wanted to see what was going to happen next? No, it was stronger than that. If only he was the man they thought he was, the stainless-steel image he projected, it would all be a hell of a lot easier.

Maybe he would have to be that image somehow.

He sighed, and got out of bed, and started to get dressed.

IV

MR. DEATH

Cajun Country

THE DAWNING OF THE
PEACEFUL DEITIES

O nobly-born, thou hast been in a swoon during the last three and one-half days. As soon as thou art recovered from this swoon, thou wilt see the radiances and deities. The whole heavens will appear deep blue.

THE TIBETAN BOOK OF THE DEAD

20

The darkness was beginning to lighten, dawn would soon be staining the sky to the east. In deserted Chartres Street, Dain tossed his bag into his rental car, drove to Canal and Interstate 10 that would take him west toward the vast Atchafalaya Swamp that was Cajun country.

On the system of raised interchanges by which traffic avoided Baton Rouge, Dain stayed on the I-10 freeway west. The sun, rising behind the car, made incredible colors and shapes of the massed horizon clouds. Industrial smoke rising from the plants lining the Mississippi had taken on dawn tints also.

Why was he here? What did he think he was doing? He should be on his way to San Francisco; it was not his fault Maxton had showed up to vitiate his bargain with Vangie. Vangie, who had taken Marie's place in his recurring nightmare—and from what bizarre corner of his subconscious had that image come?

Who had told Maxton where Dain was? Or, perhaps,

where Vangie was? Or Zimmer? Whose bug had been on Farnsworth's phone? Who had put Inverness on Dain's trail?

Dain kept telling himself he was looking for strands that somehow stretched back to the Point Reyes cabin five years earlier, but he knew in his secret heart that the idea was nonsense. This morning he had faced the fact that he had to come here because he otherwise would feel guilty about Vangie's very real danger: because whoever had led Maxton to Vangie in New Orleans might now lead him to Vangie in Cajun country.

The phone rang. Maxton was sitting on the edge of his bed in robe and slippers, yawning, but he made no move to pick it up. When it kept on ringing, a cheap busty blonde wearing a very sheer expensive lace negligee came out of the bathroom. The fresh bruises on her full, soft breasts and rounded belly looked a soft gray through the sheer material. She picked up the phone. There was another bruise on her cheek, ugly and dark.

"This is Mr. Maxton's room," she said in a soft southern voice with a secretarial inflection. She listened, handed the phone to him.

"Yes, this is Maxton . . ." He suddenly leaned forward tensely on the bed. His face, voice, eyes were very hard, his jaw set. "What the fuck do you mean, Dain and the girl together? That isn't possible. He's right in the next . . ." He broke off, said, "Hang on a second . . ."

Maxton dropped the receiver on the floor and erupted through the balcony door to the terrace. He threw the door to the next room wide. It was empty, Dain's suitcase was gone. Maxton whirled away, stormed back to his own room and the phone.

"You're right. He's gone. Do you know where . . ." He listened. "Vangie's parents, huh? Yeah. Give me a second."

He snapped his fingers, the blonde opened the drawer of the bedside table, gave him ballpoint pen and paper. He sat down on the bed to write the directions.

"Lafayette . . . Breaux Bridge . . . Henderson . . . Follow the levee to . . ." The blonde was on her knees in front of him, busy fingers undoing the sash of his robe. "Right turn or . . . I see. Over the pontoon bridge. Gravel road . . . mmm-hmm . . . All right . . . crossroads store. Road ends. Yes, I've got all that."

He broke the connection, dialed three digits. The blonde's hands were inside his pajama pants, stroking him erect. He said to the phone, "Trask? We're going after that bitch, you and Nicky be ready to roll in ten minutes . . ." Trask must have said something, because he listened for a moment, then snapped, "No, I want to be there to watch her die. Before she does, I'm going to . . ." He caught his breath and his threats against Vangie died as the blonde took him in her mouth. He told the phone, "Make that twenty minutes," and tossed it aside.

The Lafayette bus ran west along the I-10 causeway on trestles high in the air. The causeway had been built about twenty years before on a Southern Pacific Railroad bed laid in 1908. Even now it was the only road that cut across the vast Atchafalaya Swamp. On the empty seat beside Vangie was the attache case; her arm lay protectively over it like the arm of a mother cradling her infant. Her face, reflected in the window, seemed superimposed on the wetlands below the causeway.

She wanted to cry. Poor scared Jimmy, she'd talked him into stealing the bonds to get back at Maxton for what he'd made her do, and they'd grabbed the money and run. And now Jimmy was dead. She was alone with the bonds and she would be too afraid to ever do anything with them.

Because of Dain. Treacherous, betraying Dain had made her believe he was giving her time to work on Jimmy, then . . . She'd be more afraid of Dain than of Maxton, because Dain could find her again, except by now he'd be flying off with his blood money in hand . . .

Dain had pulled off to the side of that same causeway and was out of his car to lean on the steel railing and stare. The Atchafalaya had struck him like a blow, as if somehow here was his destiny, as if here he would find all his answers. He found it fitting that the eye of devastating Hurricane Andrew had come ashore in this area in 1992.

Now he faced his own devastation here in this breathtaking 2,500 square miles of bayous and lakes and waterways and swamps. Forests of cypress and tupelo and ash and willow and live oak—some flooded, some not. Every kind of game from bear to wild pig. Crabs and crawfish and bass and catfish. Cottonmouths and gators and snapping turtles to take off your fingers while the mosquitoes flayed you alive.

How Marie would have loved to be standing here with him right now on the edge of this unknown, hot, wet, tropical world! Probably Vangie, who'd been born here, was feeling that same lift of delight right now . . .

Dain straightened up abruptly. For the first time in five years he had thought of Marie as Marie, not as icon. In his last nightmare, it had been Vangie blown away by the hitman's shotgun. What the hell was happening to him?

Dain shivered in the warm dawn air, turned back to his car. He had a lot of miles to go and had no real idea of what he would do when he got there. Wherever there was going to be.

The bus stopped at the Lafayette depot with a hiss of air brakes. Vangie was first off, minus her blonde wig and slanty eyeglass frames. A few steps away from the bus she spun around in a series of uninhibited circles, attache case in hand, long raven hair flying out from her head. She was suddenly ravenous.

The Ragin' Cajun was a workingman's sort of cafe, big and boxy, the walls mostly bare except for beer ads. She chose a table near the back facing the door to see anybody coming at her. At the next table were two Cajun men in work clothes, with seamed outdoor faces and callused hands cut and scarred from trotlines. How many Sunday mornings as a little girl had she eaten in this very cafe with her papa and *maman*?

When a pudgy teenage waitress brought her the mandatory cup of fragrant chicory-rich coffee, Vangie didn't even have to look at the menu. Ten minutes later she was tearing into eggs and sausage patties and grits and hot biscuits smothered in country gravy, washing it all down with her third cup of coffee.

A man about her own age, very husky, very Cajun, dressed in work clothes, put coins in the jukebox, punched buttons with the speed of long familiarity. He was thick and square, with laughing eyes and black curly hair and a wide shiny nose on which the pores were visible. Just as he started past Vangie's table she leaned back from her cleaned plate and drew a big breath of contentment.

He glanced at her appreciatively, then did a double take as his eyes slid up across her face.

"Vangie?" he exclaimed. "Vangie Broussard?"

She looked up at him, tears sprang to her eyes. She said in a voice full of wonder, "You, Minus?"

"Dat's me," he admitted.

"How long has it been?"

"Dat mus' be ten year. How your *maman* and papa?"

"I just got off the bus."

"You ain't seen 'em yet?" He grabbed her arm, dragged her to her feet. "Den me, I tak off de morning work, drive you home to see dem . . ."

The beat-up old '75 Ford 250 pickup with the 4 x 4 option went along the dirt track on top of the high levee. There was pasture to the right, a narrow twisting bayou, well below flood stage now, to the left. When it reached an intersecting T-road of gravel, the pickup went down across the bayou on a one-way pontoon bridge, very narrow, its tires thumping, drumming on the bed of the bridge. On the far side it plunged into thick forest on a narrow road shaded by the hardwoods. Vangie was looking about in unalloyed delight, her face very open and innocent.

"I'd forgotten how much I love this old swamp!" She half turned toward Minus on the wide vinyl seat patched with long strips of silvery duct tape. "I'm goin' back to the old camp on my papa's fishing ground off Bayou Noire, and just fish and hunt and trap crabs . . ."

Half an hour later, the truck broke out of the forest. It went along the gravel road to a narrower dirt track coming up from the low slow brown reach of the Atchafalaya River to form a "T." There was a little country store with a faded BROUSSARD'S sign on the front and a converted houseboat tacked to the rear as living quarters. Toward the road were rough dearhound kennels.

They bounced down the dirt track; it dead-ended at the riverbank, below which a couple of boats were pulled up on a narrow earth landing area. Minus stopped on the gravel apron in front of the store with a squeal of worn brake shoes.

Vangie got out with her attache case, stood looking up at Minus through the still-open doorway. "You come in, see Maman?"

Minus shook his head, tapped the watch on his wrist.

"Gotta work. *Ce soir* I be back, we all drink some beer."

Vangie gave him a big grin. "*Tu dis.*"

She slammed the door of the pickup, stood waving as it made a U-turn and went back the way it had come. She hesitated a moment, then trudged across the gravel turnaround toward the store with an almost frightened look on her face.

21

Vangie climbed the rough unpainted wooden steps worn smooth by countless hunters' boots, crossed the narrow plank *galerie* to press her nose against the screen door. No one was visible. She pulled it open, entered, it slammed three diminishing times behind her, tinkling the attached bell. She set down her attache case carelessly beside the cash register on the front counter as a woman called from somewhere in the rear of the store.

"You wait one little minute, *non*?"

Vangie started at the remembered voice. "Sure."

Just as it had been during a thousand daydreams in a hundred strip joints over the past decade. Shotguns and rifles upright in a cabinet behind a front counter that held fishing lures, hooks, nets, line, rifle and shotgun shells. From the ceiling hung rows of muskrat and nutria traps. Below a small black-and-white TV blurrily showing a lively Creole talk show, a large screened box stood on four legs. It contained thousands of live crickets for sale as bait; a light inside kept them actively chirping and jumping against the screen sides.

"Not a single thing different," muttered Vangie to herself.

She bent over the cricket box to wrinkle her nose at the remembered acrid smell. She straightened, belatedly went back for her attaché case, wandered down the aisle toward the rear where the voice had come from. There was a showcase with hard candies and tinned fancy cakes and a giant glass jar of pickled eggs on top. She sucked a piece of candy as she moved past another case filled with buckets, tubs, tinware, white-ash hoops for hoop nets, netting for gill nets and trammel nets, wire poultry netting for crawfish traps.

Through an open doorway in the right wall were three rough wooden steps down to a small damp room where a row of live-bait boxes took up the space except for a plank walkway around them.

Maman, in her mid-forties and blessed with remnants of Vangie's same beauty, was bent over one of the bait boxes with a small scoop net in her hand. She was a warm, vital woman with a lined, bright, open face, wearing a cotton dress of no particular style. She glanced up at Vangie in the door frame at the head of the steps, then back at her work with a small wry welcoming smile.

"Too much *tracas* for little-little money, *tu dis*?"

"Yeah, I know," said Vangie softly. "Jesus, do I know."

With a twirl almost like Vangie's when she was dancing, Maman spun around at the sound of Vangie's voice. A slow radiant smile illuminated her features. She dropped her little scoop net, darted toward her daughter with open arms.

"Vangie! So beautiful you have become!"

They met at the foot of the steps; Maman enfolded Vangie in her arms. Vangie felt a flush mantling her features, embarrassed and ashamed to be bringing her big-city trouble to this place.

"Ten years you gone," exclaimed Maman, stepping back from their embrace. Her eyes twinkled. "You bring me some pretty little grandchildren, *non*?"

Vangie gave an uneasy laugh. "Um . . . not quite yet, Maman."

Maman held her at arm's length, impressed and pride-filled. She looked over Vangie's shoulder, saw the attaché case.

"A secretary to an important man, my Vangie?"

"Ah . . . *non*, Maman. A . . . singer. And a . . . a dancer . . ."

"Singer? Dancer? Maybe I see you on the TV?"

"Uh . . . not quite yet, Maman." She added uncomfortably, "I'd . . . like to stay for a while . . ."

"Stay? Of course you stay!" Maman gestured toward the front of the store. "Ten year ago you walk out dat door, you. Now you back, Maman gonna keep you, not let you go!"

She nodded happily to herself and bent again over the live-bait tank. She deftly scooped the dead shad from the surface with her little net and tossed them aside, casting sideways glances at Vangie and speaking with her eyes on her work.

"You think Maman not know how hard it is to make your way in dat outside world, dere? You got some trouble, Vangie, you tell your *maman*, we fix it up real quick, *non*?"

"Yeah, I got trouble, Maman . . ." She paused, added, "No trouble with the law, trouble with some men who want . . ." She paused again. "They don't know where I am, so I just need a . . . place nobody outside the parish knows about, okay?"

Maman winked at her gaily. "Okay, you," she said.

They both laughed. Vangie spoke in a new tone.

"*Et* Papa? Where's he?"

Maman laid aside her scoop and straightened up. She looked at Vangie with great love and pride in her face. She took her daughter's arm. "Out checkin' de set lines, where else? Dat catfish, he been runnin' real good, him."

"Where?" demanded Vangie eagerly.

"Bayou Tremblant, by dat *boscoyo* knee of cypress where Dede catch de ten-poun' bass on dat little-little perch hook." They mounted the steps together. "We got time for one *demitasse* of *café*, *non*? Den you go surprise him, you."

Vangie only nodded silently, her eyes blurred with tears of relief and love and release and safety. She was moved beyond anything she could have imagined. Arms around one another, they went toward the living quarters at the back of the store.

Dain stopped the car nose-up next to a couple of others on the steep grassy side of the levee above the Breaux Bridge boat landing. As he got out and locked it he could see, downslope beyond him, a concrete boat launching ramp and a U-shaped dock with a dozen outboard motorboats moored. On the *galerie* of the store a couple of loungers paused in their checker game to look at him and make comment with appropriate gestures.

He went down the bank on his slippery leather-soled oxfords to the edge of the water, moving warily, obviously out of his element. Stepping onto the dock, he stopped dead. Inverness was sitting in a flat-bottom scow moored to the dock, grinning at him like Brer Rabbit from the briar patch. Dain walked out with deliberation, seeking his stance.

Inverness was going to be a complicating factor, for sure. He was a cop, with a cop's ways. On the other hand, maybe without him Dain would discover nothing at all in this unfamiliar world—he would be as competent in this environment as he was in any other. Dain stopped on the dock above him.

"Back to San Francisco, huh?" said Inverness ironically.

"Change of plans, but how about you? I thought you'd accepted Zimmer as a suicide, pure and simple."

"We still need Broussard's statement. Since she's Cajun, I figured she'd hightailed it for home. Most of 'em do when they think they're in trouble. Course I'm not telling you anything new, since you're here too."

"A manhunter's intuition," said Dain, ironic in turn, then he had to chuckle. "It was her name. Broussard. Cajun. Originally, the Acadians. Run out of Nova Scotia by the British in the seventeen hundreds. French descent. Still speak a patois. Evangeline."

"Yeah," said Inverness. "Settled in the bayou country to farm, but they got flooded out every spring so they embraced the swamp—fishing and hunting and moss-gathering and fur-trapping. Very in-turned, family very big with them. For a city boy, you know a lot about Cajuns."

"For a New Orleans cop, you know a lot about swamp folk."

"I'm not married, got no family, so I fish and hunt. That means the bayou country. For damn near five years, every weekend and holiday and vacation I can wangle, I'm right out here."

"Couldn't the Lafayette parish police get her statement?"

Inverness grinned. "This gives me an excuse to get out into the swamp. That explains me, but what about you?"

"She's worth money to me," said Dain easily.

"Ah, yes. Money money money. The older I get . . ." He didn't finish the thought. "Anyway, I think Broussard's folks run a little general store somewhere out of Henderson. But since Broussard is one of the four most common Cajun names, don't make book on it."

"I don't make book on anything," said Dain, "not any more."

"If I'm right, the easiest way to their store is by boat—almost all their trade is with swamp people working the bayous." He jerked his head. "Get in. May as well look for her together—it's a hell of a lot of backwoods out there."

Dain started to unfasten the painter from the stanchion on the dock. "If we don't find her?"

"I've got a motel room at Lafayette for the night."

Dain jumped down lightly into the boat, shoved it away from the dock. A slow eddy caught the prow, swung it out into the river. Inverness was priming the motor.

"What if she takes off into the swamp instead of talking?"

"Then we'll get to go in after her," he grinned happily.

Maman's old-fashioned iron cookstove and oven, once wood-burning, had been converted to butane gas. There was a chipped white enamel sink, and an ancient white enamel fridge with the cooling coils bare on top instead of being fitted in underneath.

Vangie and Maman sat at the minuscule table, finishing their coffee and fresh *beignet*. A gumbo already simmering on the stove filled the room with rich dark smells. Vangie leaned back, replete, licked the last of the powdered sugar off her fingers and half stifled a satisfied little belch.

"Oh, Maman, how many years since I've had your *beignets*!"

Maman drew a deep breath, sniffing. "Tonight, gumbo!"

"Guess I'd better go meet Papa before he starts back, him." Vangie stood up. "But I have to see the dogs first!"

"And you gotta change your pretty city clothes, you," said Maman. "Your old clothes still fit you, I bet!"

The stately blue and white bird stood motionless knee-deep on the fringe of the bayou. A far mosquito whine got steadily louder, but he ignored it to dart his head suddenly down into the water. He came up with a small wriggling silver fish speared on his bill just as the flat-bottom scow bearing Inverness and Dain appeared around a bend in the stream. He crouched, alarmed.

Dain was in the prow of the skiff, craning down the bayou at the spindly-legged bird bursting off the water on huge flapping wings, a doomed minnow wriggling in its bill. A heron? A crane? Inverness would know—Inverness probably knew as much about this swamp as any outsider ever would.

Which made him turn and start to yell a question, but his words were lost in the staccato beat of the motor. Inverness, in the stern, just pointed at the outboard motor and shrugged. Dain pantomimed turning it off. Inverness frowned, turned it down to trolling speed.

"For Chrissake, it's a Louisiana heron," he snapped.

But Dain said, "Why didn't you ask the guy you rented the boat from just where the Broussard store was?"

"You had me stop for that? Cajuns are very big on minding their own business and everybody is first cousins. Unless you speak their patois, better just look, not ask."

He speeded up the motor again. Every sunken log had its colony of turtles to either slide into the water with barely a ripple or do a sudden scrabbling noisy belly flop. One had a snow-white egret standing on its back; bird and turtle fled at their approach, one up into the air, the other down under the water. Bright-feathered ducks unknown to Dain zipped by on whistling wings. Fish swirled in the shallows when the boat's waves touched their exposed backs. He glimpsed a lumbering black bear in the brush along the bayou, several small swamp white-tailed deer, and a little shambling ring-tailed fellow with a pointy nose he thought was a raccoon but actually was a coatimundi.

A thick-bodied snake Dain took for a water moccasin swam past with whipping sinuous motions. Beauty was edged with death here, which he realized was what he had come to seek in his own life. As if feeling his thoughts, Inverness suddenly flipped the motor into neutral. It popped and spluttered as they watched the life going on around them. There was a strange, almost luminous look on Inverness's face.

"I tell you, Dain, come retirement, I'm right out here for good—living off the land. This is just about the last place a man can do it—be entirely on his own, trade what he catches or shoots or traps for whatever store-bought stuff he needs like hooks and lines and shells and flour . . ."

"You don't like people very much, do you?" asked Dain.

"Show me a cop who does."

Dain could think of one, Randy Solomon; but even with Randy, it was sort of despite himself.

Vangie had her fingers through the chicken wire at the deerhounds' enclosure, scratching the long floppy ear of a sad-faced, dewlapped liver and white hound. She was dressed for the bayou, tight jeans and a cotton long-sleeved shirt with her hair tucked up under a billed gimme cap.

"This bluetick looks good," she said as the floppy-eared hound crowded the wire for more hands.

"Your papa say he de bes' deerhound we ever have."

Vangie came erect. There was disbelief in her voice.

"Better than old Applehead?"

By mutual consent, they turned away toward the river. Maman almost giggled. "You know your papa. Every hound de bes' one he ever had, him."

The dogs pressed against the wire behind them, clamoring,

tails wagging, heads alert, as they left to descend the switch-back dirt path from the top of the riverbank. Near the boats was a big sunken live-box where the fish taken on the setlines were kept until they were sold.

"I look for you two soon after sunset," said Maman.

Vangie hugged her, unwound the chain painter of the flat-bottom scow from around a tree, pushed it out, then with a final push jumped lightly into the prow. The ten-year lapse might never have been; she walked expertly back to the rear as the current moved the boat downstream and away from the bank. She sat down on the rear seat, primed the out-board, started it. Her mother stood watching on the shore. Vangie put the motor in gear, started off with mutual waves between the two women.

Maman trudged up the path to level ground. Vangie's boat was just disappearing around a bend in the river down-stream. The diminishing whine of the motor faded away as she went back into the store, picked up the attache case and carelessly stuffed it under the front counter before going back to tend her gumbo.

At Henderson's Crossroads, a big four-door sedan came along the blacktop road and stopped just short of the steel bridge. To the left a seafood restaurant was built over the water, with the inevitable checker-playing geezers on the *galerie*. To the right another road went off on the levee par-allel to the bayou.

Trask, behind the wheel, said, "You wanna ask which—"

"We ask no one anything," snapped Maxton. "I'll drive from here on. I have directions. First, over the bridge, then take a right along the top of the levee . . ."

22

Inverness got back into their boat, went to the rear seat. Dain cast them off, jumped in as the old Cajun who wasn't named Broussard turned away with a wave of his hand.

"Third time unlucky," Dain said.

Long afternoon shadows were reaching across the swamp. Inverness was setting the start lever on the motor. He shrugged.

"If we don't find 'em tonight, we'll come back in the morning by car, get Vangie's statement, be on our way . . ."

The boat had started to drift downstream. Inverness was about to start the motor, but Dain held up a hand to stop him.

"Unless somebody gets her first. Zimmer wasn't a suicide."

"What the hell are you—"

"Some hard boys from Chicago were all over the Vieux Carré looking for them yesterday. Last night, Zimmer ended up dead. Maybe Vangie couldn't have done it, but a couple of strongarms could have stuffed him in that bathtub easy enough.''

"Without marking him up? A man fighting for his life?" Inverness shook his head doggedly. "No way."

He turned back to the motor, but Dain spoke again.

"You shove him in the tub, grab him by the hair, hold his head under." Inverness was watching him, so he added appropriate gestures. "He grabs your arm, fighting you, but this gives your backup man a chance to slash his wrist. Clean, one stroke. Now he's bleeding to death, even while he's fighting for air." Another gesture. "Zip! The other wrist. Then you let go of the head so he bleeds to death instead of drowns. Instant suicide."

"You seem to have given this a lot of thought," said Inverness slowly, as if ideas and questions were moving ponderously about in his mind.

Dain said, "Their room had been searched."

"Dammit, that I don't believe! My men would have noticed if there had been anything—"

"Your men weren't looking."

Inverness turned back to the motor, seemed to address it.

"You have anything else?"

Dain gave a low chuckle. "My hunter's intuition."

Inverness looked back at him, started to chuckle with him, then suddenly got serious, with an odd expression on his face.

"You trust that really?"

The door crashed open against the wall, the two attackers were framed in it. One of them, sunglasses, curly hair. The other, ski-masked so no hair showed.

Details of only shadowy recall previously. Was memory coming back, after five long years?

"With my life," Dain said fervently.

The big sedan came to a stop on the gravel at the dirt turnoff to Broussard's Store, about a hundred yards shy of the deerhound pen. No one was visible, nothing was moving.

"So, whadda we do?" asked Trask.

"Wait," said Maxton.

"For what?" asked Nicky from the backseat.

"Dark."

The shadows were getting long across the brown reach of Bayou Tremblant. Vangie's boat had been pulled into shore a bit downstream from the bend where Papa had run out his trotline. The water was slow enough here for the line, known locally as a float line because it was supported at intervals by cork floats, to run out at a right angle to the current.

Papa was in the blunt prow of his flat-bottom scow, Vangie on the stern seat. Papa, a short fierce bristling man, very French, was pulling them along the line, checking the hooks hung from the main line at three-foot intervals on shorter, lighter lines called stagings.

Almost every hook had a catfish on it. Papa removed them, tossed them into a big wash bucket full of water. Vangie was rebaiting each hook, using the heads of large shad as her cut-bait. Both were quick and expert at the work. Vangie's face was intent but serene, Papa was grinning with delight as he pulled them along the line.

"De bes' day I have all spring, Vangie."

"I've brought you luck, Papa," she said gaily.

"Havin' you home make Papa so happy he wanna bust, him."

Vangie was silent, thoughtful. "It's good to be home, Papa, but I hate to see you work so hard."

Papa laughed. "Not hard, do what you love. It doan make much money, but what you wan' Papa to do?" His laughter had turned to indignation. "Go drive a truck? Pump 'pane in New Orleans? Work on a oil rig with *les Texiens,* him?" He shook his grizzled narrow head. "Time all you got b'longs to you, just you alone. So you gotta use that time lak you wan'."

In a sudden terrifying moment, Vangie realized that she had never really planned out what she would do with the bonds. She'd stolen them more to get back at Maxton than for the money . . . Oh, some fuzzy thoughts about tropic isles, the great cities of Europe, the pyramids along the Nile,

Japan, Hong Kong, *freedom*—but mainly it had been, at first, just *taking* them, and then just *getting away* with them. Not much beyond that.

Maybe poor Jimmy had been right. Maybe they should have cashed them in and just started running and living and loving with the money, until Maxton eventually, inevitably caught up . . .

But no, she'd thought only of escape. Now Jimmy was dead. He would never escape. She had the bonds but was afraid to cash them.

No. Not afraid. She knew now, without hesitation or question, what she would do with them. She would cash them somewhere far away, then send her parents the money. If Maxton *did* ever catch up with her, he would never be led back here to the bayous and to them.

"What if someone *gave* you money, Papa? A lot of money?"

"Doan want a lotta money," he said with fierce pride. "I do my life damn good, me! Got all I need. Your *maman*, good hounds, good fishin', good huntin', dis bayou . . ."

They had worked their way across the channel to the far shore. He let the cleaned and rebaited line drop back into the water. Vangie watched him hungrily, as if trying to figure out the secret of life that he had and that she had lost.

"Dat de las' hook," he said happily. "We go home now."

It was dusk. The three men watched Maman as she removed the last of the dried laundry from the line. She picked up the big wash basket and, leaning sideways to counterbalance its weight, went to the back door of the living area and disappeared. Two minutes later she emerged with a brimming bucket of scraps for the hounds. They flowed around her in an excited river of silky tan and white backs, yelping and barking and whining, ravenous as only dogs can be.

"That old broad don't never stop working," said Nicky. "Probably outlive us all."

"Wanta give odds on that?" asked Trask, and laughed.

She returned to the house and the lights went on. Maxton

got out of the car, followed by the other two. They walked down the road to the store, climbed the creaky wooden steps to the equally creaky *galerie*. Maxton stopped, Nicky and Trask went through the screen door, it slammed its three diminishing times behind them, tinkling the bell.

Maman trudged up from the rear, beaming. Her expression changed when she saw the two men and Maxton outside.

"Cold beer," said Trask.

Maman jerked her head. There was suspicion in her manner. "In de back. In de cooler 'gainst de back wall."

Trask went down the aisle out of sight. Nicky took out some folding money, offered her a $50 bill, thereby keeping her at the front of the store.

"Got nuthin' smaller, you?" she asked.

Nicky dug around in his billfold, came up with a twenty.

"For three of them," he said.

Maman made change. Trask came up the store holding all three icy bottles of beer in his left hand, the necks between his curled fingers.

"We'll drink 'em here." said Nicky.

"Mebbe you leave dem empties in de crate on de porch, *non*?"

On the *galerie* they gave Maxton his beer, and all three men moved to the front edge of the porch beside the steps. They could not readily be heard from inside. They stood in a row in their town clothes, facing out, drinking their cold beers.

"I went through the place," Trask said. "She's alone in there now, but the clothes I saw on a fucking blonde snatch at the New Orleans bus depot was lying on the bed."

"Blonde, huh? A wig and she gets past you," said Maxton in a low snarly voice. He stopped and spread his hands. "No matter. She's been here, we're here now, we'll ask where . . ."

A car came down the dirt track from the gravel to stop in front of the store. Two Cajun fishermen got out and crossed toward the trio on the *galerie*. Sunset was flushing the sky over the trees to the west with delicate violet and rose pink.

"Nice sunset," said Maxton to the fishermen as they started up to the steps.

"Tu dis," said one.

They went by, into the store. Maxton said, "Get us another round of beers, Nicky. It looks like we'll be here a while."

Papa's scow, silhouetted against the gold and crimson sky, was towing Vangie's empty boat across an open area of marsh. Vangie, in the prow of Papa's boat, was twisted around forward so the wind was in her face. The motor was a thin steady throb; a big heron flapped by over them in spindly dignity. Vangie looked up at a trio of wood ducks whistling by overhead, then looked back at her father. She laughed. He laughed. There was sheer shared delight in both of their faces.

Beertown was a tavern in Henderson where students from the University of Southwestern Louisiana in Lafayette came to drink beer during the school year. There were fishing nets with cork floats strung on the walls, a couple of open muskrat traps on display, a warmouth bass mounted behind the bar, a juke and a shuffleboard and a lot of undistinguished country music, which is why the college kids liked it.

School was out for the summer, so it was once more Cajun country. At the bar a group of young bucks, Minus among them, was drinking beer. The bartender, Ta-Tese, was their age and obviously one of them.

"Eh la bas, Minus," he said. "Your roun'."

Minus checked his watch, nodded. *"Tu dis."*

Ta-Tese got fresh beers all around from the cooler, plunked them down on the bar. He winked at the other Cajuns.

"Why you honor us comin' roun' here to do your drinkin'?"

Minus drank from the bottle neck like they all did.

"Dat Vangie, she back from de big city."

Cojo exclaimed *"Pensez-donc!"* in wonder. "Dat was one pretty girl, her. What she lak after all dese years, man?"

Minus couldn't resist making a whistling mouth and waving one hand as if he had just slammed it in the door.

"Poo-ya-yi! Dat some woman!" Then he laughed and punched Cojo on the shoulder. "An' she invite me to come out to de store tonight, drink beer wit her and her folks." He set his empty bottle on the counter, slapped some money down beside it for the round of beers. "Henderson is closer to Broussard's Store an' Vangie den Lafayette is. And *dat's* why Minus honors you by comin' round here tonight fo' a beer."

He started for the door laughing at their envious faces. Until she had dropped out at the age of sixteen, Vangie had been just about the hottest number their high school had ever seen.

23

The Cajuns emerged from Broussard's Store in the deepening dusk, one carrying a six-pack, the other a paper bag. Maxton, Nicky, and Trask were over by the edge of the porch, putting their empties in the wooden crate left there for that purpose.

They covertly watched the others depart.

"Nicky, stay out here in case anyone else comes."

Maxton and Trask went in, their entry jingling the little bell merrily. Maman hurried from the living quarters, went behind the front counter. Her face was flushed from cooking.

"You want a couple more beers, you?" she asked brightly.

"We want your daughter," said Maxton.

Maman leaned on her elbows and locked her eyes on the network sitcom feed now coming in on the blurry little TV, thus further concealing the attaché case with her body should any of them come around behind the counter.

"Go off ten year ago, her," she said.

"Come back today, her," said Maxton harshly.

"We want your daughter Vangie, goddammit!" yelled Trask. He loved this stuff. It excited him.

"No see her, ten year."

Maxton slapped her explosively across the face. Maman cowered back against the wall, her hands up to protect herself from a beating. Maxton made a disgusted gesture and went back toward the living area. Trask took over, carelessly.

"Tell us now, you old sow, or I'll hurt you bad."

He reached for her, and clawed hands flashed out to rip down his cheeks. Trask reeled back, yelling, his face pouring blood as Maman ducked under his arm and was gone. He crashed after her, toppling merchandise to right and left. Maxton emerged from the living area.

"What the hell's going on?"

"Fucking old bitch clawed my face."

"Well, at least you were right about the clothes, Trask—I remember that outfit from Chicago. Now go find the old lady. She can't get by Nicky on the front and I'll cover here."

Crouching behind a rack of hunting clothes, Maman jerked down the circuit breaker. Instant darkness.

Maxton's voice wobbled with earnestness. "Goddam her!"

Red and green running lights glowed out to the side of Papa's flatboat as it approached the landing. The wake curled palely in the near darkness. He turned the throttle, the motor dropped in pitch, the boat slowed. He reached back to keep Vangie's towed flatboat from running over them as he cut the motor and the keel grated on the bank. Vangie jumped ashore.

"We put the fish in the live-box, Papa?"

"Tu dis," he grinned.

He heard the mooring chain clink as Vangie wrapped it around the tree, could dimly see the open padlock in her hand.

He shook his head. "No, de chain hol' her, good-good." He had a big rich laugh for such a small, feisty man. "Bet Maman got one great big gumbo waitin'!"

Maman was in the bait room using both hands to hold a large scoop net submerged in one of the live-bait tanks. A sudden flashlight beam hit her square in the face. She crouched, tensed like a trapped bobcat, did everything but hiss.

In a satisfied voice, Trask called, "I got the old bitch."

And the scoop net full of live wriggling shad slammed into his face. He crashed down on his back, flashlight flying, as Maman ran right over him up the stairs.

The dim battery-powered light in the cricket box at the front of the store had not gone out with the other lights. Maxton saw Maman scuttling from the bait room, a dark figure moving between him and that dim light. She ducked around behind the front counter, grabbed the attaché case, jerked open the screen door—and ran right into Nicky.

Trask stumbled up to grab her with savage pleasure.

"She's fucking *mine*!" he exclaimed.

Nicky hissed, "Someone's coming."

Trask slapped a hand over Maman's mouth, dragged her to the back of the store. Her eyes gleamed over his hand like those of a ferret in a trap. Maxton put the attaché case on the counter.

"Just keep quiet," he said to Nicky in a low voice. "With the lights out, they'll probably go away."

Papa's approaching voice said, " . . . an' catfish gettin' more a pound than they ever got."

"That's wonderful, Papa," said Vangie's voice.

Maxton hissed at Nicky, "That's her! Quiet . . ."

Vangie stopped abruptly. "The lights are out, Papa."

"*Fous pas mal*. Dat Maman, she in back makin' supper, her."

Without hesitation he went up the steps and across the porch. Maxton could see Papa's silhouette appear in the pale oblong of the screen door. Papa came in, tinkling the bell. Vangie was coming warily a few steps behind him.

Maman twisted so her mouth was momentarily uncovered.

"Prenez garde!" she yelled.

Trask's hand jerked her head savagely the other way, there was a loud snap and it remained over at the grotesque angle. Her eyes were wide and staring. Nicky jumped Papa, but her cry had alerted him, he was no easy prey for the strongarm. They went over sideways into the cricket box, smashing it to pieces.

Papa found breath to yell, "Vangie! Run!"

She grabbed the case as Maxton grabbed her. Kicking and clawing fiercely, she twisted free, slammed the screen door wide and was off the edge of the *galerie* with the attaché case. Maxton tried to do the same, his left foot came down in thin air, and he did a tremendous front flip off the edge of the porch.

Papa had a grim two-handed bulldog grip on Nicky's ankle, but Trask slammed him beside the head with his gun butt, followed him down, smashing again and again until Nicky dragged him away.

"C'mon, for Chrissake, the old guy's finished."

Vangie slid down the bank in pale moonlight like an otter down a mud slide. There was mist over the water. She jumped into her father's boat, snapped shut the padlock on the chain around the tree, ran down to the stern. Hand-over-handed up her scow on the towrope. She threw in the attaché case, jerked open the slipknot on the towrope.

"Here! She's here!" yelled a badly limping Maxton when he saw her below just about to jump into the flatboat.

Without even looking back, Vangie dove into the water. The boat started to swing free. Maxton tried to scramble down the bank, fell, slid and rolled right down to the water's edge. Nicky and Trask, on the bank above, started firing wildly over his head at the drifting scow, even though Vangie was nowhere to be seen in the concealing river mist.

* * *

Her sleek head broke water on the far side of the scow so it was between her and the shore. She reached up for the gunwale, but it splintered and flew apart. She grabbed a breath, ducked under again so she didn't see two more slugs hole the side of her outboard motor. Maxton, flat on his back in the mud, was yelling hysterically at his cohorts firing over his head.

"Quit firing, quit firing, you fucking apes!" He struggled to his feet as they slid down the bank, waved his arms wildly. "Get after her, for Chrissake!"

Neither man moved. They weren't about to dive into that cold fucking water in the dark, there were gators and snakes and turtles, oh my . . .

"The boat, you stupid fuckers! Use the boat!"

They scrambled for Papa's fishing scow. Nicky grabbed the prow. Trask tried to unwind the mooring chain from around the tree. Nicky shoved. Nothing happened. Trask took out his gun.

"She locked the fucking chain to the tree."

Maxton said, "It doesn't matter," in a subdued voice. They turned to look out over the mist-covered slow brown river. There was nothing to be seen but mist. "She got away clean."

Actually, the flat-bottom scow had wedged itself up against a cypress knee. Vangie's forearm and lower leg came up to hook themselves over the gunwale, she rolled up into the boat. It sent out silent wavelets, Vangie herself was silent, listening to their distant voices echoing off the sounding board of fog.

"Hell, I hit the motor a couple times," said Nicky's voice. "She ain't going anywhere with it."

Vangie saw the holes, with cold fingers loosened the clamps holding the motor to the transom. She was shivering in the night air. Maxton's echoing voice transfixed her.

"What about her folks?"

Trask said in bragging tones, "I took 'em both out."

Vangie sat down abruptly on the bottom of the boat, terror

and despair washing over her in great waves. She started to sob even as Maxton's voice came again.

"Terrific work, Trask! Let's get out of here before someone finds 'em."

Suddenly all fear was gone. She stood up, knuckling her eyes like a little girl, but her face was a mask of hatred. She jerked lose the gas line, with one wild heave sent the motor into the water with a heavy splash.

Maxton's distant, muffled voice demanded, "What was that?"

"Me, you fuckers!" she screamed into the fog. "I've got the bonds! Come and get me, I'll be waiting for you! Especially you, Trask!"

24

When Minus turned into the dirt track to Broussard's Store, his headlights swept across three fishermen just getting into their big four-door sedan. They spun gravel and came right at him, lights on bright. Minus had to slew over to one side of the dirt track, his horn braying angrily, so their fenders could clear his by scant inches.

He yelled curses after their retreating taillights until his Cajun good nature prevailed. Then he shrugged and started up the steps to the store. He stopped. The place was dark.

"Vangie?" No answer. He went further, craned forward cautiously like a cat in a doghouse. "*Eh la bas!* You, Vangie!"

Still no answer. With sudden decision, he grabbed the screen door and pulled it open.

Inverness kept the motor barely chugging as their flatboat went down the broad river. Dain was twisted around so he could shine a flashlight low under the fog ahead of them. He found it quite remarkable that Inverness could navigate at all in the drifting mist. His light picked out Papa's moored boat.

Inverness cut the motor entirely. "This is the one."

"That's what you said at the last three landings."

"I'm bound to get it right eventually."

Together they pulled the boat up, followed their flashlights up the bank to the level ground by the store.

"What the hell?" said Inverness.

His light had picked up Minus, slumped against the fender of his pickup with his face in his hands. At the same moment a sheriff's car came roaring down the dirt track.

"Whatever happened," said Dain hurriedly, "you'll want to talk to that dude before your country cousins bottle him up."

The cop car slowed to a stop in front of the store, its revolving roof light casting a pulsing intermittent blue glow over the scene. Dain was already halfway up the front steps.

"Hold it right there, mister!"

Inverness whipped out his shield. "New Orleans police. Working a possible homicide case that might connect with this."

Dain used a ballpoint pen to pull the screen door open enough to get a shoetip in. If the girl was dead, it would once again be his fault. No wonder she had been replacing Marie in his nightmares!

The first thing he heard was the triumphant chirping of a thousand crickets. His flashlight showed him the smashed box, the little crickets leaping everywhere, flooded one of them like a spotlight on an entertainer. The cricket began to perform, sawing away. It was sitting on a dead and broken and blood-splattered Cajun face. Vangie's dad. Had to be. Jesus God.

The full charge of buckshot swept him back against the table. A widening red pool began to spread beneath his chest . . .

He had to handle it. Another new memory, jarred loose from his subconscious. Dain followed the flashlight beam down the store, sweating with the nightmare image of his own death.

The shotgun had killed Eddie, had left only Dain.

A woman was sprawled facedown over stacked soft drinks in old-fashioned wooden boxes, head at an unnatural angle. Dain's light moved down her and up again, and away.

Eddie saw the shotgun belch yellow flame to smash Marie back and up and out of this life . . .

Vangie's mother. He leaned against the wall, fighting nausea. Another siren—an ambulance this time. Nobody in this slaughterhouse would need an ambulance. His moving eye of flashlight stopped on the half-open door to the living area.

No sign of the bonds here in the store, and . . .

Jesus, no! Let the cops find Vangie.

He pushed the door open silently, looked down a narrow hallway to a kitchen. His flashlight showed a table, two coffee cups, a plate with a few *beignets* still on it, two smaller plates sprinkled with powdered sugar. The coffeepot on the stove was warm, as was the cast-iron pot of gumbo. The oven was cold.

No bodies. Praise God, no bodies.

Back up the hall. Bedrooms. One was obviously her folks' room, the dressertop crowded with framed family portraits dimmed by age. A gilt-backed hairbrush with strands of gray-shot black hair in the bristles. An age-slicked cane rocker with a thick missal in French on a small round hardwood table beside it. Hand-hooked antimacassar covering the table.

No bodies in here, either.

Last room. He drifted the door open with his flashlight. Tossed across the rough bunk bed were Vangie's miniskirt, blouse, pantyhose. Her shoes on the floor. No blood on the dress.

A strange voice said, "Thank God."

His voice. He backed out, went back up the hall.

Vangie was not dead in this place.

And no bonds were here, either. The place wasn't torn up enough for someone to have searched. It had to be Maxton and his two goons who had killed her folks. *Had* to be. So the bonds didn't really matter any more, did they? Unless

Vangie was still alive. Which it suddenly seemed she might be. Which meant she might have escaped with them.

If so, Maxton would still be after her. And Dain would still have to do something about it. *He*. Him. Not Inverness, not the other cops. *Him*. If he could get to her first and talk her into giving the bonds to him, he was pretty sure Maxton would accept them and give up the search. Maxton wasn't the sort of guy would enjoy slogging through a Louisiana swamp looking for an exotic dancer he once had slept with.

In the store, Dain started back up the aisle toward the pale rectangle of screen door. Two black shapes appeared in it.

The door crashed open back against the wall and a bulky man was silhouetted by moonlight behind him. A sawed-off shotgun was in his hands. A second bulky shadow crowded in behind him.

"What'd you find?"

The cop, a second one behind him, was staring at him almost suspiciously. Dain shook his head and went by them out the door.

Two police cars were angled in, both with their cherry-pickers revolving, a sheriff's car and an ambulance were pulling up behind them in the yard. Cops and medics crowded their way into the store as Dain jumped down off the *galerie*.

As he came up, Inverness was asking, "But these three men you saw definitely didn't have Vangie with them, is that right?"

"J'ai dis que non." Minus had been crying.

Dain walked Inverness off a few steps.

"Her folks, dead. No sign of Vangie. I want to find her."

He looked back at the store now blazing with light. A uniformed cop was just jumping down from the *galerie* and starting their way. He turned quickly to Minus.

"If they didn't have her in the car, where is she?"

"Mebbe she already went out to her papa's ol' camp on his fishin' groun' befo' dey got here." He knuckled his eyes again. "When I drive her out here, she say dat where she wan' go, her."

"You know that part of the swamp?"

"Fo' sure. Dat on de Bayou Noire."

The cop arrived to lay a not-unfriendly hand on Minus's shoulder. "Captain, he wanta talk with you, *cher*."

Dain yawned involuntarily. For the first time in five years, he was exhausted, dying for sleep. Inverness said, "We'll go back to Lafayette—to my motel." He gestured after Minus when the cop was out of earshot. "Tomorrow we'll hire him to guide us out to Bayou Noire."

It was dawn. At the boat marina Maxton was asking the tall, stooped, chicken-necked proprietor about a crawfisherman's flatboat, very wide of beam, with a slightly tapered prow ending in a blunt nose. Maxton was dressed for the swamp, as were Nicky and Trask, lounging on the dock beside their disorderly heap of gear. The skinny old Cajun gestured as he talked.

"Sure, dis de kine boat I rent dem, go anywhere dat boat go." His chuckle turned into a cough that curled him like a shrimp. He straightened up, red-faced. "Dat Minus, he tak dem out in dat swamp first t'ing today, not even light yet." He opened his mouth and laughed. His teeth were discolored from chaw tobacco. "I t'ink dey after somep'n big, dem!"

Inverness was at the outboard to the rear, Dain hunched in the center seat. His body ached as though he had a fever. Minus, in front, watched the channel ahead of them. Their gear was neatly stowed. Lashed right on top of their crawfisherman's flatboat, on the left side, was a pirogue, a narrow, canoe-like rowboat. Dain wished he could stretch out in it and rest, long enough to think. His mind felt jumbled, confused.

When Minus pointed, Inverness cut their speed, swung the flatboat off the open waterway into a very narrow, tree-shadowed bayou. He blazed a sapling with a hatchet, then swung into midchannel and speeded up again.

They were gone quickly, their motor noise died out. Peace and calm descended on the bayou. A turtle started to clamber up on a half-submerged cypress when the departed motor sound grew stronger again. He slid back off the log.

Another flatboat with three men, but without a pirogue atop it, came from the same direction as the first. It went down this same narrow channel. Its motor died away. Its waves stopped washing the shore. The turtle clambered up on the log again to sprawl luxuriously in the warming sun.

Inverness was isolated by the motor, and Minus was brooding, depressed, shaking his head from time to time as if talking to himself. Dain knew that game, only too well. If only I had gotten there quicker night before last . . . if only . . . if only . . .

If only Maxton hadn't come to New Orleans. If only Vangie had given Dain the bonds so Maxton wouldn't have killed Jimmy, and probably Vangie's folks. At least it looked like she had gotten away clean with the bonds. Now he had to find her, and get them back from her, before Maxton did both things.

But how could Maxton find her? They probably knew where she was, Maxton didn't. But the swamp had a way of changing all equations. Despite its beauty, it was full of death. A blue and white streak of kingfisher darted through nodding reeds near shore just as a cardinal was struck down in midflight by a swooping sparrow hawk.

Inverness seemed infected by the same pervading atmosphere of gloom. They stopped to eat the sandwiches they had bought at the marina, and he made another of his hatchet blazes on one of the small trees flanking the narrow waterway.

"I'm not the swamper that Minus is," he almost apologized. "I want to be able to find my way out of here if something goes wrong. Anything can happen to any of us at any time."

As if to prove him right, a Louisiana heron, carefully stepping through long grass onshore, suddenly darted its head down to spear a foot-long red-bellied water snake, shook it to snap the neck. The head flopped uselessly as the heron ate it with greedy gulps, long gullet jerking with each swallow.

They worked their way up a series of sloughs where the water shoaled until the propeller roiled mud. When Inverness killed the motor their echo lingered a moment before it was abruptly cut off. Minus reacted with a swift turn of the head toward their wake. Inverness tipped the motor up to clear away water lilies and yellow flag twisted around the propeller shaft; Dain and Minus broke out the push poles.

And there it was again: beauty and death. A mother wood duck and her brood swam away from them past a half-sunken log. The log swirled, the last duckling in line disappeared. The log immediately sank beneath the brown water. The ducks scattered for shore. But a second, then a third, then the final duckling went under one by one as the gator struck from below. The frenzied mother was still beating her wings and squawking loudly for her brood as Inverness found deeper water and started the motor.

Late in the day and deep in the swamp, the bayou was split by a small island. Minus gestured to the right-hand channel, then pointed to a beach on the island backed by a clearing.

"We camp there!" he yelled over the motor.

Inverness swung the flatboat, cut the motor just before they nosed up onto the muddy bank. Again Dain heard that odd echo as if another, distant motor also had been cut. Minus had already leaped out into the sucking ankle-deep ooze. Dain joined him and together they pulled up the boat. Minus seemed to be coming out of his depression.

"We leave de flatboat here tomorrow, go on by pirogue. Dis here boat, we have to go roun' on de open water couple mile ahead. Bayou too shallow for it. Dat take a extra day. Wit de pirogue we be at de fishin' camp demain—dis bayou take us right to it."

An hour later night had fallen, their tent was up with the mosquito flies closed, Inverness was at the cookfire making supper in a blackened frypan, and Dain was holding a flashlight steady for Minus. The Cajun was knee-deep in the water tying short lines with hooks baited with bacon squares onto sturdy branches of the overhanging bushes. As he secured each weighted hook and line, he dropped it into the water.

"Mebbe we get us some catfish fo' breffus," he said.

He and Dain scoured the pots and dishes with wet sand and poured boiling water over them, then waited for the coffee to boil in the big battered blue enamel pot. Inverness was inside the tent, his silhouette moving against the nylon as he pumped up the kerosene mantle lantern. He picked up what looked like a heavy belt in silhouette, put it around his waist, cinched it tight.

Idly watching his shadow actions, each of them listened to the sounds of the night, the rustle of a small mammal in the bushes, the bass carrunking of bullfrogs, the thin whine of mosquitoes, the thrum of a nighthawk passing in a rush of wings.

It all sounded peaceful, but Dain wasn't fooled any more. Nothing lived unless something else died.

Inverness came out, hung the hissing lantern on the tent pole. Dain squinted at the sudden white light. One silhouetted action was explained: a .357 Magnum in a tooled leather holster now hung at the lawman's lean hip. Dain poured steaming coffee into a thick white mug. Minus lumbered to his feet.

"I go check dem bush lines we set," he said. At the edge of the lamplight, he turned back. "*Tu sais* somebody been followin' us all day? Stoppin' de motor when we stop ours, startin' up again when we start ours?"

Neither man answered him. With a shrug he went off down toward the river, flashlight in hand.

Inverness, looking after him, slowly sank to a woodsman's squat with his back almost touching the front tent pole. Dain watched him, his eyes sharp and hard. Inverness shook his head in wonder.

"Who in hell could it be?"

Dain said, "I have a pretty good idea, but why ask me? You're the boy's been blazing a trail for them all day that even I could have followed."

25

Neither man shifted his position, but the gauntlet had been thrown. There was a subtle tension in their poses, yet from a distance they still could have been a couple of old friends discussing the day's events in the camp. The fire crackled, sending sparks swirling up into the darkness.

"Why would I do a thing like that?" Inverness asked lazily.

"For the same reason you ran us all over this swamp day before yesterday when you knew damn well where the Broussards' store was. So the killers could get there first."

"You think I wanted her folks—"

"No, I think you wanted Vangie caught because you're on somebody's pad and were told to want her caught." Dain sat up, drew up his knees, hooked his arms around them, feeling as if there were cobwebs on his brain. "She wasn't there and things got out of hand and the old people died."

Inverness shifted his position while remaining in his tireless wide-kneed squat. His voice did not match his face, which was tense, watchful, perhaps even a little regretful.

"And whose pad are you suggesting I'm on?"

"Whoever told you I was in New Orleans. I think you're even more interested in me than in Vangie."

"You think too much, Dain."

"Five years ago—"

"I don't know anything about five years ago."

Dain got control. "Five years ago a contract was put out on me because I was too good at finding out things. My wife and child died. Five years ago you soured on mankind, took to the swamps. Is there a connection? I get the feeling there is."

"Don't be a fool," said Inverness scornfully. "If you want to find someone to pay for your family, go after the guy who put out the contract."

"He died. That leaves me with the man who brokered the hit and the men who carried it out. It's taken me five years of looking, but I think I've finally hit a raw nerve."

Inverness chuckled. "Christ, Dain, you're really out of your tree. What's the word they used to use? Overwrought? Having the vapors? Which one am I supposed to be? The guy who brokered it or the guy who carried it out?"

"I didn't say that. But hitmen aren't thugs, you know— they're specialists."

"Like me."

"Like you," he said stubbornly.

He knew Inverness was right, he was reaching, there was a hollow feeling in his gut he'd never had when he'd been playing chess. Paranoia. But he couldn't stop himself. It was like he was a kid again, that feeling of helplessness from childhood, the unnamed fears that playing chess had conquered. Five years ago he'd quit playing chess, but had kept them at bay by playing other, more dangerous games. Now, all finished.

"Why did you drag me up to view Zimmer's body?" he heard himself asking like a betrayed kid. "You aren't even a Homicide cop. And Maxton. Somebody told Maxton where to find Vangie so he could get to her before I did, and I think . . ."

Inverness stood up in one smooth movement, his head touching the hissing kerosene lamp so it danced on its tent pole hook. It cast moving light and shadow down over his face.

"I've had enough of this crap."

Minus entered the rim of lantern light holding up a massive wriggling catfish. "Lookit dis catfish was on de—"

Inverness, startled, spun toward Minus. His boot grated on a fallen branch, a silver ring glinted on his left hand.

A bulky man, a sawed-off shotgun in his hands, was silhouetted in moving shadow by moonlight through the trees outside the cabin. His heavy boots grated on the bare plank floor. A silver ring glinted on his finger.

Dain wasn't ready. He gaped in total astonishment even as the .357 Magnum boomed, blowing Minus backward, arms flying, fish flying, blood spilling. Belatedly, he reacted, kicking the coffeepot and already rolling as it hit Inverness in the gut. The gun roared again and dirt jumped where his chest had been.

He was zigzagging out of the firelight as the Magnum roared three more times, chipping wood from a tree in front of him, blowing a branch off a bush just beside him, splattering mud at his heel. He was out of the light when the final shot brought a cry and a loud splash.

Inverness flipped out the cylinder, shaking out the spent brass. By the hissing lamplight he reloaded methodically, his movements casual, unhurried. A minor thrashing in the brush flared his nostrils and sent him into his predator's crouch; but then he relaxed, got down the lantern and walked to the sprawled body of Minus. He sighed and holstered his gun and grabbed the dead Cajun by an ankle.

He dragged Minus down to the water, heaved him as far in as he could one-handed, then, still keeping the lantern raised high, used his boot to shove him out far enough for the slow surge of current to take him. The body slid downstream into darkness.

Crouching, Inverness checked the edge of the stream for the deep muddy marks where Dain had run down into the water. He edged forward a foot at a time until he was satisfied.

"No blood," he said aloud.

He came erect, still holding the lantern up high, staring out into the darkness of swamp and swirling muddy water.

"Dain!" he shouted. He lowered his voice slightly. "You don't have a boat or a gun or a knife. No food, no drinkable water. All you've got is a choice. Me or the swamp."

Across the narrow arm of waterway, below the far bank of the bayou, Dain stood submerged in thick swamp water up to his neck. His intent face was touched by the light, but he had smeared mud across it so it reflected nothing.

He was motionless, unblinking, watching the enemy whose voice was coming across the water.

"Your wife was part of the contract, Dain, but for what it's worth, I'm sorry about your kid. You called that one about right. I've been a straight cop since then."

Dain stood in the thick brown water in stunned silence, not believing what he had heard. Was it this easy? Or this hard? Did the enemy at last have a face, a name?

He'd sought this confrontation, prayed for it, had trained for five years for this moment. He'd thought he'd created a killer to face this professional killer—and here he stood neck-deep in the muck and the other guy had the gun.

So who was he now? A computer nerd, a chess groupie, a games freak who'd gotten his wife and child killed. Trying to undo that unspeakable evil, he'd gone right on to a new game even worse. A game that was relentlessly killing, one by one, every poor bastard who crossed his path. Except Inverness, who, lantern high overhead to create a white core in the darkness, would have made a beautiful target for a man with a gun. Dain, of course, was empty-handed. He could have howled like a wolf with the agony and the irony of it.

Inverness was declaiming to the swamp as if it wore Dain's face. Fucking Demosthenes yelling at the ocean. He sickened Dain, revived his hatred. If he could hold on to that . . .

"When I was told you were on your way to New Orleans, I thought you were after me . . ."

Who told you, bastard? Who who who?

"It was my idea, not Maxton's, to try and scare you off. When that didn't work, I thought you'd made me—so I wanted to get you out here in the swamp where killing you wouldn't make any more stir than swatting a skeeter. I figured showing you Zimmer would make you come running out here to save the girl.''

What about poor Minus, you fucker?

As if he heard the thought, Inverness said, ''I needed Minus to guide us so you wouldn't get suspicious. I figured he'd go after you, but he startled me and so I took him first. Just as good. We gotta talk, don't we? Just you and me.''

Dain almost answered. He *wanted* to—wanted to explain himself, wanted to know why this killer was diabolically yoked to him, wanted answers to the questions tormenting him more than he wanted revenge. He started to clear his throat to yell across the narrow channel, then grabbed hold of his mind, let the other man's spate of words stay him.

''It's just you and me and the swamp, Dain. The girl, Maxton—they don't matter. It's you and me who share the nightmares. You and me who gotta talk. Or maybe we gotta fight.'' He gave a short laugh. ''Maybe I'll fuck up again . . .''

He paused, holding the lantern aloft to make a white-hot halo around him, peering earnestly into the darkness where Dain, shivering in the thick water, almost answered that almost seductive voice. It was that short laugh that stopped him.

That and the loathing that had swept through him at mention of the nightmares. *His* nightmares. They were all he had, and the killer even wanted to take those away from him.

''What do you say, Dain? I can't bring back your wife and child, but . . . can't we let the past die, go on from here?''

Was Inverness asking forgiveness? Maybe, after all . . .

What the hell was he thinking of? This was a *hitman* asking forgiveness, asking Dain to speak, to show himself, standing there with a lantern in one hand—and a gun in the other. A gun he had methodically reloaded after killing Minus.

Forever the amateur, Dain, his thinking screwed up by what he'd learned tonight. An amateur with a patchwork body that ached to give in to the swamp, and maybe fever, a body that wanted to just slip under the water and . . .

Inverness would be counting on that. But goddammit, Inverness wasn't the only killer in this swamp. All day Dain had watched things die, none of them willingly. Hatred and weakness rose like bile in his throat—and he was silent.

Right now, silence was the only weapon he had.

It worked. Inverness had talked too much, and realized it.

"You'll be dead by nightfall tomorrow, Dain!" he yelled, as if suddenly enraged that he wasn't able to end it right now. "If the fucking swamp doesn't get you, I will!"

He turned away from the bayou, just a pale aureole moving away into the night, dropping Dain back into total darkness. The mud on his face had dried. He could feel it cracking as the tenseness left his features. He patted water on it noiselessly with his hands. He waited.

With Inverness gone, the swamp that was waiting with him gradually came alive again. The dark air again was filling with its humming, croaking, cackling song. Dain almost sang along with it. *Inverness was afraid of him!* He'd tried to kill Dain twice and had failed both times. He was the professional and Dain was the amateur, but the slaughter was working on him in a way it wasn't working on Dain.

That gave Dain an edge. He felt he could stand there in the heavy water of the swamp all night if he had to. Which is when he sagged and his head went under. His groping hand caught a branch trailing down into the water from the bank, he pulled himself erect, spluttering, fighting his gag reflex, a tremendous urge to cough and snort. Inverness was still not that far away.

On his way back to the tent, Inverness passed the twenty-pound catfish whose thrashing had startled him earlier. It was still flapping its tail and gasping in the grass. He picked it up and carried it back to the water, threw it in. Almost, he thought with sudden self-anger, as if placating some god of the predators—the only deity he would have acknowledged if any gods had existed at all.

Was Dain after all tough enough to have known Inverness was trying to lure him, and so had kept silent out there in the swamp? How in the fuck had he missed with all six shots?

Come to that, how the fuck had he missed killing Dain five years ago after putting three charges of double-0 buckshot into him and burning a cabin down around him?

Or had Dain been hit after all tonight, but hadn't started bleeding until he was in the water?

Back at camp, moving slowly and thoughtfully, Inverness killed the lantern and went into the tent to wait out the dying of the fire's dim light.

It was very late and through drifting tatters of mist a gibbous moon showed the tent flaps were closed. The fire was dead except for one or two dully glowing embers. An owl swooped across the clearing on huge silent wings. A fish broke water. A raccoon came hesitantly out of the brush to begin nosing around the front of the tent.

On the side of the flatboat where the pirogue was lashed, the very top of Dain's head broke water very slowly. He stood, mouth-breathing, water streaming off his flattened hair and down his face, for a full two minutes, waiting, listening. Four baby raccoons trundled out to join their parent in foraging around in front of the tent. All else was silence and darkness. Safety.

He turned to work on the ties holding down the pirogue, unfastening them one by one. Out in the bayou behind him a fish jumped. He had it all planned out. Steal the pirogue, head for Vangie's fishing camp as quickly as possible. Maybe she would have guns there. If not, get her away immediately, out into the swamp where Maxton and his men couldn't find her.

Inverness would be coming after him first, but would be blazing that trail for the others to follow. He had no illusions about Inverness being able to find the place. Inverness knew the swamp well enough to have gotten a clear idea from Minus of the camp's location on Bayou Noire. But Dain doubted the pursuers would have another pirogue. They would have to go the long way around, giving him time to make Vangie safe.

And to prepare for whatever destiny faced him in this swamp. He wasn't going to be a rabbit cowering in its burrow when they came. More a tough and wily badger they'd have to dig out. A badger with teeth and claws and a will to live.

All the ties were loosened. He reached for the pirogue and began moving it off the flatboat with infinite care.

Torchlight hit his back and Inverness fired down the beam of light from the brush where he had been waiting for five cramped and silent hours. The slug hit Dain in the back by the top of his shoulder blade, just below his trapezius muscle. He was driven forward by the blow, splashing and stumbling, his clutching nerveless hand flipping the pirogue over the top of him as the fading thought went through his mind, *Rabbit, not badger after all . . .*

As he went under, two more shots in rapid succession hit the water just where his head had disappeared and Inverness went crashing through the brush to the water's edge, charging out after the pirogue. But it was drifting more rapidly now, just too far for him to reach. He kept the beam of his flashlight on the overturned craft, seeking any sign of Dain's head breaking water, trotting and ducking and slogging along the narrow muddy overgrown shore to keep even with it.

At the tail end of the island he stopped, gun in hand, staring after the drifting pirogue. Finally he turned away. He knew he'd gotten Dain this time, and the pirogue wasn't going anywhere. He could go down and pick it up in the morning while waiting for Maxton to show up.

Maxton. Maybe he ought to grab Maxton and the two goons and take them back and turn them in for killing Vangie's folks and Minus . . . It would square him with his superiors for rushing off into the swamp without leave . . . maybe save his pension . . .

Fuck. What was he thinking of? There were still the bonds. Maxton wanted them and he wanted the girl—probably to kill her, if what happened to her folks was any indication. If Inverness brought them in, sure, he'd have his pension. But if he just killed them and sank them in the swamp, he'd have the bonds. Just him. Nobody else knew about them except Maxton.

Of course if Dain were still alive, Maxton and his men would also be useful, no, essential, until Dain was

"Goddam you!" he said aloud to himself, then realized he was really addressing Dain. He was starting to get superstitious about the fucking man, as if he had supernatural powers of survival or something . . .

He started resolutely away back up the islet toward camp.

He had shot Dain in the back. With a .357 Magnum. Dain was dead, dead dead dead as fucking Jesus. He wasn't going anywhere except the mud at the bottom of the channel, thrust there by some patient gator to ripen until he could be torn into proper bite-size pieces and eaten.

Fucking Dain was dead.

26

A delicate palette knife of dawn slid through the flooded sentinel trees, laying watercolor washes of gray over the gradations of black. Here and there a bird called, something in the water splashed. Far off a Louisiana panther made a dark sawing sound, then screamed like a woman in labor.

Two flooded hardwoods leaned their heads together over the bayou, their leaves in whispered conversation, their feet in the water. One of them forked some distance above the ground. The fork held a nest containing three greenish white eggs. What looked like a large water snake swam rapidly to the base of the tree, started to slither up the trunk.

Suddenly it was a bird, a sinuous-necked sleek-bodied bird called a snakebird. Its webbed feet had strong climbing claws. When it reached the fork, it perched on one of the branches and preened its wet feathers to redistribute the oil that made its feathers waterproof. Then it sidestepped awkwardly over to settle on top of the eggs.

A dingy patch of mustard yellow showed far below, in the tangle of brush and driftwood caught between the bases of the trees. Minus had been deposited there sometime in the night by the gentle but persistent currents. His dead eyes stared up the trunk at the snakebird far above. When dawn broke, his shirt became a bright eye-catching gold.

The upside-down pirogue drifted up, carried by the gentle current against the same tangle of driftwood and brush as Minus. It clung there. It rocked, sending out ripples. The snakebird started up in alarm, then settled back again.

Inverness, untroubled by bad dreams, had slept until well after sunup. In finally killing Dain, he had killed his doubts. By the light of day, last night's secret and half-formed fears seemed silly. Dain had been shot in the back with a .357 Magnum, his lungs had filled with blood, and he had died. End of story.

Inverness breakfasted leisurely on a small catfish from one of Minus's brush lines, then set out to fetch the pirogue before Maxton showed up; it would save them a day. A mile below the island he abandoned outboard for push pole: the water was shoaling rapidly. He rounded a curve in the bayou, and a snakebird flapped down from one of a brace of flooded-out hardwoods with a loud miffed squawk, swept over the water away from the flatboat.

In a tangle of driftwood and brush at the base of the tree was Minus, lying faceup and bare-torsoed; the crabs had been feeding around the bullet hole in his chest. Inverness stood in the flatboat looking down at him. The logical place for the current to have deposited him. All fine so far.

But this was the logical place, also, for the current to have deposited the pirogue and Dain. Inverness had fully expected both to be wherever Minus fetched up, or at least the pirogue if Dain with his perforated lungs had sunk.

He raised his head, looked around the swamp, contentment oozing away. No pirogue in sight, swirled against some other deadhead by a vagrant eddy of current.

Last night Minus had been wearing a bright yellow shirt. Now it was gone. Only Dain could have taken it. But how the fuck could the man have survived being shot with a .357 Magnum? How had he survived being shot thrice with a shotgun and left to die in a burning cabin?

He checked the bole of the tree, the brush pile near Minus for sign just to be sure. Yes. A fresh indentation that could have been made by the pirogue's prow; and there, the brush was crushed. He could almost picture the scene. The boat, suddenly a human hand would have broken water beside it, groped, found Minus's face as something to get purchase on, closed about it . . .

Yes, that was the way it would have gone. Another minute would have gone by, then Dain would have dragged himself partway up out of the brown water. Would have lain there, gasping, facedown, across Minus. One arm hanging uselessly from the bullet that had entered his back and must somehow have exited high enough up in his chest to have missed heart and lung. But still he would have coughed raspingly, startling the snakebird. When he had, fresh red wetness would have spread from the wound.

So he would have taken Minus's shirt to use as a sling to immobilize the arm, also perhaps as packing to make the wound bleed less. Then he would have righted the pirogue with his one good arm, gotten in, poled away. One-armed.

Jesus, it wasn't over yet. Inverness knew he would not sleep tonight, no matter how many men Maxton had with him.

The Chinese water lilies produced vivid purple flowers that nodded above pads lying flat on the surface like green plates. On one plate was a small green frog. The frog tensed at an uneven sucking sound and a harsh, rasping exhalation, leaped for his life as a muck-covered push pole was driven down into the lily pads from above. The pole found bottom. Beyond it, the side of the pirogue slid by.

So did an hour. Now Dain poled through a hyacinth-choked neck of bayou that looked like solid earth—what the Cajuns call *prairie tremblant*. Here in the open, merciless sun beat down on his unprotected head. He poled one-armed, his useless arm tied to his side with a sling made of Minus's bright yellow shirt. More of the shirt, ripped from the tail, had been stuffed right through the bullet wound from front to back. This crude bandage was soaked with new blood. Sweat stood on his unshaven, sun-reddened face, his eyes glittered feverishly.

He had done all that as soon as he had found Minus, knowing his infected wound would soon make him even more feverish, then had used a trick from his two years of convalescence after the first try on his life: narrowing the focus of his mind to a single thing.

Then it had meant taking this step, resisting the pain of that flexing movement, using them to block out the pain and guilt of his family's death brought about by his own stupidity. Now it was a single laser of thought: follow the bayou. He might lose *why* he was following it in the fog of fever; but he was hoping he could hang on to the action: *follow the bayou.*

He forgot about the bonds, and he had to block out the knowledge that he was now half an invalid, more a liability than an asset to Vangie. He had one overwhelming concern: get to her, warn her they were coming. He had to beat them there. He still had to try and make her safe while preparing for his own final confrontation with Inverness.

If he didn't die on the way.

Beyond the *prairie tremblant* was a small lake dotted with stands of cypress. Water hyacinth broken free from the main body drifted in clumps and patches on the otherwise clear water. In the middle of this sudden dazzlingly open expanse, the pirogue was a toy canoe, Dain a toy soldier leaning motionless on his push pole. The toy figure slid down the pole to the bottom of the small tippy craft, almost capsizing it.

Little waves moved out in concentric rings from the pirogue, became mere ripples, ceased. Under the noonday sun the surface of the lake was glassy and still. A shoal of fingerling shad came up to just below the surface, camouflaging their presence from below with the pirogue's shadow.

Dain stirred, edged his head painfully over the gunwale of

the pirogue so he could look down into the water with dazed eyes. He could see minnows swimming there. The water looked cool, inviting. The minnows looked like they were having fun.

But he couldn't give a fuck about them, whether they lived or died. He had to follow the bayou.

His hand went down, burst the surface of the water to scoop some up, dash it over his head. Another, then another. His wound gave him an almost overwhelming thirst, and he knew he was dehydrating. But to drink unfiltered swamp water was to invite dysentery and disaster. No matter how weak, how disoriented, he had to keep going—by nightfall he would be totally irrational. Already his periods of lucidity were getting shorter.

Follow the bayou.

He splashed more water. Rested. Below him, the little shad returned. Dain grunted getting upright again. The pirogue tipped, almost sending him into the water. Concentric circles of waves became ripples and died, but they had sent a message out to a warmouth bass. It came up from below in a rush, shot right out of the water beside the pirogue as it struck one of the shad, dropped back in with its typical triple tail-splash as it swallowed its victim, dashed after another.

Dain's pole descended into the water. The pole found bottom. Dain grunted, the clouds scudding across his mind again even as the pirogue slid forward. On the far side the little lake narrowed back into twisting bayou again. At its mouth was a fallen tree with two dozen turtles sunning themselves on one of the limbs that rose out of the water.

Follow the bayou. Why? Don't know. Do it.

As Dain's pirogue approached, one of the turtles, then another, then the rest in bunches scrambled and slid and splashed off their perches back into the illusory safety of the water.

When he had passed, still following the bayou, they returned. They had hid from him but his passage had meant nothing to them.

*   *   *

Her flatboat was pulled up in front of the cabin, Vangie was on the bank, checking setlines for fish. Papa had chosen his site well. His fishing camp was on what had once been a peninsula sticking out into vast flat marshlands stretching to the edge of Fausse Point Lake. A mile back from the tip, the bayou once had cut a narrower, separate channel to the marsh, thus forming an island. On one side was the marsh, on the other the narrow bayou which meandered through thick woodland to empty into the marsh.

The camp gave a good view over the open marshland. The rest of the island, behind the raised, cleared area where he had placed his cabin, was deep woods. It was a peaceful scene, but inside Vangie was churning. All she could do was hide here. She could not go to the police: she had stolen $2 million. She had to count on the fact that although Maxton was a ruthless and powerful man who wanted to watch her die, he was from the city. Eventually, even he would give up.

Dain was out of the picture once and for all, thank God, the blood money for giving them to Maxton heavy in his pocket. With him gone, she could survive here until things quieted down. Then she could slip away, with the bonds . . .

She had arrived trembling with terror, but it was her second day here, and she had finally stopped leaping at every crackle in the brush. She could check her setlines. The very familiarity of the place and the work helped calm her.

Stay alive. It was what she wanted now. Try to forget about Maxton. This place was hard to find even if you were a Cajun. But she couldn't forget the bonds, and she knew Maxton wouldn't either. She had fled empty-handed, and Papa never left any guns here at the shack. Which meant that if Maxton ever did find her, it would be three armed men against her bare hands.

But he couldn't find her. And the police had no reason to be looking for her. They would have accepted Jimmy's death as a suicide, her parents' deaths as random—they knew nothing of the bonds.

Her parents. She wanted to cry, but she couldn't. She wanted to smash things, throw things, grieve—but she couldn't. How could you grieve when your parents were dead because of you?

Some animal sense made her suddenly raise her head to look up the bayou. She stood up abruptly. Far, far up the narrow waterway, just coming into sight around the last turn, was a pirogue. Even at this distance she could see that the man was poling one-armed and had the other arm in a gaudy yellow sling.

Vangie drew in her breath. Dain! Here! He had set up Zimmer for the kill; she didn't see how he could have, but maybe he'd had some hand in getting her parents killed, also. And now he was here to set her up for them. The Judas goat. Maxton and the other killers would not be far behind.

Goddam him! Weapon or no weapon, she'd see about that.

She started walking rapidly back toward the cabin.

Dain poled his erratic way toward the distant camp. The wetness soaking through his bandage was no longer red, but pus-yellow. It took all of his willpower to stay focused on that cabin. *Follow the bayou.* He had made it! He was here!

Where? Why?

No. Hang on. Just a few more shoves with the pole . . .

The prow of the pirogue sliced into muddy earth, stopped. He poled three more times before realizing he was grounded. He let go of the pole and fell sideways out of the pirogue into the muck and shallow water with a loud splash.

It felt wonderful there. Cool and soothing. Mud bath. Mummy would be mad, his Sunday clothes . . .

Don't lose it. He was here. He got to his knees. Crawled ashore, dragged himself erect. Stood swaying on the muddy bank, getting his first look at the fishing camp.

The two rooms formed a stubby ell of unpainted, hand-split cypress boards around a framework of young cypress trees. Stilts held the floor off the ground, even though the cabin stood on a ridge that was itself above flood stage. The roof was peaked, shingled by two tiers of overlapped cypress boards. A two-section stovepipe stuck out of the wall beside it at a crazy angle. The foot-square glassless windows at either end of the cabin were netted against mosquitoes, their exterior wooden shutters laid back against the walls.

The handmade door also stood open, almost invitingly. Very invitingly, in fact. Even as he thought it, the cabin began to distort, to stretch and contract as if made of rubber or Silly Putty. Dain kept his eyes fixed on it as he moved; by the time he had reached the bottom of the three mile-high steps it was yawing mildly as if at sea in the middle of a storm. There was nobody in sight. Who was he expecting?

"He . . ." He lost it, tried again. "Hello?"

There was no response. Dain went up the steps with agonizing slowness. He paused on the stoop, swaying with the rhythm of his own ragged breathing.

But he had remembered why he was here.

"Vangie?"

He called her name and she came around the door frame from inside the cabin, yelling formlessly, high on rage, already swinging a heavy wooden paddle. It caught him in the stomach, doubling him over, driving out all his breath. She swung again, this time against his useless shoulder, knocking him off the side of the porch like a sack of flour.

White-hot pain shot from his shoulder through his entire body. Even his teeth, his toes hurt. He landed on the grass with a thud that drove his wind out and consciousness away, thinking he was saying aloud, *Christ, Doc, that hurts! I don't know how many more times I can take you cutting me . . .*

She stood looking down at him, face flushed as much from emotion as from exertion.

"Goddam you, you got my parents killed! You got Jimmy killed! Now you come here . . ."

He was staring up at her, his eyes open, obviously conscious, but with a strange passivity.

"I know why you came here! To lead Maxton to me, you fucking Judas!"

Still no response. It was as if he were defenseless, defeated by her mere words. But she knew he was hearing her, was conscious, was seeing her. A new fear struck her.

"You fucker!" she screamed. "Don't you dare fucking die on me before I can kill you!"

Then she threw the paddle aside and leaped down off the porch after him.

One of the two rooms was for living, the other for storage of gear. Rough wooden shelves nailed to the walls held canned goods. At one end of the room was a hand pump over a half fifty-gallon oil drum, cut longways with a blowtorch and braced with sawhorses to serve as a sink. Also a potbelly iron stove and a wooden table with four chairs. In the other end were two bunks with sheets, blankets, pillows.

Vangie backed in through the open doorway, dragging the unconscious and filthy Dain, who outweighed her a hundred pounds, by his armpits. She dumped him on the floor beside one of the bunks. Grunting and heaving, she got first his torso up on the bunk, then swung his legs up, leaving him lying twisted and half on his side.

From the table she got a huge glittering Bowie knife, tested the blade on the ball of her thumb as she crossed the narrow room to the recumbent man. Razor-sharp.

In the sixteen years of her life spent in the swamp before she had fled to the bright lights and the big cities, she had killed hundreds of animals, thousands of fish. Gutted them, skun them, filleted them. She was no stranger to death. It didn't bother her to kill. So easy here. What difference it was a man, not an animal? One slash across the throat, like bleeding a hung deer . . . Or a single thrust up through the solar plexus under the sternum to the heart . . .

Dain was already almost dead. A falling-out with the others? Something in the swamp that had gotten him? To know what had happened, she would have to get a look at the wound.

And whatever had happened, Dain alive was an asset. If they were coming after her, maybe he could be a hostage.

Dead, he was just something to bury.

She knelt beside him, slashed the sling, then tore his shirt down. She stared at the wound with the scrap of yellow pus-caked cloth stuffed through it. She bent over it, sniffed, jerked erect.

"Jesus," she said aloud, "is that ripe!"

The swamp had not done this to him. It was surely a bullet wound, heavy caliber to have ripped through with such power. Steel-jacketed because a hollow-point or lead-nose bullet would have taken his whole shoulder off. If for some reason Maxton wanted to kill him as much as she did, he might be useful to delay them until she could get away.

She left him there unconscious, his wound uncovered, went back into the kitchen area, pumped a pail of water, set it on top of the stove, and lit the already laid fire. Without a backward glance, she went out through the open doorway. He was going to die anyway. If something came in and got him while she was gone, it would save her a lot of trouble.

Then she thought, I might do it myself when I come back.

But not right this minute. She recovered the paddle she had whacked him with, went down to his pirogue, shoved out into the bayou. She paddled easily and expertly back upstream, in the direction from which he had come.

Fifteen minutes later she swung the pirogue in toward a dead buffalo fish she had remembered was on the bank. As the prow drove into the mud three feet from the dead carp, a swarm of big green-bellied flies rose up, buzzing angrily. The side of the fish was moving in a slow steady seethe, almost as if it were still alive. Vangie crouched beside it, big Bowie knife in hand.

It was dusk when she returned to the cabin. Dain was breathing noisily. She thumped a tin can down on the table. Pumped up the kerosene lamp. A match flared, the mantles flamed, then steadied to pour out white light. She lowered the glass shield of the lantern, left it on the table.

On the stove, the water was boiling ferociously. She wrapped her Bowie knife in a towel and dropped them both into the boiling water, dropped in two more towels as well, took the bucket off the stove. Only then did she turn to look at Dain for the first time since returning from her foray.

His eyes were open, glittering in the lantern light, but his voice was rational.

"What am I doing here?" he asked.

"Dying," said Vangie.

27

Dain was declaiming, waving his good arm around as he did.

" 'By my troth, I care not; a man can die but once; we owe God a death.' "

Vangie pumped up the lantern some more, brought it over to set it on a chair near the cot on which she had dumped him.

"That's Shakespeare," said Dain.

"Terrific."

He lapsed into silence as she made her preparations. First she brought a tarp from the storeroom, managed by rolling him first one way and then the other, to get it under him and over the bunk. When she went to work with the knife there would be a lot of blood, water and pus to contend with.

Next she got out the first-aid kit Papa had always made sure was in the camp. Sterile gauze and adhesive tape and, thank God, an unopened bottle of iodine. She'd need plenty of that.

She lugged over the bucket of cooling boiled water, set it on the floor, fished out the towel with the Bowie knife in it, holding it gingerly in the steaming towel, tossing it from hand to hand so she wouldn't scald her fingers.

"You're going to die sane," she said. "You're going to feel it coming." Her eyes narrowed, her face got mean, she burst out, "You son of a bitch!"

She pulled up the second of the two chairs, sat facing him. She opened the hot towel, took out the Bowie knife, poised it above the infected wound.

"Grab onto something besides me or I'll kill you before I want to."

Her arm jerked. Pus squirted. Dain gave a single yell and was silent. She worked with the blade, wiping sweat from her face with her sleeve from time to time, rinsing out the wound with the boiled water and sterile towels when she was finished.

"Fun time," she said to the silent Dain.

And poured about half the bottle of iodine into the opened wound. He screamed again, then was silent again. She felt his pulse; it was racing. Better than not going. She had no way to check his blood pressure, wouldn't have known what was good and what was bad even if she'd had the proper instrument.

Finally, it was time for the coffee can full of seething maggots from the dead carp. She sat down on the edge of the bunk and very carefully began packing the fat squirming white creatures into Dain's infected wound. When she had used enough, she wrapped it with gauze and used adhesive tape to bandage it.

Miles away in the swamp, two flatboats were pulled up on the edge of a broad, lakelike waterway. In a small clearing were the hunters' two tents, their flaps closed. On a little natural raft of vegetation just below the low bank, a bullfrog carrunked away, swelling its throat to drive a ball of air back and forth over its vocal cords and create its thrumming sound.

Without warning a raccoon killed it with one savage

crunching bite. The coon began backing off the raft of vegetation with the dead frog in its mouth. As it did, a bobcat on the bank gave a sudden high scream.

Maxton's voice yelled, "Jesus Christ, what's that?"

The coon had dropped the dead frog to flee. A powerful flashlight began playing wildly over the inside of one of the tents. The bobcat slunk into the underbrush with the frog.

"Your conscience, maybe?"

The tent flap opened and Inverness looked out. Maxton's pale face appeared beside his in the narrow V-shaped opening. He was still waving the flashlight around.

"It . . . it sounded like . . . a woman's scream."

"That isn't until we get to the camp," chuckled Trask from the other tent.

Inverness could feel the pressure building inside. He just wanted it finished. He just wanted fucking Dain dead. Maxton and the two creeps could do what they wanted to Vangie. He let the flap drop back again.

"Go to sleep, Maxton. You'll need it. I smell rain."

Through the small mosquito-netted window on the east side of the fishing shack, dawn was staining the horizon with a narrow crimson line. But neither of them was awake to see it. Vangie was crowded into the same narrow bunk as Dain, his head resting partially on her breast and partially on her shoulder. His wound was tightly bound with fresh white gauze.

"No," he said suddenly in a conversational voice. Vangie's eyes opened. He began throwing his head from side to side. "*Run*, Albie!" he cried. "*Ru . . .*"

He subsided. She put her hand on his forehead. It was cool to the touch. The fever had broken in the night. Just some nightmare . . . But Dain thrashed again, almost throwing her off the bunk with the violence of his movements. She saved herself only by putting one foot on the rough plank floor.

"Marie! Look out!" He paused for a moment. Then, a loud cry, "Vangie!" Softer voice. "They're . . . coming . . ."

She leaped out of the bunk, ran on bare feet to the table,

pumped the dying lantern bright again. She sat down heavily and, hunched forward, regarded Dain intently, an almost frightened look on her face.

She shivered. "Why me . . . in his nightmares . . ."

When he had begun bucking like an out-of-control stallion, her old perverse reactions took over as they had so often in the past. She'd started to feel sorry for him. Yesterday, she'd wanted to kill him. This morning, when he had been bucking beneath her, she'd wanted to fuck him. It was as old as mankind, deny death with an act that affirmed life, sometimes created it. But here and now, with this particular man, her body's reaction seemed a betrayal and made her angry.

"Goddam you," she exclaimed, "if you're going to die, I wish you'd do it."

Dain made no more movements or outcries. Vangie's head gradually slumped to her forearms, crossed in front of her on the table beside the slowly dying lantern. She slept again.

Midmorning, rain pouring from a leaden sky. Vangie was coming from the marshland in the pirogue through the driving storm, wearing gleaming raingear. Two cylindrical chicken-wire traps in the bottom of the boat were crawling with live crawfish.

Inside, Dain awoke to the sound of rain drumming on the roof, swung his feet to the floor and tried to sit up. On his second try he managed to stay upright. His right arm was immobilized under its gauze wrappings; he gingerly scratched at it. His color was better, he felt totally rational.

"Be a hero," he said aloud to himself. "Stand up."

He tried. Fell back on the bunk. Tried again. This time he managed to get to his feet, swaying but upright. He began a very slow progress across the room. Rested, hanging on the back of a straight wooden chair. Panting. He looked at the inviting bunk a continent away. Started back again. Made it.

Sat down. Rested. Stood. Started back toward the table. Made it. Back to the bunk. Stayed upright.

Again. And again and again and . . .

The door was jerked open and Vangie was blown into the cabin by hurled sheets of rain. She set down her bait bucket full of live crawfish as the door slammed behind her. Only then did she see Dain on his feet, halfway between bunk and table.

The color left her face and her mouth fell open in astonishment. Perhaps Dr. Frankenstein's face had worn a similar expression when the monster he had stitched together actually sat up and was alive.

She snatched the Bowie knife off her belt and held it low and in front of her like a knife fighter in a bout.

"You son of a bitch!" she shrieked at him.

Dain stared at her quite mad face. There was a calmness and detachment in him that was almost animal, perhaps the contract of death that naturalists have noted between prey and predator, perhaps the detachment that often comes to people who have suffered pain or been tortured for long periods of time.

"I'm starving to death and this thing is itching like hell," he complained to her.

Vangie didn't know what to do. She was ready to kill him and he was acting like a character in a TV drama. She covertly slid the knife back in its scabbard, picked up the bucket of crawfish and set it in the half-drum sink and started pumping fresh water into it as if the knife had never been in her hand.

"That's, ah, not, ah, not surprising," she told him. "I packed it full of live maggots last night, and repacked it this morning before I went out. Maggots eat only dead, infected flesh, leave the healthy flesh alone."

Dain paled and sat down rather abruptly at the table. He stared at her, looked down at his shoulder, back up at her. He made a "whew" mouth and blew out a long breath as she carried the water and crawfish over to the stove.

But then stubbornness entered his face. He said in a bleak voice, "We've got four men coming in after us."

Vangie sat down as suddenly, as heavily as he had, as if all her strength had suddenly drained out.

"*Us*, you bastard?" Then belatedly, she added, "Four? I thought there were only—"

"Actually, only three of them are after you and the bonds. Maxton and his strongarms. The fourth one is after me. But I'm sure he wants his cut of the loot, too."

"Maxton," she said scornfully. "You sold Jimmy out to him, you sold me out to him. Did you sell my folks out, too? What did they ever do to you, you fucker? I wanted to save them—"

"Maybe they didn't want to be saved."

Vangie burst out, "Goddam you!" and launched herself across the table at him, eyes flashing, fingers clawed to rip his face. He kicked back his chair as his undamaged arm swept her right off the table. The impact knocked her breath out, so she sat on the floor blinking up at him and gasping.

"Hell, they don't have to come in after us," said Dain. "We'll do each other in."

Vangie's panting eased. Dain held out a hand to her. After a hesitation, she took it, allowed him to help her to her feet. She crossed to the kitchen area and got busy preparing the crawfish. He spoke suddenly and harshly to her back.

"I don't give a fuck whether you believe me or not, but I didn't sell you out, lady. Five years ago, someone blew away my wife and son—"

"Marie and Albie?" she exclaimed before she could stop herself. She got quickly busy lifting the lid to check the steaming crawfish, so she wouldn't have to meet his eyes. "I heard a lot about them last night when you were asleep."

"Nightmares. I have a lot of them ever since . . . I've been trying to find the men killed them. That's why I do the sort of work I do for the sort of people I do. What's your excuse?"

She actually started to justify herself to him. "The bonds were going to save me from . . ." She stopped, added defiantly, "And my folks from working themselves to death . . ."

Dain said, softly, "Well, maybe we can save each other."

She shot him a glance but said nothing. Her silence was more palpable than words, an acquiescence she could not yet acknowledge. He spoke to this unspoken acceptance in her.

"Remember down by the river that afternoon I told you I'd stirred someone up by coming to New Orleans to look for you? That was a New Orleans cop named Inverness.

He'd braced me the night before, when there was no legitimate way he could have known about me or known I was in town. I figured it had to be connected somehow.''

She said stiffly, ''Was it?''

''Yes, but not the way I thought.'' He began to prowl the room. His strength was rapidly returning now that the infection was down and the fever gone. ''I don't know if he's the one tipped Maxton where you were, but he's one of the men who shotgunned my family. So he *has* to kill me now.''

''Because you know what he did?''

''Because he knows I'll kill him if he doesn't.''

Vangie turned to face him, leaning back against the edge of the steel-drum sink. His implacability was good, she could use it, use him like a missile against her enemies. Maybe. He might even be telling the truth.

''If he's after you and Maxton is after me, why are they teamed up together?''

''I don't know how or why, but I know he was blazing trees to lead Maxton here. It only makes sense for him to help Maxton get the bonds and kill you, so Maxton will help him kill me, and so will give him a cut of the bonds.'' He paused. ''You'd better know it all, Vangie—Inverness killed Minus, too.''

''Oh God,'' she said softly, ''another one.'' Another death on someone's conscience, whether hers or his he wasn't sure. She added, ''Don't they think you're dead?''

''*They* might—Inverness won't. He's a hunter, he'll be reading sign, he'll know.''

Vangie got out a couple of thick white plates and some silverware. She avoided his eyes.

''And you, you fucker, you led them right to me.''

''Not me—Minus. He told Inverness where he thought you were, how to get here—thinking Inverness was a straight cop. I did too, until Inverness started leaving a trail for Maxton to follow. I couldn't lead anyone anywhere, you know that. I'm worthless in this swamp.''

''You got here,'' she said.

''Minus said that in a pirogue you just had to follow the bayou. I did. I thought I could save you. Then I just had to get here or die, it was as simple as that.''

"Nothing's ever that simple," she said ruefully, as if
sorry he had made it and she had saved him.

"Now we have to face them," he said as if she hadn't
spoken, "or die."

"We can run."

He just shook his head. Their eyes locked for a long moment. Then she turned away, took the steaming fragrant
bucket of crawfish off the stove.

"Four men," she said. "By pirogue or flatboat?"

"Far as I know, flatboat. It makes a difference?"

"The storm. Without pirogues, they have to cross the
open water—maybe ten miles of it. This wind won't fall
until morning, the waves until afternoon, and even then they
can't hit us in daylight. So we've got until tomorrow night."

"Why not in daylight?"

"They'll expect guns to be here."

"Why aren't there?"

"Swampers wouldn't steal anything else'd steal guns."

In the marsh it was very dark, though still only five in the
afternoon. The rain was pouring down, the tops of the overstory trees that dominated the rest of the forest were being
whipped and tossed by the wind. The two boatloads of
hunters were just nosing into shore where the wide waterway they had been following entered the vast open expanse
of marshland lake.

They cut the motors, grounded the boats, the four men
jumped out to pull them up. Maxton grabbed Inverness's
sleeve.

"Why are we making camp in the middle of the afternoon?"

The big policeman just walked off. Maxton hesitated, then
trotted after. They shoved through wet underbrush, broke
free. Maxton stopped, appalled at the violence of the open
marshland.

The sky was a vicious indigo piled with black clouds.
Lightning flashed and flickered constantly. Muddy massive
whitecaps piled up out in the open water, sweeping across
the surface with relentless precision to finally tip and froth

and break into dirty white sweeping crests. The wind howled, rain raised two-inch welts on the surface.

"Understand? The wind probably will die down through the night, but the waves won't fall off until tomorrow sometime. If we try to cross before they do, we've got a damned good chance of capsizing and drowning. That's why we're making camp with three hours of nominal daylight left."

Maxton began in a congested voice, "We'll try now, god—"

Inverness just turned away. "Give it a rest, Maxton." He *knew* goddam Dain was alive, and that belief filled his mind, left him nothing with which to worry about the girl. "You'll get her. She can't run *and* she can't hide—not from me."

Vangie leaned back by the light of the hissing pressure lantern, and patted her tummy. If she'd been alone she would have belched. There was just a heap of discarded shells and claws on each of their plates. At their elbows were thick white ceramic mugs of steaming coffee.

"Dain, we can't stand and fight. We *have* to run!"

Dain's face became stubborn, almost mulish.

"We run, we die. We stay and fight, maybe we live."

"Without weapons against four armed men?"

He jammed a finger against his temple, suddenly angry. "We've got *these.*" He swung an arm around the room. "We've got everything here." He pointed at the door. "We've got everything out there. I want to—"

"That's what this is all about, isn't it? What you want."

"It's what you want and need, too, Vangie," he said.

"Don't be so goddam sure of that, either."

As she sloshed off the plates, Dain sighed and started to clumsily take off his pants one-handed, almost immobilized by his own thoughts. Vangie was now at the door, shoving it open a crack as if to assure herself the storm was real. Rain poured through the narrow opening, Dain could hear the howl and rush of the wind. She let it slam again, turned to him abruptly.

"All right, goddam you, I'm in."

Jesus! He was doing it again! Doing to her what he had

done to Marie with his bland, big assurances all would be well . . .

Don't be so goddam sure of that, either.

That was the trouble, he was always so goddam sure about what the women he was involved with wanted. They were never real to him *as human beings* until it was too late, until he had fucked them up. Only then, when dire results from his actions had destroyed them, did they become real. Only when they were icons that he could worship.

Did he have that much hostility toward, fear of, some constant "they" out in the real world? Five years ago, playing games—chess, detecting games on the computer and out in the field—while nurturing his fears and grudges behind a mask of geniality. But it was the women who paid, because he led the "they" right to the place where the women were either trusting . . . or hiding . . .

His game had always been practicing his form of worship of those unreal icons. But outside this profane religion of his they had been real enough, his ladies—real enough to die, to be threatened now again with death.

He had done it to Marie, now he held her dead body up like a crucifix between him and Vangie so he could keep Vangie unreal, too, until it was too late.

But she *was* real. Right here, right now . . . Getting undressed with the lack of self-awareness about her body that most dancers and athletes end up having. Dain, until that moment as unconcerned as she about stripping off his shorts, stopped dead, caught by her beauty.

She stopped also, feeling the full weight of his intensity. There was a sudden unexpected tension between them. All of a sudden, Dain couldn't take his eyes off her.

She turned to look at him, then released the pressure in the lantern. As it hissed out, the light began to fade. She crossed to him instead of to the other bunk, cupped his face with her two hands, looking down at him in the dimness.

And he was real to her, too. Whatever, whoever he was.

"Jesus, Dain," she said softly, "I don't even like you! But tomorrow we might both be dead."

In a hoarse voice, he said, "Or they might."

Because he felt sudden, blinding, total lust, as he had so

often and just as suddenly for Marie—and had not felt even once in the five years since her slaughter. He could not make of Vangie an icon as he had of Marie. To do so would be to destroy her also. No! She was real, here and now. Real . . .

He pulled her hot, naked body against him almost roughly. She gasped as he began licking one already erect nipple. His body jerked as if from a jolt of electricity when her hands cupped his scrotum and closed around his distended member.

As the lantern died, they became lovers in the night.

28

Dawn filtered through the thin mist drifting up off the water. By its light a young marsh rabbit hopped out of its burrow between the roots of a big fallen oak tree near the water's edge. The woods were wet, but the rain had stopped. As soon as the sun was up, the swamp would be steaming.

The rabbit began scratching its ear with a hind foot, the leg audibly thumping the ground with each movement. The vibrations raised the spade-shaped head of a five-foot cottonmouth that was just sluggishly stirring on the far side of the fallen oak. It was nearly a foot in circumference and was a slate-gray color that blended perfectly with the bark of the tree. It bunched into a tight coil almost experimentally, then slithered slowly forward, tongue darting to get the news.

Dain and Vangie walked down the meandering track her father had cut through the undergrowth and saplings during dry weather so he could put out setlines and crawfish traps from his boat during the spring floods. Dain's arm was in a sling Vangie had made from an old pillowcase, but his color was good and he moved well. They were walking side by side but not close enough to touch one another.

"I figure twelve hours before they get here," she said.

"Good. Gives us twelve hours to take inventory, plan, pick the killing ground . . ."

"You're so damned . . . *casual* about it . . ."

"Live with death long enough, you get casual about it."

"Especially someone else's," she said in a neutral voice.

As she spoke, the cottonmouth's arrow-shaped head shot forward between the roots to bury its fangs deep in the rabbit's shoulder, just for an instant. It drew back, re-coiling, waiting. The rabbit writhed, stiffened, jerked, died.

Why did he kill it, Mommy?

I'm afraid that's what he does for a living, Albie.

Could he kill me?

There's nobody around big enough to kill you, Tiger.

If the rattler in the desert three years ago had struck Dain when he danced with it, Vangie's parents wouldn't be dead. Jimmy Zimmer wouldn't be dead. Minus wouldn't be dead. But Albie and Marie still would be. To avenge their deaths he had trained, planned, shut down every other aspect of his life. Until last night with Vangie.

Vangie was watching, mesmerized, as the snake glided forward, unhinging its jaws to open them amazingly wide. The inside of the snake's mouth was an absolute, dead white, which had given it the name cottonmouth. It was swallowing the dead rabbit whole, walking its distended jaws up around the body as if the rabbit were entering a tunnel.

For those moments there was nothing else in the world for her. No love last night with him; no dead lover, no dead parents, no men bent on their destruction a few scant hours away across the marsh.

Suddenly it seemed to Dain that for five years he had been willfully evoking certain emotions—pain, the feeling of loss, the need for revenge—mainly for the pleasure of satisfying them. And telling himself he was being true, being steadfast to holy memories. To the icon he had made of Marie.

Would she have wanted that? Did he want that? Last night

he had more or less returned to life, in Vangie's bed and in her body; against that reality, deliberately continuing the motif of the past was something like viewing a snuff film again and again. The pornography of violence.

He realized almost with wonder that if he could walk away from this right now, and never look back, he would. But he couldn't. Vangie couldn't. The past was vengeance. The present was survival. The future was . . .

Vangie said in an almost dreamy voice, "He'll probably lie up there for three or four days, digesting. Sluggish as an old hog in a wallow."

Dain returned to the snake, that now looked like just another tree root. The rabbit was gone, a slight bulge in the long curved sinuous body.

"How long would a man live if he was struck by that thing?"

"Depends on the size of the snake and where he gets you. Bigger they are, the more venom they pump. Get hit in a hand or a foot, you'd probably survive—'specially if there was a doctor only a couple of hours away. But one like this hit you close to the heart, you'd only have a few minutes."

He nodded thoughtfully, started away up the path. The future was their present now.

"No guns," said Dain. "One knife that's worth a damn, that Bowie knife of yours. So we have to—"

"You never quit, do you?" asked Vangie.

"You know how to survive in the bayou, I don't. When you start picking up signs they're coming, maybe even when you just *feel* they're coming—tell me. I'll need to know how much time we'll have. We have to pick the killing grounds, attack them when they think they're attacking us."

Vangie said, hesitantly, "How . . . do you know if you can kill someone or not?"

"I don't know," said Dain. "I've never done it."

"But I thought you were . . ." She stopped. Her face hardened. "They murdered my parents."

And my wife and son, thought Dain. But suddenly it wasn't enough. Carry it far enough, you just became them. Better to stick with simple survival, them or you—

"*Look out!*"

Vangie grabbed his arm and jerked him to one side. Head down, watching the trail, he had been just about to walk into a line strung across the road between two trees, eight feet above the ground. At three-foot intervals were loops eighteen inches long, made by gathering and tying off the primary line. Heavy fishhooks had been threaded through the bottom of each loop. Hanging from one of these hooks was a decomposing sparrow hawk.

"Tight line," explained Vangie. "Left over from fishing."

"Eight feet up in the air?" demanded Dain.

"You have to remember that during flood stage, the tight line was just about six inches off the water, so the hooks, with bait on them, were about a foot below the surface. Now, of course, with the water back down almost to normal—"

"And the hawk?"

"He didn't have anyone to grab his arm."

Dain nodded, a thoughtful look on his face. His body was still full of unexpected jolts and betrayals, sudden weaknesses, but since the fever had broken his mind was clear.

"Let's get back and start planning our assault," he said briskly. "We're going to need those old muskrat traps from the storeroom . . . and I'm glad you didn't jettison that gasoline can along with the outboard motor . . ."

They moved off through now sun-shot woods starting to steam in the muggy heat of morning.

All four of them were sweating with the humidity by the time they had broken camp, striking the tents and packing up all of their gear. Nicky and Trask were starting to lug it all down to the boats, but Inverness stopped them with a wave of his hand.

"Leave all the gear and equipment here, we'll all go in one boat. It'll make us less of a target and we'll move faster."

Maxton said, with a show of bravado, "Frontal assault, right? Before they can run?"

"And get picked off in the boat, Maxton? Not likely. No

frontal assaults, get that through your heads, all of you. We sneak up on 'em after dark, and if we're damned lucky—''

''What the fuck, Inverness, first waiting for the god-damned storm to end, and now this! They could be long gone by the time we get there.'' Maxton was building up a nice anger at the more cautious hunter. ''The girl ran with nothing but the bonds—and you told me yourself that Dain wasn't armed.''

''You want to take the chance there were no firearms at the shack?'' He shook his head. ''They're not going to run from us.''

''What the hell is it with you and Dain, anyway?''

''He wants me dead,'' said Inverness. He was suddenly hard as strap steel. He moved in on Maxton, hulked over him. ''When I got word he was in New Orleans, I thought he was after me and let you know he was there. Now I'm lead-ing you to the girl so you can get your fucking bonds and your fucking nasty little revenge. In return you're going to help me get Dain for good. I've already killed him twice but he didn't stay dead, so—''

''You're *scared* of him!''

''You're goddam right I'm scared of him, the same way I'm scared of a cottonmouth coiled under a rock. Five years ago I killed his wife and kid, and he knows it.''

''Why didn't you just kill him in New Orleans?'' asked Maxton. ''A mugging. A hit-and-run . . .''

''Better out here in the swamp where nobody'll wonder where he's gone. What are you bitching about? Because of me you'll get your fucking bonds *and* the girl.''

''We keep fucking around, she'll be gone by the time we get there.'' He shook his head in disgust. ''From what you tell me, you killed Dain again the other night. So I say we—''

''He's alive and that fishing camp is his goddam rock. He's going to be coiled and waiting for us. That's why we go in after dark when he's cold and sluggish.''

''You're as fucking crazy as he is,'' said Maxton; but he stamped off down to the boat without further argument.

The mist had burned off, the steaming had stopped when the leaves and foliage had dried. On the open cleared knoll, a dozen muskrat and nutria traps were laid out in the bright sunlight. Vangie was on her knees greasing them, making sure the traps didn't slam shut on her hand as she tested them one by one.

Dain came down off the little verandah of the cabin. Awkwardly, because he had trouble keeping the gunnysacks open, he began stuffing them with the traps she had greased.

"I've cut the two-by-fours for the cleats to go up on either side of the door, but you'll have to nail them up. I can't do it with only one arm."

Vangie suddenly stopped working to look up at him, shading her eyes with one hand. "I can't believe this! We're actually trying to plan ways to kill four men!"

"No, four men are planning to kill us. We're trying to survive. There's a difference."

"Easy enough for you, with nothing in this world that you care about."

Dain started to speak, to tell her about his insight that morning: that only simple survival, not revenge, would have a chance of getting them through this. But instead he surprised himself by saying, "I care about you, Vangie. A lot."

She tried to reply, stopped; she couldn't handle that one. She didn't know what it meant, didn't know what she wanted it to mean, didn't know if she felt a similar sentiment in return, whatever the hell sentiment it was in the first place. She settled for ignoring it completely.

"You found Inverness easily enough after five years—"

"He found me."

Surprised, Vangie said, "How?"

"That's one of the many things I want to ask him when we get together again."

"Think he'll answer?"

"If he doesn't kill me first. I didn't even recognize him as one of the hitmen. No premonitions, no sudden flashes of evil—I *liked* the guy. Thought he was just a cop doing his job. If he hadn't kept pushing himself at me, I never would have known who he was."

"He *wanted* you to recognize him? That doesn't make sense."

"Not wanted—*needed*. If I recognized him, then he would be justified in killing me. I think that does make sense."

"For a hitman?"

"He's a complicated guy," said Dain, "and he's missed me twice. It's spooking him." He shoved the last trap into the gunnysack, said roughly, "But even so he's not going to make any easy mistakes this time. C'mon, let's get these into the woods and get them set."

Vangie nodded, grabbing the second sack, then said abruptly, "Listen, Dain, last night was just . . ."

"Just last night," said Dain quickly, "I know. But . . ."

"Yeah," she said. "But."

They both looked around, as if fixing this place and this moment in their minds. Then they started down the road dragging the gunnysacks behind them.

It was still daylight when they shoved off into the channel toward the lake, all four men in the one boat, all of their gear except their weapons far behind them in the camp. They had motored this far, then had lain up here until late afternoon. Inverness did not start the outboard right away.

"We can use the motor getting across the main body of open water, but we'll have to row the last three miles. Surprise and darkness are our best weapons."

"Jesus, Inverness, you keep acting like this is going to be some sort of war," said Maxton. "The boys and I think Dain is dead and the girl is unarmed—"

He had to break off because Inverness had started the motor to head for open water, and couldn't hear him anyway. Maxton settled for cursing Inverness under his breath.

Vangie had just finished nailing up cleats of staggered lengths of two-by-four to the wall on either side of the door. She had used spikes so they couldn't be torn out of the wall by anything smaller than, say, a fire-crazed stallion. Dain dropped a five-foot length of two-by-six horizontally into the cleats. This made it a bar across the door which would prevent it from being swung open from the inside.

"Perfect!" he exclaimed.

He hugged Vangie momentarily with his good arm, removed the two-by-six and carried it off the porch to stash it under a bush where it couldn't be seen but would be readily accessible.

"Okay. Now, where's that vat of tar your dad used for treating the fishing nets?"

Vangie pointed. "Around that way—at the edge of the woods. But what good will a vat of tar do us?"

They started walking off across the open area toward the woods on the far side of the knoll.

"I don't know—yet," said Dain. "Maybe none. But . . ."

The venerable cast-iron vat, over six feet in diameter and three feet deep, was set under a sycamore tree below a lip of the knoll. It looked full of water.

"There's a couple of feet of tar under all that water from yesterday's storm."

The huge old relic had a hollowed-out place beneath it where a fire could be laid to bring the tar to a boil. Dain was delighted by it.

"We'll bail it out and fire it up. If we could—"

"*Listen!*"

Both were instantly still. Only then to Dain's ears came the very faintest of mosquito whines from out in the marsh. It stopped even as he heard it.

"Outboard?"

"Yes. Your friend Inverness misjudged how far the sound of a motor carries over water."

"How far away are they?"

"Three miles, probably. They'll plan to row the rest of the way in well after dark."

"So we'll have enough time to get everything ready—if we're lucky."

"And if we're not," said Vangie unexpectedly, deepening her voice to quote, "'By my troth, I care not; a man can die but once; we owe God a death.' Shakespeare," she added, then burst out laughing.

He laughed himself. "Did I . . . when I was delirious . . ."

"Yes."

"And you remembered it."

"I liked it. That part about owing a death—"

"Yeah, well, Maxton and company owe some deaths, too," said Dain, suddenly darkening and hardening.

Vangie started bailing water with an old coffee can, Dain started gathering kindling for the fire beneath the vat. She suddenly stopped, watching him drag up a large oak branch.

"Dain. I don't want to die."

"Neither do I." He gestured out at the swamp. "Neither do they."

"Then—"

"Then we have to want to not die harder than they do."

29

Dusk had come again, and the sky was ruddy with sun-set-washed cumulus. The boat grounded behind a very low ridge rising from the marsh, its blunt prow sliding up over the mud without sound. The four men got out, bent over so they could not be seen above the reeds and rushes. Trask had been stuck with the rowing for the last mile. He flexed his hands gingerly.

"Jesus, what blisters!"

"Man jerks off as much as you oughta have calluses half an inch thick," guffawed Nicky, who'd had gloves.

Maxton followed Inverness as he crawled to the top of the rise. They parted the rushes and peered through. On a spit of land a hundred yards away was the rough-built cabin. Vangie was just walking toward it, alone, careless, unhurried.

"We could wing her from here if we had a rifle," muttered Maxton regretfully.

"You're forgetting about Dain."

"Fuck Dain. He's lying dead in the swamp somewhere."

Inverness looked over at him, shook his head. "You're a fool, Maxton. He's over there. Waiting."

"And you're a fucking paranoid." Maxton swung around so his back rested on the sloping earth as if were the back of a chair. He took out a cigarette, but Inverness shook his head.

"They might smell the smoke."

Maxton shrugged, put it away again, his face mean.

"*They?* You sure are scared of a dead man, Inverness. Why'd you blow away his family in the first place?"

"I was hired. Even now a certain number of big-city cops hire out as hitmen on the weekends. You do one, two a year—good money, easy work . . ." He gave an easy chuckle. "Usually."

"You're a cold-blooded fucker, aren't you?"

Inverness just stared at him. Maxton looked away first.

Dain was crouched on the floor about three feet from the back wall, working on the end of a floorboard with a small pry bar, when Vangie finally entered the cabin. She left the door open; the windows were both already open. The big red gasoline tank from the flatboat was on the table.

"I can feel them," said Vangie, "the way I could feel you before you even got to New Orleans. Stay away from the windows in case they have binoculars."

Dain straightened up, still on his knees. "How long?"

"There'll be a moon tonight, so the first cloud that covers it after full dark will bring them in."

"Then let's finish up here."

He returned to his floorboard, Vangie began pulling the bedding off the bunks, laying it out like gunpowder trails. With the harsh squawking protest of nails being drawn from wood, Dain raised one end of the plank. Vangie began gutting the mattresses, strewing the dried moss around. He fed the end of one of the blankets down through the slot he had opened.

Vangie suddenly gasped.

"My God, the pirogue! If they see that they'll know—"

"I moved it up beyond that big cypress and covered it with branches." He chuckled. "I put the attaché case in it, too."

Vangie started to whirl toward the place she had hidden it, behind some sacks in the storeroom, then froze, her head coming up, her nostrils flaring like those of a spooked mare.

She said, "It's time."

"Okay. You shut the windows and then get into position. Let me know when you're ready."

After Vangie had gone around shutting the windows, he stood up and, on an unspoken common urge, they embraced.

Vangie said in a small voice, "Good luck, Dain."

"Good hunting, Vangie."

Somehow the phrases seemed inadequate, especially if they turned out to be the only epitaphs either would get; but what else was there to say? He watched her go out the door and around to the back of the cabin in the darkness, and ached to call her back. But it was too late for that.

There was the slightest lingering sunset over on the western horizon, but moonlight was already laying down cold fingers of light as the four manhunters wrapped rags around the tholes of the oars. Nicky and Trask were very clumsy at it, Inverness swift and adept. Nicky stood up in frustration.

"Can't we use the fucking flashlight? Can't see a—"

"*Quiet!*" hissed Inverness. "Voices carry at night."

He stuck an oar pin in the oarlock, tried it by moving the oar back and forth. It made no sound. He nodded and looked up at the sky. Clouds thickly edged with silver were massing across the face of the moon, fading its light.

"That cloud will give us twenty minutes," he said in a very low voice. "Let's move out."

Now that he could not be seen from outside, Dain had the kerosene pressure lantern on the table, by its light was pouring gasoline over the blankets and ripped mattresses Vangie had strewn about. He especially drenched the blanket trailing down under the floor. At her three measured knocks, he released the pressure of the lantern, by the dying light poured out the rest of the gasoline, dropped the can, and went to the door.

His dark silhouette darted out through the door, closed it as the lantern died. He dropped nimbly to the ground, flitted across the open knoll and without pausing hopped down over the lip of earth where he had hidden the two-by-six.

As he waited, peering through his screen of branches, he gradually became aware of the night life around him. A week ago he would not have been. That was it! Marie had always been so much more intensely alive than he; now, if he died this night, it would be knowing he had returned to life before it happened.

Was it the knowledge of death out there that made life so precious? Blind, urgent, unquenchable life? The night was alive with animal cries, whistles, songs, chitterings. First, flying squirrels emerged from abandoned woodpecker holes to soar through the dimness, chattering shrilly. Then a fox trotted by a yard from the immobile Dain without being aware of him ambushed there. An armadillo waddled across the open ground. A carefully stepping deer made little splashes at the edge of the channel.

Through the forest drifted a great horned owl. It floated across the tops of the trees, swooped down over the bayou, landed in a tree near the point of the island. Dain's eyes, accustomed to the dark, followed its flight, could pick out its dark bunched shape in the top of the tree. It looked about fiercely and gave its distinctive *hoo, hoo-oo, hoo, hoo* hunting cry.

It was glaring down at the water, its light-gathering eyes picking up the dark moving shape with its four hunched hunters. A fish broke water right beside the flatboat's gliding hull. There was a vague squeak of oar, a slight gurgle of water along the strake. The slog of the prow into mud.

Four silent shapes left the boat, melted into tree shadow. Silent was a relative term; their clumsy presence muted the life around them. The owl flew off unnoticed by these other hunters, noted only by Dain as the light began to pick up with the moon's emergence from the clouds.

* * *

Crouching in their cover together, the raiders looked across the now once again moon-drenched open ground to the cabin, dark and peaceful. They spoke in low tones, although Maxton couldn't keep the elation out of his voice.

"She doesn't have a fucking clue we're here!"

"Even so, we wait fifteen minutes," breathed Inverness. "Watch the animals. They'll always tell you if somebody's around. Did you see the owl telegraphing our presence below his tree? If Dain is watching—"

Maxton came out of his crouch and massaged his knees.

"If that bitch was wise to us, she'd be ten miles down the bayou with my bonds. Instead she's alone in there, asleep. I want to hit her now. You got us here, great, that's what you'll get your percentage for. But now I'm taking over the assault."

"I'll cover you from here," said Inverness drily.

"Like hell you will." He turned to the other two silent killers. "Trask and I will each take a window. Nicky, you bust in through the door. And remember we need her alive long enough to tell us where the bonds are."

"What if Dain's in there? What do I do then?"

"Kill him," said Maxton. "Inverness, you'll take the back of the—"

"Pass."

"You're passing up your cut of the bonds, too, you know."

"You don't get it, do you? All I want is Dain—dead. I'd be a fool to risk myself over the bonds if he already is."

"And if he isn't?"

"Then maybe you'll get lucky and kill him for me—or at least maybe cripple him up some more, I know I winged him the other night. If he kills you, I'm no worse off."

Maxton just chuckled and turned away.

"The yellow streak shows at last," he sneered, then said to Nicky, "Remember—we need her alive to get the bonds from her."

"And to have a little fun with after," added Trask.

*　　*　　*

The pilings gave just enough headroom for Vangie to lie on her back under the cabin with her head turned so she could see out from beneath it. She stiffened momentarily when, out on the moonlit ground, the moving feet of the three attackers appeared. They took up their positions around the cabin.

Gun in hand, Nicky approached the front steps, tense and crouched and ready. He silently mounted them, crossed the porch. A second small cloud started across the face of the moon, dimming its light again, so the flash in his left hand flickered for one instant to show him the simple iron latch.

Nicky jerked open the door and leaped through the opening, yelling, gun quartering the room.

Everything happened at once, in the five seconds it took for his light to show the room was empty.

Dain was already charging silently at a dead run from his place of ambush under the bushes. His two-by-six slammed the door shut as he smashed it down into the cleats Vangie had made for it. He was already spinning away at a dead run for cover.

"Now!" he yelled.

Vangie touched her already struck match to the blanket-fuse coming down through the cabin floor, rolled away from the searing heat as it went up in a whoosh of igniting gasoline.

Inverness already was drifting back from his tree-shadow cover toward their flatboat pulled up on the mud behind him, even as his quick eyes picked out Dain's dark moving shape hitting the safety of the bushes on his return.

"That goddam Dain," he muttered aloud. "Waiting."

The whole inside of the cabin was already blazing. Nicky was slamming his forearm against the barred door, but it didn't give. He dropped his gun, ran back a few paces—and the fire running up the gasoline-soaked fuse Vangie had ignited whooshed up around him.

Blazing now, screaming, he hurled himself again and again against the door.

30

The door of the cabin burst outward, the cleats ripping from the wall, and out came a screaming fireball. Air sucked inside made the cabin a sudden massive torch. The fireball rolled in the grass and then quit screaming and quit moving as inside, the shells in its dropped gun began to explode.

Maxton came running around the corner of the cabin from the far side toward their drawn-up boat, gun in hand, yelping in fear, ignoring the burning Nicky. At the water's edge, in full moonlight, panting, he ran back and forth like a dog left behind by the family car. Their boat was gone. He could just see Inverness on the water, rowing it toward the open marsh.

"Inverness!" he shrieked. *"For God's sake . . ."*

Inverness kept on rowing with long, full, unhurried strokes. Maxton ran up and down the bank in a frenzy.

Vangie rolled out from under the huge torch the cabin had become, jumped to her feet, ran for the safety of Papa's fish-

ing road through the woods. The burning cabin made everything as bright as day, and at the edge of the undergrowth
she ran right into Trask's arms.

"Got you, bitch!" he panted.

She ripped his face just as her mother had done, he staggered back, letting go of her, so she had room for a high
dancer's kick, the sort where they try to touch their nose
with their knee. Only his scrotum was in the way. He emit-
ted a pneumatic *"Whoosh!"* and Vangie ran into the woods.
He got one shot off, aiming low despite his pain, but missed.
Bent over, cursing foully, he staggered after her.

Even through his panic, Maxton heard the shot. It helped
ease his fear, he began looking around. And shit, ten yards
away up the bayou, there was Vangie's flatboat drawn up
nose-to on the bank. He trotted toward it, still wobble-kneed
from the shock of that screaming fireball rolling out of the
cabin at him.

Dain, grunting, hit him like a blocking lineman. He went
sprawling, the gun went flying.

Maxton scrabbled for it in the mud as Dain put a foot
against the prow of the flatboat and, with a great heave, sent
it shooting backward out into the channel. Maxton came up
with his gun, but Dain was already zigzagging away as he
fired. Lucky for him, no barrel-clog of mud. Two more
shots, but Dain was gone, back into the undergrowth.

Maxton whirled back toward the flatboat. It was being
carried away by the current in the same direction Inverness
had disappeared—around the front of the island. He looked
back to where Dain had disappeared, then back to the boat.

He could dive in, swim after it—he did his dutiful laps at
his health club in Chicago three days a week. But what if
Dain had the pirogue hidden somewhere, came out after
him, smashed in his head with a paddle? He would be too
vulnerable in the water, even with the gun . . .

The underbrush rattled behind him. He spun and fired
again. There was instant crashing and thrashing, then sudden
silence. Almost reluctantly, Maxton edged across the clear-

ing past the settled angry red remains of the cabin and the black ugly charred remains of Nicky.

His cocked and ready Colt airweight .38 six-shot revolver was outthrust toward a patch of shadow where he feared Dain might be lurking. He was feeling better again. He had a gun, Dain didn't. Trask obviously had winged the little bitch, would have her waiting for him. He couldn't remember how many shots he had fired, but he had a fistful of extra bullets in his pocket.

A couple of yards to the right of where he thought Dain was, the top of a bush moved slightly. He shifted his aim without making any noise.

"Dain?" he called.

The next bush moved, surreptitiously, slightly. Maxton edged closer. Hell, he'd hit him with one of those shots, Dain was trying to crawl away. But he had to make sure.

"Maybe we can deal."

Silence from Dain. A charred timber in the cabin collapsed in a shower of sparks, jerking Maxton's head around. He turned back quickly. A third bush was moving. Feebly. Yes! He went into his firing crouch.

He called softly, "All I've ever wanted is the bonds!"

No answer.

"I don't want the girl. Not any more."

Hell no, he didn't want her. Trask already had her. The top of the next bush moved slightly. He brought up his gun. Sidled closer.

Dain was lying on his back under the bushes, dappled with moonlight. He held a long willow stick in his good hand, angled up against a branch of an overhead bush three yards away. Unlike Maxton, he had kept count of the shots fired.

"Just two more, damn you," he muttered to himself.

At almost the same time, Maxton's voice came again.

"What do you say? Not you, not the girl. Just the bonds."

For answer, Dain jammed the stick hard against the bush, and so close together they were almost one, two slugs ripped through the undergrowth where he should have been. He was already on his feet and bursting out of the thicket.

Maxton was five yards away, digging a handful of shells from his pocket to feed into the gun's open cylinder. Dain's charge rocked him back on his heels, sent the bullets flying. But Maxton swung the .38 in a vicious arc—the barrel slammed down on Dain's injured shoulder.

Dain cried out with the pain, spun away, fell, rolled away from Maxton's surprisingly quick and viciously kicking feet, was as quickly on his own feet, ready. They circled like fighting dogs seeking advantage. But Dain was backing up as he circled, away from the last embers of the burned-out cabin.

Maxton sprang.

He was a powerful adversary and he had the use of both arms and a pistol as a club. They grappled, fell, rolled over and over, striking, kicking, grabbing. Dain, hampered by his useless arm and the need to protect his wound from Maxton's blows, was fading fast. His bandages were soaked in new blood.

He managed to break free, get to his feet, back up a low rise with a big sycamore tree in the dip beyond it. He was staggering. Maxton swung the heavy revolver again, Dain ducked, but the gun sight raked across his forehead. Blood ran down into his eyes. Maxton laughed.

"I'll chop you to pieces, Dain."

He feinted twice, then leaped in with another terrible swing of the gun. But Dain sprang forward inside the blow, with his last despairing strength got his good hand on Maxton's windpipe. Squeezing. Maxton's eyes began to bug out. The gun slammed into Dain's back, but because they were chest-to-chest there was little force in the blows.

Then Dain fell backward to land at the very lip of the knoll, dragging Maxton down on top of him, with a leg already drawn up to his chest so the raised foot would plant itself firmly in Maxton's belly. As the big man came down on top of him, the leg pistoned straight up. Maxton's momentum, guided by the throat grip and given terrific force by the thrust of that catapult leg, sent him right over Dain's body in a flip.

Under the wide-spreading sycamore the flat black slowly seething depths of the tar vat sent up sluggish bubbles. Dain released his grip on the throat and Maxton went out beyond him and down, screaming horribly when he landed spread-eagle on his back in the bubbling tar, still clutching his useless gun. He tried to rise, pull free, but he was already burning. Several jerky motions, still screaming, but all they did was send waves of tar from the sides of the vat rolling back over him. In a few moments, he subsided to a shapeless smoking mass.

Dain missed that part. He had passed out.

Vangie was leaning against a tree, panting, half a dozen yards off the road through the woods. She could hear the sounds of Trask's supposedly stealthy pursuit behind her, but she didn't move. Not too far behind, Trask also stopped, panting, to listen for sounds of his fleeing prey. His face was cut by slashing branches, blackberry thorns.

As he dashed sweat from his forehead with the back of his gun hand, Vangie burst in apparent wild terror from cover a dozen yards away. She was gone even as he fired—still low, still trying to bring her back alive. He was a good soldier, a good button man. He had his quirks, but he knew how to obey orders.

He plunged away after her.

But it was harder now, the moon was lower, its light dimmer. He stopped, listened. He didn't know that Vangie was sitting on the ground a few yards ahead of him around a bend in the track, also listening. She had been hard-pressed to keep from losing him. She was poised for flight, but there was nothing to flee from. She couldn't hear him moving around. She took her big Bowie knife from the sheath, nervously, put it back.

It was time. Life or death. She wondered how Dain was. Out of sight of each other, they still were fighting in tandem.

She picked up a rock from the trail, hesitated, then heaved it back the way she had come.

Trask's head jerked around toward the crashing from the undergrowth. He had been concentrating all of his attention in the wrong direction, but now he had that little bitch!

Gun in hand, he charged around the bend in the track.

Vangie was half-sitting a few yards beyond, one leg drawn up, massaging her ankle with an agonized look on her face. She screamed in apparent surprise and fear.

"I did your folks, now I'm gonna do you!"

And he charged her. There was no way she could escape him. Oh, she tried. She leaped up but cried out, fell, rolled, holding her ankle, trying unsuccessfully to scrabble away from him. Not this time. He was upon her . . .

But just a yard short of Vangie, in shadow that made it even more invisible, was one of Papa's tight lines—eight feet above the ground where Trask would never see it unless he was looking up. Instead of the original hooks on the stagings, now at their three-foot intervals were strung the muskrat traps Vangie had been greasing, each one open and set.

Trask, charging, yelling, gloating down at his prey helpless at his feet, ran face-first right into one of the gaping traps. She had led him to it as carefully as a mother bird feigning a broken wing will lead a fox away from her nest.

The trap's powerful spring snapped jagged steel teeth shut on his face with a vicious metallic snap. He screamed and danced, jumped and jerked—and his wildly swung gun hand smashed into a second trap, which snapped shut around it, crushing the fingers, piercing the wrist. The gun fell.

Vangie came up off the ground in a lithe drive of piston legs, right at him with her huge gleaming Bowie knife in both hands, cutting edge down, held the way a Mayan priest might hold the knife to rip open the chest of a blood sacrifice. *He was the one! The one who had killed her folks!*

Her face distorted with the killing lust, she slammed the blade down into the center of the screaming man's belly in a long disemboweling slash like a hunter gutting a hung deer. She cried out formlessly as she did it; a splash of hot blood hit her across the face as her attack carried her right past the flopping, shrieking man.

Vangie dropped her knife and staggered a few steps away

into the woods exactly like a drunkard, then collapsed. She slumped there in a huddle, unmoving, sobbing.

For ten years her life had been without consequence, without meaning. Now she had killed two men. She had stolen $2 million. Her folks were dead because of her and she had mourned them with a knife. She could never again be whoever she had been for those ten years.

She cried for who she had been and for who she had become. She cried for Dain, for her folks, for Jimmy.

She didn't cry for Trask.

Finally cried out, she fell silent. After a time, animal, bird, and insect noises began again, tentatively at first, then soaring in a triumphant discordant chorus to greet the first predawn lightening of the forest.

31

There was the faintest of pale gold horizontal slashes drawn on the utmost horizon. Everything below was a cold gray blanket of ground mist, the big cypresses rising from it here and there like sentinels. In the woods, just the woolly polls of the overstory trees stood above it like tight-packed heads. On the bayou a flatboat drifted in the gray world where air and water were barely separate, as if floating in a dream.

Inverness came abruptly erect on the seat. Looked around in an almost dazed manner. Splashed water in his face. Even the splashes were muted, distant, dreamlike. He began to row.

Vangie appeared at the mouth of the road walking list-lessly, shoulders slumped, face innocent as a sleepwalker's. Trask's pistol dangled from one hand by the trigger guard. Overlaying the scents of the morning swamp was the sweetish smell of barbecued meat, not entirely pleasant. She shuddered when she realized what it was.

Dain was limping toward her across the open ground past the rectangle of ash and charcoal, still faintly warm, that marked her father's cabin. He looked pale, drawn, dragged off center by pain, bloodstained from his reopened wound. She knew she couldn't look much better.

They stopped three feet from each other, not touching. Vangie finally reached out to lay a hand on his good arm. Only then did they come together, clasp each other fiercely with nothing of lovers in it, only the intimacy of warriors who have survived the battle. They finally stepped back. An uncontrollable shudder ran through Vangie, somewhat like the sudden diminishing little gasping intakes of breath after a fit of hysterics.

She said tentatively, "You ought to see the other guys?"

"What other guys?" he said in the same tone.

Wonder was in her voice. "It's . . . over? Truly all over?"

"Yes. For you it's all over."

A final shudder ran through her. "Inverness?"

"Strategic withdrawal. He'll be back."

Vangie made an aborted gesture back toward what she had left hanging from the tight line in the woods. "I . . . I don't know if I can . . . again . . ."

"If I could get out of it, I wouldn't either," he said. "But you can get out. You must get out. I couldn't stand it if after all of this you . . ." His voice had harshened; now he said in softer tones, "Go bury your dead, Vangie."

They started walking slowly down toward the water, Dain limping, his good arm around her shoulders for support.

"Will you be all right?" he asked.

She didn't answer.

"Please. Take the bonds and run."

"I'll have to," she said finally. "If I'm still here when he comes back, he'll have to kill me, won't he?" Right along with you, she seemed to be implying, though she didn't say it. "But if I'm back in civilization, shocked, explaining that I was camping out in the bayous, I didn't know my folks had been murdered, I've never heard of any of you . . . Then I'll be safe."

"Take the gun."

"I have the gun." She gestured with it. "You hid the pirogue with the bonds in it. He can't follow me in a flat-boat, he has to go the long way around. So don't worry about me."

Couldn't you worry about me? he thought. Just a little? He'd wanted her to leave, but hadn't really expected that she'd do it.

It was dawn but the sun had not yet broken through the haze. At the rear of the island, where the bayou had cut its ancient channel, Inverness's flatboat drifted soundlessly out of the fog to ground with only a whisper of keel against mud. With an almost incredible swiftness, Inverness was up over the gunwale and into the bushes.

He kept going swiftly but carefully, slipping from cover to cover, stopping often to let the birds tell him what or who might lie ahead. Totally alert, he was the hunter in his element.

As they shambled down toward the water, Vangie was shocked at how much weaker Dain was. How was he going to stand up to Inverness? He might already be dying; he'd sustained a terrible amount of damage.

"What about you? You can't just stay here and wait for him."

"He has to end it. End me. To him I'm a nightmare that isn't over when you wake up."

"He killed your wife, Dain," she said cruelly. "He'll find Trask, I used the knife on him. That ought to slow him down . . ."

Dain nodded. "That's his only failure as a hitman. It's our only edge."

"What? I don't understand."

"His imagination. He's got a vivid imagination."

"If that's your edge, use it. What are you going to do? What's your plan?"

"Delay him, that's the plan." That wasn't what she had

meant. "I'll get you as much time as I can. I'm not strong enough to fight him, he's too wary to be tracked down, and I'm not good enough in the woods to ambush him. So—"

"So you have to make him come to you."

"When he does, how will he do it?"

"Under cover of this fog. He'll row around to the rear of the island, work up through the woods afoot, probably along Papa's fishing road . . ."

Dain gave a short mirthless laugh, started coughing at the end of it. "The man . . . who won't . . . die . . ."

He was coughing up blood. She didn't know if he was talking about Inverness or himself. She couldn't leave him here in this state, she couldn't stay with him, she couldn't take him with her.

Inverness stopped with one foot raised and a hand extended to push aside a branch. He had heard, reduced by distance, robbed of words and given mere tones, the raised voices of Vangie and Dain. He began to trot through the woods toward them, turning into the fishing road when he crossed it, because the going was easier and faster.

And stopped dead, a horrified look on his face. Trask's gutted body, still held by the deadly traps, had dragged the nylon tight line down so he was held up in a sort of grotesque half-curtsy. One arm was held out head-height by its trap, his legs were bent in an awful parody of a ballet dancer's *plié*. He had been neatly disemboweled. As for his face, in *its* trap . . .

Inverness edged around the body, unable to look away, then was free of it. They'd been thorough. One burned to death, one gutted. Not a squeamish pair. He wondered what they had done to Maxton. Not that he cared too much. There was nothing squeamish about the survivors of this world, and he was a survivor.

Now shunning the open meandering road, he picked his way as quickly as he could through the heavy undergrowth flanking it. He pulled up short a second time: there had been a distant shot.

What the hell? That didn't make sense unless . . .

Unless he remembered the butchery on Trask. Whoever did that didn't have many compunctions. Two million in bonds . . . Just Dain and she left . . . He had been just sort of assuming they would face him together, he would kill them both, take the bonds . . . But maybe only one would be left to take out . . .

Suddenly he was sprinting ahead, crashing through the forest, careless of noise. Two more shots had sounded far ahead of him.

32

Ten minutes later he was at the edge of the woods, scanning the clearing. Burned-out cabin, just a heap of charred wood now. Beyond that, the blackened thing that once had been Nicky . . .

He moved around the perimeter, saw the tar baby in the vat. The person inside would have been burned away leaving only a shape of cooled tar, like the ancient Pompeiians caught by flowing lava while fleeing Vesuvius. Had to be Maxton. And Dain had done it with the use of only one arm.

A couple of minutes later, Inverness parted the bushes near the water's edge to look out cautiously at the landing area and the thinning fogbank beyond. The mud was trampled, marked with footprints and keel marks. After a long reconnoiter, he stepped out. Looked up the bayou, stiffened.

Up about where Vangie had first seen Dain poling down toward the fishing camp in the pirogue, Vangie was now poling away from the camp in the pirogue. Alone. The craft was too shallow for Dain to be hiding in the bottom of it.

She reached the bend of the bayou and passed from his sight.

Alone. Which meant that Dain was either waiting for him somewhere in ambush—or the argument he had heard had been genuine, the shots real, and Dain was . . .

He turned back to the landing area, crouched, reading sign. He chuffed, an almost silent exhalation of air. Splattered across the churned muddy verge was blood. Fresh blood, his touching fingertip confirmed.

Then his eye picked up a glint at the water's edge, and he gave a small exclamation of surprise. He lifted Trask's gun from the mud. Sniffed the muzzle. Looked quickly around, like an animal about to take a drink, then broke the gun. Two unfired shells. He closed it very slowly, a puzzled look on his face.

Patiently, he started over the ground again with his eyes, minutely seeking everything he had missed the first time. Gave a little grunt of satisfaction, waded out to midcalf. Tromped down into the mud and water was *something,* paper, man-made. He reached down, brought it out.

A sheaf of soaked, trampled, mud-smeared bearer bonds. He thumbed them. Half a dozen, twenty-five thousand each: a hundred and fifty thousand bucks. Dropped in the struggle, probably when the shots had been fired.

He started back out with his head moving, scanning the bushes, the trees, the bayou, the open water of the marshland . . . With a muttered exclamation he threw the bonds aside and went into a firing crouch, his right hand whipping out the .357 Magnum from its holster on his right hip with practiced ease.

The fog had lifted enough so he could see Vangie's missing flatboat forty yards from shore and slowly being carried further. One of Dain's shoes rested on the gunwale as if he were lying faceup, partially across the seats. His good arm was hooked over the far side of the boat so his hand was obviously trailing in the water even though Inverness could not see it.

Inverness slowly put his Magnum away again, even more slowly settled into his woodman's tireless squat, his eyes fixed on the drifting boat.

His posture was patient but his head was spinning. Dain. Dead? Everything said he was—blood, bonds, gun, the departed Vangie. But . . . this was Dain. The man he couldn't kill. But Dain had trusted her and she'd shot him with Trask's gun and had dumped him in the boat and set it adrift so Inverness would see it and be delayed by it.

Or maybe she hadn't. Time would tell.

Three hours later the fog had burned away and bright sunlight flooded everything. Inverness still was hunkered in the scrub by the shore, staring out at the drifting boat. His arms were now wrapped around his knees. The boat was quite a bit further away, but was slowly turning around and around in a big leisurely eddy. Dain's good hand was indeed trailing in the water, submerged about halfway down the bared forearm.

He could only really make out Dain's boot, a little of the hair of his head, and that arm trailing in the water. The arm made it Dain, not a dummy made up with moss and Dain's clothes to fool him.

During those three hours the body hadn't moved an inch.

With abrupt decision, he stood, trotted off toward the fishing road through the woods. Half an hour later he arrived back at his flatboat, seized the prow, and shoved off into the bayou as he leaped aboard. Unshipped the oars, swung the prow, and began rowing away with long steady strokes. In action he was as quick, as sure as he'd ever been. Then why couldn't he . . .

Goddammit, now he was going to deal with Dain.

It was high noon, so there was no shade. Dain's flatboat drifted in its eddy of current. From around the tip of the island came Inverness's flatboat to the beat of his steady rowing. A dozen yards from the boat in which Dain sprawled, faceup to the sun, he rested on his oars so his boat coasted to a stop. He sat, staring. Waiting. Not quite ready to deal with Dain after all.

If Dain was not dead, only dying, the heat and sun would finish him off. Waiting could only benefit Inverness.

He waited.

Waited until the sun had started its climb down the western sky. Just sat there on the middle seat of his boat, legs drawn up and arms clasped around his knees. From this close he could see Dain sprawled, bloody and lax, across the seat.

Enough.

Inverness suddenly jerked out his .357 Magnum, then once again just sat there with it in his hand, resting the hand on his thigh, the gun pointed at nothing. He yelled.

"Dain!"

No reaction. Man—or body? He raised the gun, aimed with his elbow resting on an upraised knee. Hesitated. Dain was dead, he knew that now, and he was about to shoot the body. Blow its foot off. To see if perhaps the man was only faking it. And if he shot the corpse, wasn't that somehow an admission that Dain had won, even in death? That even his *corpse* could spook Keith Inverness so badly that . . .

With sudden resolve he re-aimed. And fired. A chunk of gunwale six inches from Dain's boot splintered as the heavy slug passed through it. Dain's boot did not move.

Inverness lowered the heavy gun with a satisfied look on his face. He'd made his test without having to shoot Dain's dead body. Dain hadn't won. Keith Inverness had won. Because nobody had the balls to remain motionless when a bullet missed his foot by six inches that way. Not when he would know the next one could blow his foot right off.

There was still a final act to perform. And even that . . . worried him. He had to dump Dain's body into the water so the gators would get it. Did some edge of doubt still linger?

"Goddam you, Dain," he said earnestly to the corpse, "even dead, you fucker, you . . . you *vex* me."

He laid the gun on the seat beside his thigh, grabbed the oars, gave a couple of strong pulls to send his boat bumping clumsily against Dain's. The impact knocked Dain's boot off the gunwale. A cloud of green-bellied flies swarmed angrily up off the bloody mess under Dain's filth-encrusted shirt.

He picked up his gun again, but it was only reflex. This was obviously a corpse. He used his gun hand to brace himself on Dain's gunwale so he could, kneeling on the seat, stretch across the sprawled body to feel the carotid artery for a pulse.

He was free at last of that five-year-old shadow across his life. Maybe even the bonds might not be lost to him. Vangie would have to bury her folks, go through a public period of mourning. Which meant she'd have to hang around Cajun country long enough so it would not look odd when she left . . .

Perhaps she would choose suicide . . . so easily arranged . . .

He was so deep in his thoughts as his fingers thrust deep into the side of Dain's throat after the nonexistent pulse, that he didn't even see Dain's good left arm, trailing over the side of the boat, begin to rise.

In the iron grip of his hand was the huge cottonmouth, grasped just behind the head. The snake's mouth, gaping in rage, showed its dazzling cotton-white lining. Its fangs were raised and ready. As the arm rose and crooked, the massive, foot-thick, five-foot body came writhing up out of the water, flowing, flowing, flowing almost endlessly upward.

Inverness, startled by the pulse he had not expected to find, off balance, was trying to get upright enough to get his weight off the gun hand and shoot. But he was out of time. By then Dain was ramming the huge diamond-shaped head up tight against his straining, corded neck.

The gleaming fangs sank into the flesh, the poison sacks pulsed. Inverness leaped back, shrieking, spraddle-legged in the flatboat, jerking away from the snake so wildly that its entire five-foot length flowed and writhed in air, supported only by its fangs sunk deep into the side of his neck.

His gun went flying so both his hands could find the snake, rip it away. The snake hit the water with a long splash, undulated away as Inverness sank down on the seat, blood running down his neck. Dain sat up in the other boat to watch him with cold interested eyes.

"My God," said Inverness. "Oh my God."

"It's a high-protein venom that literally rots out the blood vessels so internal hemorrhaging begins," said Dain. "You're bleeding to death inside even as we speak."

Inverness put his face in his hands and spoke through his spread fingers. "It hurts. Oh Jesus it hurts."

"It's meant to. Your lymph glands are swelling up trying to churn out enough antibodies to save you, but there aren't that many antibodies in the human body. You'll start getting excited, your pupils will dilate until the light hurts them . . ."

Inverness raised a haunted face. Sweat was pouring off him. He croaked, "My lips are numb."

Now that he was here, watching one of the hitmen actually dying, simple survival wasn't enough for Dain after all. He wanted at least to *know*. Who. Where. Maybe *if* . . .

"Who hired you to kill me and my family, Inverness?"

"Pu . . . Pucci . . . Mario . . . Pucci . . ."

"No. The middleman. The other shooter."

Inverness tried to swallow. Put a hand up to his neck, sweating like a man with motion sickness. His face was ghastly. His voice was querulous.

"The . . . middleman called me, I flew up from New Orleans. The other hitter had . . . directions . . . I had . . . orders . . . take out everybody in the place . . . Didn't know . . . woman and kid . . ."

His head slumped, but Dain reached from boat to boat, grabbed his shoulder, shook him.

"Who, Inverness? Where?"

"He called me again last week . . . after five . . . fucking years . . . told me you were coming after me . . ." His voice started to fade again. "Hoping . . . I'd . . . take you out . . ."

Inverness was twitching, losing motor control.

"*Who?* Goddam you, give him to me!"

Inverness coughed rackingly. A little blood came from his mouth. But defiance along with death had entered his eyes. His lips twisted into some semblance of a smile.

"Fuck you, Dain . . . I'm . . . giving *you* . . . to *them* . . . The other shooter is . . . still around . . . He'll blow you . . . all to shit . . ." He gave a choking laugh. "The laugh's . . . on you . . ."

He fell silent, folded down on himself, went away from

there. Dain looked down at him for a long moment, nothing showing in his face. He finally spoke.

"Is it, Inverness? Hell, *you're* dead!"

The sky was pale, sulfur-colored. The water was a mirror. Five minutes later Inverness, stripped of keys, wallet, and money to make identification harder should he ever be found, splashed into the marsh.

Most likely a gator would discover him before dark, thrust him deep into the mud, ripen him up . . .

But hell, old Inverness would like that, wouldn't he?

Hadn't he just loved this old swampland?

V

SHENZIE

Don't Call It 'Frisco

THE DAWNING OF THE WRATHFUL DEITIES

O nobly-born, not having been able to recognize when the Peaceful Deities shone upon thee, thou hast come wandering thus far. Now the blood-drinking Wrathful Deities will come to shine.

THE TIBETAN BOOK OF THE DEAD

33

Eight days later Dain emerged from his room at the Imperial Motel in Lafayette, his arm in a neat black sling. It was here he and Inverness had stayed the night before going into the swamp after Vangie, and their rooms had been held for them. He crossed to his rental car parked directly in front of the room, tossed his suitcase into the open trunk, went over to the adjoining room and emerged with Inverness's suitcase. He tossed that in also, slammed the trunk lid, and went off toward the office.

Inside, the clerk looked up from his accounting when Dain put the keys for both rooms on his desk.

"Mr. Inverness and I will be checking out."

"Certainly, sir." The clerk got out both bills, ran them through the computer to get the final totals, handed them over. "These include all phone and laundry charges."

Dain was here doing this only because he didn't want any loose ends. He wanted it finished. He didn't want anyone coming around a week or a month or a year from now to ask him questions he couldn't really answer. End it here and now, cleanly, so there would be no sticky strands tying it to him later.

It had been eight days since he'd dumped Inverness's body into the Atchafalaya. The identities of the other hitman and the man who had set up the hit had died with him. So be it. But could he just walk away from it? Could death still be looking for him though he no longer was looking for it?

Of course he could. The dead were dead, blood had paid for blood. He would not be working for the mob any longer, would no longer be moving in those circles. He could make a new start of sorts. Let Doug Sherman go back to book-selling full-time while he became the sort of P.I. who took any and all clients through the door. Randy would help him get referrals . . .

He went through the invoices item by item with the clerk fidgeting in the background, just so there would be no surprises. He hesitated for a long time over one item on Inverness's bill, then folded them up and put them in his wallet. He felt as if he had been kicked in the heart.

"These look in order. Put Mr. Inverness's room charge on the signed credit card charge he left with you—I'll pay for mine with cash."

From the motel, Dain drove to an auto supply store, bought a towbar, drove back to park half a block from the motel, went into the lot, got Inverness's car without being seen by the clerk, and drove back to his own car.

He arrived at New Orleans in midafternoon with the Inverness car on the towbar behind him, drove to the government housing developments near the Superdome, and dumped it at the curb. Driving to New Orleans International Airport to turn in his rental, he figured the abandoned car would be in a bump shop by nightfall, unrecognizable by dawn.

He fought hard against thinking about Vangie, speculating where she might be or what she might be doing. She had brought him alive again by accepting him into her body, he had set out to save her life, she had saved his. She was involved in life, she *was* life.

The urge to run to her, try to build his new life around that vitality, was almost overwhelming, but he had no right to do that. She had a new life to build, and the bonds with which to do it. A new life having nothing to do with hootch dancing in cheap strip joints.

The sign over the clock read NEW ORLEANS INTERNATIONAL AIRPORT. The clock read 7:32. Dain had just paid with cash, and the attractive blonde in the blue uniform with little silver wings over her left breast gave him his ticket to San Francisco. She had nice dimples and bold eyes.

"Your SFO flight boards in twenty-eight minutes, sir."

He went through the detectors, stopped at a bank of pay phones on his way to the gate. He was once again carrying his leather-bound *Tibetan Book of the Dead,* which he set on the metal shelf below the phone as he waited for his call to be picked up.

"Douglas Sherman here," said the phone.

"Dougie! It's Dain."

"Dain?" He paused. "My God, I was starting to wonder—"

"I'll be getting in tonight, going to the loft."

"Did . . . everything go smoothly?" Sherman asked cautiously.

"Not really," he said. "I found the fugitives and I found the bonds, but . . . I don't believe we'll be collecting our fee from Mr. Maxton."

There was a long pause. "Maxton is—"

"Not going to pay our fee," said Dain firmly. "I also ran into one of the gentlemen from Point Reyes. I'll tell you all about it at the bookstore in the morning."

He started away, then looped back to the phone. He had realized he didn't want to take the shuttle bus from SFO back to the city when he got home. And he wanted to tell Shenzie all about it. Cats understood things like revenge very well indeed.

The call was a short one.

"Randy? This is—"

"Hey, Hoss, where the hell are you?" demanded Solomon's big voice. "Why the hell haven't you—"

"Still in New Orleans, catching a flight home in . . ." Dain checked his watch. "Eleven minutes—"

"I'll be waiting at the airport."

Dain gave him flight number and arrival time, then added, "Can you bring Shenzie, too? I really—"

"Sho nuff," said Randy with his big booming laugh. "He's right here with me on the couch, watching TV."

Dain's window seat looked out at moon-silvered clouds far below the plane. His face was exhausted and drawn. He thought he was too keyed-up to sleep, but then he was dreaming.

He was in a strange apartment in a hot steaming tropical land, using his computer to identify those he sought. He was nude, sweat-drenched. In thirty seconds he would have them, their identities and locations would leap from the screen at him . . .

He heard voices, as if through steel wool.

They . . . they all . . . dead?

Yeah. We'll check if he has any notes here, a computer . . . then we'll burn the place down . . .

There was a loud *pop!* and a flash of light, and the computer blew up with an acrid puff of electrical smoke. One leg of the computer table collapsed, the whole setup slid to the floor. He had spent hours in the intricate tracery of their tracks, now it was gone, all gone in a puff of smoke.

Dain threw himself on the bed, arms and legs flung wide. On the opposite wall was a familiar Magritte. The door of the bathroom opened. Vangie emerged, like him nude in the blanketing heat. Suddenly he had a massive hard-on, the biggest erection of his life.

She stepped up on the bed astride him, looking down at him in anticipation as his exciting view of her dark sexual nest made his hard-on even more distended. She lowered herself onto him with exquisite slowness, impaling herself on that enormous organ. Her body accepted all of it, she immediately began fucking him frenziedly, immediately reared back in ecstasy, immediately collapsed shuddering against him, all within a few seconds and long before he could come himself.

Then she lifted herself off his still-erect member, planted a kiss on its engorged tip as if kissing a rose, winked bawdily at him, and was gone.

Randy was waiting by the loading gate at SFO, his face a huge grin as passengers streamed around them off the plane. He examined Dain keenly and gave his big laugh.

"You look like you got a tale to tell, Hoss."

He told it on the way into the city, Randy behind the wheel, Dain beside him, Shenzie in his carry case on the backseat, meowing in his pissed-off way at being cooped up so long.

"Hell, if Inverness was a cop, I oughta be able to find out who he saw when he came to town—"

"Five years ago? And he wouldn't have come as a cop."

Shenzie meowed yet again, insistent for attention. Dain started to reach over the back of the seat with his good arm to open the case and stick his hand in.

"Hey, man, don't let him out in the car!" Solomon said in alarm. "I did driving down, he like to took my ear off."

Dain nodded and took his hand from the case. To their left the lights of the tough little town of Brisbane were scattered like children's jacks down the eastern slope of San Bruno Mountain; ahead and to their right beyond an arm of the bay was the pale unlit mass of Candlestick Park.

"Only thing you ain't told me, what happened to the bonds?"

"Vangie kept 'em. She paid enough for them." He added, "I also didn't tell you, I think I might know who brokered the hit."

Randy shot a look over at him, eyes gleaming ferally. "Let's go get the fucker."

Dain shook his head. "I don't want to do anything about it, Randy. I'm just so goddamned tired of it all . . ."

"There you go again, goddammit! Didn't you learn nothin' five years ago? Right now you don't look in good enough shape to handle a can opener for the cat food, but that fucker, whoever he is, he'll just keep coming at you, Eddie. He'll figure he's got no choice. Why don't you tell me who he is and where he is, and go home and get some sleep. When you wake up—''

"I can't do it that way, Randy. Hell, I'm not even sure of my facts. It's just a maybe. I can't stomach any more killing on just maybes.''

Randy's face was taut, his skin and eyes were glistening.

"You lemme talk to the fucker, we'll get sure. Remember what happened last time you tried it alone.''

"It happened because I wouldn't let go of an investigation. This time I'm letting go before it gets started.''

Randy sighed in exasperation. "Where've I heard that one before? Look, Hoss, all I'm saying, you're pretty beat up right now. Things'll look different in a few days after you've had some rest. Then you and I'll get together—''

"I'm not going to move on it, Randy. That's final.''

And there it remained as Randy left the freeway for Bryant Street, ran down through the night-quiet South of Market streets to the Embarcadero. He pulled up in front of Dain's darkened, dilapidated pier.

"I'm probably wrong about him anyway,'' said Dain.

"Meanin' you think you're right about him.''

Randy shook his head, got out to pull the suitcase off the backseat as Dain got Shenzie in his carrying case. When Randy's taillights had winked out of sight, Dain used a key on the small door beside the loading door, went in, entered the open freight elevator, left Shenzie there to go back outside for his suitcase.

The creaking, swaying lift clanked to the top floor. Dain hit the hallway light switch, then opened the fuse box to unscrew one of them. All his actions were rendered more difficult, more deliberate, by the fact that he had only one arm to use. And by the fact he was reluctant to do them at all.

Two trips to get suitcase, cat, and *Tibetan Book of the Dead* to the big steel door of his loft. He balanced the book on top of the suitcase, got out his keys, paused.

"What are the odds, cat?'' he asked softly.

Shenzie meowed, also softly.

"That bad, huh?''

Dain silently unlocked the door, opened it a scant half-inch on the blackness within. Took a deep breath. Then jerked the door wide and went through in a knee-high dive, obliquely so he would pass instantly out of the light.

Three shots exploded almost together from the darkness.

Dain's voice said, "I was hoping you wouldn't be here, but . . . just in case . . ."

Two more shots at where his voice seemed to come from sang and ricocheted. The light switch was clicked in a frenzy.

"I took out the fuse, Dougie-baby," said Dain.

There was a long pause, then Sherman's voice said, "How . . . did you know that . . . I . . ."

"Your unlisted phone number was on Inverness's phone bill at the motel in Lafayette."

A flashlight stabbed the darkness where it seemed Dain's voice had come from. It picked up only weight-lifting apparatus. A five-pound weight spun right up its beam like a Frisbee. There was a crunch, a cry, the light hit the floor and went out.

Dain's voice, now cold and inexorable, said, "I looked because he had to call somebody who was also in touch with Maxton for Maxton to have followed us into the swamp. I didn't think it could be someone local in New Orleans, but I didn't expect it to be you. Once I knew, and thought about it, of course then it all made sense. But if you'd just left it alone tonight . . ."

Another muzzle flash, another bullet whining ineffectually. Sherman was a silhouette against the light, jerking first one way, then another, gun extended, trying to pin down Dain's voice.

"Who better than you to keep tabs on me, down through the years—hell, I begged you to. My go-between! Just as you'd been Pucci's go-between, down through the years. You even kept in touch with Inverness—you're a very careful man, Dougie . . ."

There was another shot. Dain laughed from elsewhere.

"When I told you I was going to New Orleans, you panicked and called him. Hoped he'd kill me but you tossed in

Maxton just to make sure. Know what happened to Maxton, Doug? I boiled him alive in a vat of hot tar."

Sherman's gun hand was silhouetted against the doorway light. The knife edge of Dain's hand broke his wrist in a karate chop. Sherman screamed, dropped the gun. Bent, clutching his shattered wrist, panicked as a fire-trapped horse, he ducked back out of the light.

"Inverness died of snakebite . . . Not a good way to go. Those last minutes of agony, knowing it's coming . . ."

"Can't you understand, I . . . I was *frightened* when you went to New Orleans . . ."

"Yes, Dougie," said Dain softly, "be frightened."

There were running steps, Sherman burst out of the darkness and through the doorway and away down the hall, holding his splintered wrist. How had he ever thought it would be amusing to tweak the tail of his own tame tiger? He'd told himself it was only smart to know Dain's every move in case he got close to the truth in one of his investigations.

Then he had, and . . .

At the elevator, Sherman had just seized the rope that would draw the bottom door up and the top one down, when Dain's foot was planted on the bottom one. He had grabbed up his leather-bound *Tibetan Book of the Dead* from on top of his suitcase in passing.

Sherman backed away, face stricken, absolute terror in his heart, until he ran out of room at the rear of the elevator.

Dain stood in the doorway, planted, solid, somehow more menacing because of his black sling than he would have been with the use of both arms. He held his leather-bound book in his left hand, spine out.

"Dain . . . please . . . after all these years . . ."

"You put a hitman on me in New Orleans—after all these years. You sent Maxton and his goons after me from Chicago—after all these years. You were waiting here in the dark to kill me—after all these years."

"Money . . ."

"Yeah, money. Inverness said it always came down to money. That's what it was always about, wasn't it? You had original Magritte paintings, for Chrissake! You don't make that sort of money selling books. I really was naive and stupid. You were Pucci's drug distributor for all of Northern California, weren't you? All along?''

"Dain, you have to believe me—"

"It wasn't Pucci ordered the hit on me—it was you!" Dain was advancing on him now. "He wasn't at risk—you were! Did he even know about me?"

"Of course he did, he . . . he ordered . . .''

"*You* ordered."

"I didn't . . . I never expected Marie and the baby . . .''

A sudden shriek, *"Inverness said his orders were to kill everybody in the cabin!"*

Sherman also shrieked. *"Dain!"*

But Dain was upon him, towering over him, all the more terrifying because he was speaking in a rational, almost quiet voice totally at odds with the tension in his face and body.

"You knew only the three of us would be out there in that cabin, Doug. And you told them to slaughter us all."

"Please! Dain! For God's sake, man, pity . . .''

Dain brought his arm back and across his body like an ancient warrior with a broadsword, then swung the hard narrow spine of the book like that warrior's blade. Not at Sherman. In martial arts he had been trained to think of striking something a foot beyond his real target.

The edge of the book struck the side of Sherman's neck with a rending sound. Dain, panting, turned away from the carrion huddled in the corner of the elevator.

"There's your pity, Doug," he said.

Shenzie started to meow, and some of the shock left Dain's face. He screwed the fuse back in tight and shut the fuse box door before going back down the hall.

"Let's get you out of that box, Shenz."

He carried Shenzie into the loft, turned on the lights—and scattered words and images from the last few hours came clamoring unbidden through his brain. Questions. Answers. Probabilities. Inevitabilities.

A coherent whole.

He sat on the bed for a long time with the carry case unopened beside him. A vast shudder ran through him.

Of course. If the middleman had come after him, why would the hitman be any slower off the mark?

Finally he shook himself, reached into the cat carry case for Shenzie. Fondled his furry little head. Chucked him under the chin, scratched him under the collar. Still no purr, of course, but at least he withdrew his hand to vocal protest.

"We'll have you out of there in no time, cat," he promised. "Just one phone call to make first."

Dain dragged Moe Wexler, the electronics genius, away from his reality cop show on TV, got some precise advice from him, then asked him to do a little job. Moe sighed and said he would have to go down to his shop in the middle of the night and it was going to cost Dain plenty, and Dain said that was all right, he had plenty, and he would meet Moe there.

The next part was going to be difficult and dangerous. But if he had to go, Dain figured, he would be going in good company. Shenzie had always wanted to be an engineer and he would be able to see some engineering problems get worked out at first hand.

Especially if Dain quite literally blew it . . .

The eleven o'clock news told the hitman he was safe. An explosion had gutted a semi-abandoned pier on the San Francisco waterfront. Fortunately there was a firehouse next door, so they were able to extinguish the resultant blaze before the flames had a chance to spread to adjacent structures.

One unidentified body had been found in the wreckage, at this hour police and firemen were sifting through the rubble for clues to his identity and for the source of the blast . . .

The shooter tapped his remote to blank the screen, and went to bed feeling totally safe and at peace with himself for the first time in five years.

34

It was one of those unusual San Francisco summer days, a sparkling sunlit morning without fog. Randy Solomon bounded zestfully down the outside stairs of his beautifully restored old Victorian on Buchanan, whistling. He turned downhill toward Fell and his car parked half a block away.

Standing on the sidewalk waiting for him was Dain. No sling this morning; both arms were free. Solomon checked his forward momentum, momentarily appalled.

"You were the other hitman," said Dain simply.

His face was pinched and drawn; another sleepless night. Randy had recovered; his face was placid, beaming. He mimed holding his arms out from his sides.

"You a tricky enough dude to be wired, Dain?"

Dain opened his arms wide for the frisk. "Doctor said I could take the sling off today, so I did, that's all," he said.

"So, no wire." Randy gave his big laugh. "So it's just us, sorta *mano a mano*, huh?"

"Something like that," said Dain. "After all, I've been looking for you for five years."

Randy nodded.

"Lots of activity gettin' you nowhere. Sure, I was the second shooter. Who the hell else could it have been? I been waiting five years for that penny to drop. When you said last night about Inverness bein' a cop, I thought you knew then."

"I didn't," said Dain. There was none of the heat and hatred he'd shown the night before with Sherman. Only a sort of sadness. "You're right, I should have known. It only made sense—a couple of murderous cops working together. You had the directions to the cabin—I'd given them to you myself. Inverness had the instructions from Sherman—kill us all."

Randy laughed his *basso profundo* laugh, spread his hands.

"Always tellin' you how I couldn't stand old Dougie-baby, where'd he get his information, shit like that, when all the time him and me . . .''

"You'd worked for him before," said Dain, more a question than a statement. "Paying for your house."

"Couple of times," Randy agreed. "Do a hit locally saves travelin' on the weekends."

"It was you who blew up Grimes on his boat."

Randy chuckled again. "You sure you ain't wearin' a wire, Hoss, seeking all these admissions, like?"

"No wire," said Dain. "Just trying to understand."

Randy was suddenly irritated. He looked around the quiet early-morning street. No one else had come from any of the houses on the block. No cars had started up at the curb. Randy had always been an early one in to the office. Dedicated cop.

"What's to understand? Killin' people's the easiest way I know to have a nice retirement." He swept an arm around to encompass the city. "Shit, they kill each other every day—over what TV show to watch and what corner to sell crack from."

"But . . . but I was your *friend*. Marie was your friend. Albie was your friend. Even Shenzie was—"

"Can't be friends with no cat, Hoss."

"But all you had to do was—"

"You wouldn't let it alone. I had set up the accident on Grimes's boat, and you just kept peckin' at it. So me and Sherman decided . . ." He broke off, said, "That was old Dougie's body they drug out of the loft, wasn't it?"

"His body," said Dain. "I called him from New Orleans, told him I was on my way back and would be at the loft last night. I wasn't going to do anything about it, but I had to know one way or the other." He suddenly quoted, "'Was me, I'd be plannin' a whole lotta other people's deaths.'" He met the incomprehension in Randy's eyes. "It's what you said to the doctor at the hospital that night. Whatever part of me was still alive heard it . . . It kept me going all those years . . ."

Randy shrugged. "I don't remember it." Then he was suddenly intense, with an edge of anger again. "But you shoulda listened closer, Sherlock. I said that's what I'd of done. Me. Not you. Hell, you was just a nerdy chess player in those days."

"Still am," said Dain, and meant it. "Playing around at life, playing around at revenge . . . Who else but you would have put that second bug on Farnsworth's phone? I never told you about the bonds but you knew about them in the car last night from the airport and I *still* didn't get it . . ."

"Yeah. Beefed up yo' body, got all ready physically for the war, but up here"—he tapped his forehead with a finger— "and here"—he slammed a fist against his own washboard gut—"you're still a fucking nerd."

His anger boiled over, he put a hand on Dain's chest and shoved him back a couple of steps. Dain gave without pushing back. Randy nodded as if his point had been made.

"You know I killed your fucking kid, you know I helped kill your fucking wife, you know I planned to blow you and your fucking cat all to hell, and what do you do? You think it all through an' you come here for a fucking confrontation."

He whirled, jabbed a finger at the flat roof of the Victorian across the street.

"Why the fuck aren't you up there with a sniper rifle and a scope, layin' the cross hairs on my chest?"

He shoved Dain again, harder this time. Dain went back a few more paces, still not trying to defend himself.

"Because you're a fucking nerd, same as you ever was." He gave his big booming laugh. "You ain't figured out shit. And you got no proof of anything." He was suddenly curious. "What really tipped you off it was Doug and me?"

"Him, a phone bill. You, the remark about the bonds—eventually it sank in. And how scared you got when I almost took Shenzie out of his carry case in the car. So up at the loft I checked and sure enough—there was a wire running from his collar down into a lump of molded *plastique* in the case with a detonator embedded in it. If I'd lifted him out—"

"So you blew up the loft, figuring I'd be watching the news and figure you were all done. And old Dougie went there, tryna get you before you got him, and by accident got blown up along with the place. You're pretty slick, Sherlock. But not slick enough. 'Cause you don't want revenge *hard* enough. You gonna *talk* me to death. Only people don't die that way."

"I'd quit wanting revenge at all," said Dain. "I was going to let it go with Doug, even after I knew he'd been the go-between. But he wouldn't let it alone. Just like me five years ago. And it got him killed, just like me five years ago."

Randy made as if to step around Dain toward his car, then checked himself again.

"Like I told you in the car last night, he couldn't leave it alone. I can't leave it alone. I ain't safe long as you're alive. But the difference between you and me, Sherlock—I know the way people die is somebody kills 'em. So I ain't gonna talk you to death."

"What are you going to do?" asked Dain in a strangely flat voice.

"I'm gonna give you time to have a lot of fun wonderin' when it's gonna happen. Then, one of these days, just when you figure I've forgot all about it, you'll turn around and, wham! You ain't there any more. Nobody'll ever suspect me, 'cause see, Dain, the whole world knows I'm your best friend. Hell, I'll cry at your funeral.''

He laughed his big booming laugh again, went jauntily down the street and across the grassy strip to his car, went around to the driver's side and unlocked it, opened the door. Dain bent down to pick up something he'd put down out of sight beside the roots of a tree, then just stood there with it in his hand to watch Solomon get into his car.

As Randy slid in under the wheel, he checked the back from automatic cop's habit. And froze. On the seat behind him was Shenzie's cat carrying case with a big red satin bow tied around it. A bow with bright gold letters stamped into it:

FROM A FRIEND. MEOW.

''*No!*'' he screamed.

Utter terror distorting his features, he tried to get out of the car before Dain pushed the button on the transmitter. Moe Wexler had been up almost all night putting it together for the detonator in the *plastique* Randy had put in Shenzie's case.

Randy didn't make it.

With a great *whoosh!* of sound and a burst of flame, his car went up with him only halfway out of it. Black smoke poured up into the unusual summer morning without fog. Dain just stood there, watching, tears on his cheeks.

''You turn around, Randy, and wham!'' he said in a soft, sad voice, ''you aren't there any more.'' He started down the street, murmuring to himself, ''Nobody'll ever suspect me. I was his best friend. Hell, I'll cry at his funeral . . .''

Cautious people had begun venturing out of their houses with stunned faces, but by then Dain was gone.

From force of habit, he went around to the back door of the little bungalow in Mill Valley, started to let himself into the kitchen, stopped dead, key in hand. The door was unlocked. He had locked it after leaving Shenzie off last night before going back to Moe Wexler's shop in the city. And Shenzie hadn't come to greet him as he usually did . . .

Nightmare. Yet another hitman was in the house, someone else he had to kill . . . forever and ever, yet another murderer to murder . . . And the iron grip of the past on his heart would never ease, he could never die and be reborn again . . .

Set carelessly on the kitchen counter was an attaché case. One that looked very familiar . . .

Dain slid forward silently, opened the case carelessly—if he was wrong and it was another bomb, now was the time to go. He had nothing left in his life he valued . . .

No bomb. It was indeed the bearer bonds that had started it all—and ended it all.

Dain moved silently through the little house he knew so well. Vangie was slumped back in the big easy chair across the coffee table from the couch, asleep, her fierce and beautiful face relaxed and childlike. Dain felt his heart leap up as he stood looking at her.

Something in his life that he valued.

Shenzie was asleep on her chest.

Dain crossed silently to the sleeping pair, put his finger down under Shenzie's throat. He was purring, his little motorboat going even in his sleep. He woke at Dain's touch, looked up at him with big pop eyes, stretched, kneading Vangie's sweater with little front paws, then shut his eyes again, indifferent to Dain's arrival.

The kneading paws woke Vangie. Just like the cat, she looked up at Dain for a long time without moving or speaking. Finally she sat up and cradled Shenzie upside down on her lap.

"You said your cat didn't purr," she told him.

"Not for five years."

She touched the name tag on Shenzie's collar.

"Shenzie. What a goofy name."

"It means crazy in Swahili. But more than that. Goofy is right—nuts, a little out of control. He always has been—knocks your cup of tea off the arm of the couch just to see what you'll do, sleeps on the cable box on top of the TV 'cause it's warm, quits purring for five years . . ."

Vangie stood up, turning to set Shenzie back in the chair when she did. She stood in front of Dain looking up at him. They were not touching, but almost.

"I came in through the bedroom window—the latch was loose." She made a quick gesture with her hands. She was dressed in jeans and a sweater and hiking boots. "You don't owe me anything, Dain, I'm not expecting anything from you, but I want to give the bonds back to that woman they were stolen from and I don't know how, so I had to ask you—"

"Eddie," said Dain.

"Eddie?"

"My name is Eddie. Dain is my last name." He scooped her up in his arms and started toward the bedroom. He had a sudden, intense erection, as he used to get with Marie at unexpected moments, as he'd had in his airplane dream. "We have to check out that loose lock on the window."

When they came the first time it was absolutely together, and both cried out when they did. And then cried, real tears, because both of them could finally let go of their losses.

Dain woke alone in bed, stretched luxuriously, felt automatically for Shenzie's little head on the pillow beside his. Shenzie wasn't there. Noonday sun through the branches of the pine tree outside the window made the bedroom a green cavern, like the bedroom in his dream. He could smell coffee. New Orleans coffee, thick and rich with lots of chicory in it.

Everything came back to him, everything, all of it.

He pulled on his shorts and padded barefoot out into the living room. Vangie was on the sofa, coffee mug in hand, staring at the half-finished chess game on the coffee table that for five years Dain had been physically unable to put away.

She looked up when he came into the room. She was wearing one of his shirts, the tails came down almost to her knees.

"My *pa-pére* taught me to play this game," she said. "My grandfather. Is this one of those chess problems he used to tell me about?"

"No," said Dain. "This is just an unfinished game . . ."

Without visible hesitation, he pulled up a chair across from her and sat down. He leaned forward, studying the board.

"It got interrupted and Marie and I never got back to it."

Vangie moved a piece. Dain countered. With a sudden soft thud, Shenzie landed on the corner of the coffee table and sat watching the play intently. His black tail with the white tip was twined loosely down around one leg of the table.

"He wishes he had hands," said Vangie.

"So he can be an engineer when he grows up," said Dain.

"Check," said Vangie.

The three of them studied the board intently for a long while, Dain seeking a way to avoid checkmate. Then Shenzie reached out a tiny black and white hand and knocked over one of Dain's pieces. It happened to be his king.

He and Vangie laughed together. He felt as if he were coming up to the surface of a sunlit sea after a very long time in cold green depths where no light ever penetrated.

They went back into the bedroom to celebrate again what they had found. As they celebrated, Shenzie went to sleep in the middle of the chessboard, the pieces he had knocked aside littering the tabletop like miniature overturned grave markers.